praise for
of one pure will

"In the eerie fiction of Farah Rose Smith we see a vital, unsettling voice, meticulous in the darkly intricate phantasmagorical labyrinths she presents. She guides readers through a world of unusual birds and curious machinery, uncertain dreams and weird moments you must experience for yourself. *Of One Pure Will* provides an excellent introduction to her work for new readers while her regular readers will be delighted to have so many of her finest stories collected together in one volume. From the titular "Of One Pure Will" to a "Delirium of Mothers" or "Rithenslofer (The Corpses of Mer)" these are elegant tales of chilling beauty that accomplish much in their frequent brevity. Dance, art, waves and pain, whatever she turns our attention to, she consistently transforms into something just short of a majestic poem rumbling, ominous raven-stuffed storm clouds at the periphery of your imagination. They'll linger with you long after you've put this book down. Not to be missed!" —Bryan Thao Worra, Science Fiction and Fantasy Poetry Association President (2016-2022)

"I have become a huge fan of Farah Rose Smith. This collection of haunting, lyrical, visceral stories is a maximalist writer's dream come true. These stories will hypnotize you, transform you, fill you with longing, and set you free in a never-ending forest filled with awful possibilities." —Richard Thomas, author of *Disintegration* and the Thriller Award-nominated *Breaker*

"Written in dense and luminously poetic prose, *Of One Pure Will* reads like a series of hypnotic dream-visions. Steeped in fantastical imagery, these stories contend with humankind's capacities for cruelty and deception, pulsing with an undercurrent of weird Gothic romance.

Farah Rose Smith is a highly talented, compelling, and distinct voice in the world of dark speculative fiction." —Mike Thorn, author of *Shelter for the Damned* and *Darkest Hours*

"To read Farah Rose Smith's prose is to walk through a dark, ornate museum. The walls are covered in vivid, decadent paintings of surreal nightmares. A low cacophony of discordant music, screams, and ancient languages echo through the halls. Take the tour." —Ben Arzate, author of *Elaine*

"With her splendid collection *Of Pure Will*, Farah-Rose Smith manages to reinvent cosmic horror with an idiosyncratic world of her own. Slow apocalypses, haunted parallel worlds, charismatic monsters and shattered personalities will haunt the reader for a long time, like a delicious and rare poison. If Anais Nin had written horror instead of erotica, she could have penned down such stories. Both luxurious and unforgiving, *Of Pure Will* is an instant and welcome classic in a genre that craved both renewal and a genuinely original feminine touch." —Seb Doubinsky, author of *Missing Signal*, *The Invisible*, and *Paperclip*.

"In *Of One Pure Will*, Farah Rose Smith deftly intertwines the oneiric, the mystical, and the brutally physical. This is a dark, elegiac collection from a powerful and unique new voice." —Matthew M. Bartlett, author of *Gateways to Abomination*

"*Of One Pure Will* is a haunted mirror in a palace ballroom: it gilds and filigrees the ghosts of the familiar with an opulent darkness, populating its reflected world with shades of uncanny and elegant horror. An echoing fanfare of fever dreams, the lush density of imagination and intoxicating craft on display establish Smith as an unmistakable talent." —Gordon B. White, author of *As Summer's Mask Slips and Other Disruptions* and *Rookfield*

# of one pure will

a collection by

farah rose smith

TREPIDATIO
PUBLISHING

ISBN: 978-1-950305-97-1 (sc)
ISBN: 978-1-950305-98-8 (ebook)
Library of Congress Catalog Number: 2021945115

First printing edition: September 10, 2021
Published by Trepidatio Publishing in the United States of America.
Cover Design: Don Noble | Cover Layout: Scarlett R. Algee
Edited by Sean Leonard
Proofreading and Interior Layout by Scarlett R. Algee

Trepidatio Publishing, an imprint of JournalStone Publishing
3205 Sassafras Trail
Carbondale, Illinois 62901

JournalStone books may be ordered through booksellers or by
contacting:
JournalStone | www.journalstone.com

For Lev Earle, my most enduring friend.

contents

"TRAPPED IN A DREAM-DISEASE"
An Introduction to *Of One Pure Will*
by Jeffrey Thomas

THE WYTCH-BYRD OF THE NABRYD-KEIND
17

IN THE WAY OF ESLAN MENDEGHAST
26

OF MARBLE AND MUD
32

THE VISITOR
41

THE LAND OF OTHER
57

AS UNBREAKABLE AS THE WORLD
68

AN ACCOUNT ABOVE BURNSIDE PARK
77

AS WITH ALEM
86

SORCERER MACHINE
93

DARK OCEAN
113

ASH IN THE POCKET
117

FOLIE À PLUSIEURS
122

RITHENSLOFER (THE CORPSES OF MER)
125

IN THE ROOM OF RED NIGHT
129

OF ONE PURE WILL
140

TIME DISEASE (IN THE WAKING CITY)
144

IVISOU
150

THE RIVER
159

THE SEA HOAX
169

ELECTRIC FUNERAL
176

EVE, LIKE SHARDS OF GLASS
181

A DELIRIUM OF MOTHERS
189

THE IRRATIONAL DRESS SOCIETY
202

PUBLICATION HISTORY

ACKNOWLEDGMENTS

ABOUT THE AUTHOR

"trapped in a dream-disease"

An Introduction to *Of One Pure Will*
Jeffrey Thomas

"A theatre of pain it is, to dream without sleep. Images. Constant,
assaulting images!"
—*Of Marble and Mud*

AS an avid reader, I appreciate not only multiple genres, but multiple approaches to the creation of fiction. I hesitate to oversimplify, but to some extent a lot of fiction can be separated into a focus either on *event* or *effect*. By event I mean, of course, fiction that is primarily plot-driven. Before reading the collection before you, I read translations of two crime thriller novels by French writer Franck Thilliez. I enjoyed them thoroughly and regret that none others in the series have, as yet, been translated. Their plots are mind-bogglingly intricate, so much so that characters conducting different aspects of their investigation repeatedly get together to exchange information, and I believe this was the author's method of recapping things for an otherwise overwhelmed reader. I can imagine Thilliez at his desk surrounded by whiteboards, index cards and sticky notes, with maybe an Excel spreadsheet open in front of him. This isn't to say fiction of this type is merely a soulless formula, but there are indisputably mechanical processes at work in its composition. That is its intent. Something is being constructed in front of us; seeing those machined parts come together is the prime reward.

However, I also find great reward in fiction that de-emphasizes or even ignores the hard-edged confines of conventional storytelling. This can be because the author is more interested, for example, in immersing us in the mind and feelings of their characters, or because they prioritize establishing a rich sense of atmosphere, whether in terms of a literal setting or a psychological environment, say of anxiety or melancholy. This approach of *effect* over *event* can also have to do with the *style* of the writing; that is to say, the prose voice itself. I wholeheartedly disagree with the notion that a writer should remain invisible to the reader, just as they say an actor shouldn't call attention to the fact that they're acting. Were we to give ourselves entirely to this notion, we wouldn't have poetry, and there is writing that blurs the line between poetry and prose to wonderful effect. Separating voice from writing is like separating voice from song, and many singers have unique voices indeed, to be savored. In my personal circle of writers, I've followed with great admiration the fantastically idiosyncratic work of such prose stylists as W. H. Pugmire, Michael Cisco, Joseph S. Pulver, Sr., and D. F. Lewis. Poe didn't give us involved plots, generally, but scenes or scenarios that were vessels to be filled with his dark poetry. None of these writers are like the other, *and that is the point*, and yet they are called to mind when I read the equally singular work of Farah Rose Smith.

Smith knows, intuitively, that horror fiction, weird fiction, dark fantasy — whatever label by which we might try to categorize her work — is at heart an effort to capture the quality of that most remarkable of experiences: the dream. Dreaming is one of those experiences that each of us shares, that we are all fascinated with and confounded by...something that we grapple to understand as we grapple to understand those other seemingly mundane, universal experiences: love and death. And dreams aren't built from factory parts, but from parts of our deepest dread and yearning.

She writes of people, as one story herein says, "trapped in a dream-disease." The proceedings of her stories are nebulous, taking place at times in some "Afterworld." Characters frequently allude to some backstory, some life-changing sin or crime, hinted regret or lost love, a tragedy that we are not permitted to witness or even learn about completely after the fact, making these references all the more sinister, and all the more like some tragic event in the life of someone we encounter whose suffering we can never fully know. Side characters are mentioned or discussed but kept at arm's length, in obscuring shadows, mysterious and elusive, but ominous for having impacted the main characters in ways we can't quite grasp. Mist is a recurrent image, and it is the mist of dream, blurring the edges of these psychic wounds, keeping pain amorphous, hard to isolate and treat.

However, some objects shine clearly through the mist, like gravestones though a ground fog, and a common factor readily discerned is the theme of families, such as in the haunting *The Land of Other* (concerning a son) or *Sorcerer Machine* (concerning a sister). A related theme is that of profound loss, as in *Ivisou*, in which the protagonist obsesses over a dead friend she adored but seems to have also resented, projecting these darker emotions onto the enigmatic woman of the title, who I feel might represent the protagonist herself, in that Ivisou is said to be "the matron of reflection" and "matrician of envy." Another kind of loss is never having attained a thing of value to *be* lost, as in *As Unbreakable as the World*, wherein the protagonist expresses the desire to have a sense of meaning, saying, "to someone, I may be a sort of something, someday." Another story states, "There is a face that sleeps inside of us — always aware, never awake. Eslan has reconciled himself to this face, as one does the inevitable death of a mother. It speaks to you with the cadence of mist." So much of Smith's themes are expressed in that one passage.

There are references to God throughout, but they offer little comfort to these lost souls. They have been "deserted by God." One character says, "God is gone, and I am on the road again," while another makes the shocking claim, "I have killed God and there is no turning back." Thus, overhanging all is an irretrievable sense of damnation and doom.

For me, one of the greatest attractions to Smith's work is her feverish, surreal imagery, though she portions it out teasingly so as not to allow us to become jaded by it. We are afforded tantalizing glimpses of the Ornament, a piece of dream architecture, "a great metallic thing, like a giant screw in situ." There are nightmarish instances of body horror. There is a city "in glass, in pearl, in odd, cosmic illumination" viewed within a strange bird egg. In this collection, such extraordinary imagery is probably best represented in a story with a science fiction/fantasy feel, *In the Room of Red Night*, a masterpiece of phantasmagorical word pictures, hellishly beautiful.

First and foremost, though, with Smith we must return to the matter of voice...how one sings. Smith's prose feels like an uncanny stream of automatic writing...delirious, fevered language one might imagine issuing from a possessed person who channels the denizen-spirits of some nearly indescribable other-land. This gorgeous language flows over you like incense, beguiling and burning. It is a dense, lush poetry, and inspires such from me in my attempt to give some impression of it.

Yes, in the fiction of Farah Rose Smith we are freed from the mathematical formulae of meaning, as in dreams we are freed of reality in its more inflexible shapes. She sings from a shared unconsciousness that we all recognize by its unknowable vastness. As she says, herself, in one of the stories you are about to encounter...

"I assign nothing with the vanity of consciousness I possess, only by some cosmic misstep.

"With human eyes, I see nothing, know nothing. With the eyes of eternity, I no longer have to know."

# of one pure will

the wytch-byrd of the nabryd-keind

gold in my eyes
red on my mouth
am I glamour
or did I eat you for treasure

CLAUDIA Marr, head swinging up in pride from the cover of a black veil, sandstorm skin sculpted by moon-glow, grows on stage from ghost to mannequin on the velvet seat of her trapeze. Her long gauzy robe cascades down from the seat, swaying matter-of-factly in the prismatically orchestrated scene. All is black save for her lips, a sorcerer's shade of amethyst, filling her cupid-bow lips like a period in a stage-book of unspoken curses.

Suspended in the liquid darkness, her face is brushed by a bronze and obsidian plumage — long, unearthly feathers from a great beast of bird-dom. The audience gasps in awe, as beast and beauty dance in-flight — a symphony of silent gestures and explosions of colour. This is a celebration of beauty — of natural life. Painted woman and wilderness born perfect. Claudia runs her ungloved hand along the underside of the bird's endless neck. It coos in growing waves — sound like spells across the aisles, through the rafters, illuminating the auspicious night in organic wonder.

The bird outstretches its enormous wings, and here the act has ended. Claudia slides from neck to tail, to the granite floor of the stage. She huffs, cold cheek pressed against the floor, remnants of golden glitter spilling out from above like god-rain. She peers out to the front row, to her sweetheart, Girard Augher.

Thank you, she whispers as the lights go dark, and the bird folds up into a black, feathered crescent.

Claudia never said much about Roman Sier, other than her last view of him was in the marble room of the old Chesterton house in Fairbrook. Having overstayed his welcome in her memory, long surpassing the dents and sighs of her precocious childhood, she had swept him out as perilously as the remnants of her past revilements. But there have been many men since then. Many pains of the heart.

"Do you house the birds in such conditions?" she asks Emiel Forsa, noting the mould on the sill and the change in temperature from one corner to the next. The warehouse is a wreck from top to bottom.

"I don't keep mine in my home, no," he answers coolly. "Does Girard?"

Claudia drops her coat on the nearest seat and stands erect, her nose barely meeting the height of Forsa's chest. Her lips are red now, her hair in a Louise Brooks bob. The Spaniard leans down to meet her eyes.

"The birds of paradise, yes. He doesn't trust them to anyone."

Forsa lets out a derisive laugh. "And the bird last night, where does he find such exotic creatures?"

"I...don't know."

Forsa's expression grows dark.

"I tell you, I don't! I know nothing of it. I only took his offer."

"To use the bird?"

"He doesn't harm them."

Forsa huffs again and turns to pour himself a drink. Claudia rushes behind him, grasping his arms lovingly, leaning her head against his back.

"Oh, please, let it be. Girard is so remorseful. He wants all to be well."

He inhales deeply, placing his glass down, turning to her. "Oh, does he...?" he asks dryly. "Tell me, do you not know what he has done?"

"He has never said."

Forsa's face, painted in red, turns from her and towards his ledger. "Hasn't he?"

Eight cages have arrived on the doorstep of Emiel Forsa. Eight immaculate, iron-wrought contraptions in wedding-white. The contents are invisible, hidden behind a translucent sheath of fabric woven between the bars, glittering with microscopic breathing holes pierced by sewing needle.

"What of this offering? Who is it from?" Forsa demands of the couriers, three small Indian men in green suits, moving identically, as though their gestures were born of an experiment in military discipline and theatre.

"I'd cut out my own tongue before I'd speak it, sir! But, perchance your curiosity lingers, a note!"

The smallest courier points to a golden envelope tied to one of the cages by scarlet thread. They depart, and Forsa is left to rip and read and revile the newly acquired oppression in his midst. Gold powder paints his fingertips.

"Girard," he whispers, eyes dancing menacingly over the insipid prose of this apology. He speaks of 'longing for old days' and 'true friendship,' of 'mistakes' and 'repentance' and '*forgiveness*'!

"Huh!" shouts Forsa, tearing the letter and setting it out the window and into the wind. It is this action that stirs the hidden beasts. A quiet, rolling caw, as guttural as the stirring of a locomotive engine, rings out from the farthest white cage. Then, each gathers with their avian brother and sister to a choir of guttural moaning and croaking – the longing to see their new home.

Reluctantly, Forsa takes his penknife to the translucent fabric, tearing gently, as to not harm or aggravate the beast. He pulls the fabric out with caution, the last talent of a worn ornithologist, revealing the species within.

But what species is this? Forsa stares in shock, a touch of horror glowing from his eyes, at the opulent bird within. It has the look and size of an adult vulture, though scarlet red in plumage. Its eyes, a deep shade of turquoise. Its beak, a sumptuous grey-gold. Its feathers are dusted with a strange golden powder which puffs out into the atmosphere with every movement of the bird. It looks up at him with a trickster's curiosity.

"Intelligent one," he says quietly, moving to cut the sheath from the remainder of the strange birds.

One meets his eye with a heathen might — the largest, most vibrant. It pushes its head back to let out a harrowing cry. Forsa is frozen to the spot, ears ringing, gold dust powdering the button-sleeve of his white overcoat.

Girard Augher conducts himself with the patchwork gestures of businessmen, though Claudia remembers him before this charade. She has lingered, knowing he would make something of himself, long beyond his travails in pseudo-alchemy.

"So the key works?" he teases.

"Indeed. How is my precious bird?" she asks, embracing him slyly with a hint of mist in her eye. The man is tall, stout, balding — an embodiment of wonder in wears that wear him.

"Well rested, lovely! Fine condition, very fine. The performance did him well, I think."

Claudia smiles. He helps her remove her coat, revealing numerous long scratches on her arms. Girard notices, though he does not speak of them.

"Tell me, how is Forsa?"

She rolls her eyes. "He is a mess of bitterness, as always."

"Ah. I am glad you have been able to maintain your friendship with him."

They sit down together in the dining room. Rustling feathers may be heard from every room in shades of light and loud. The scratching of talons and militant crowing of uncounted avian beasts illustrates the evening conversation, in piercing lamplight.

"They are cramped in here, are they not?"

Girard laughs. "Only for a time. I am in the process of moving many of them to larger quarters. Then this home may begin to look like a *home*, yes?"

Claudia leers as he stares out the dining room door into the living area, where a great ivory cage sits. She knows something is bothering him. He speaks before she has the chance to ask.

"Tell me something, Claudia."

She stiffens her shoulders, listening.

"Do you consider me a *generous* friend?"

Girard crosses his arms over his chest, steeped in thought. His glasses tip as he fumbles with a stray golden fork, decorated with a phoenix on the handle.

September 19th, 1934

I have been gifted six birds that seem to have come from some unexplored region of Northern India. These birds, which have no scientific designation, have enormous scarlet plumage, variable beaks (white, black, grey-gold), and glossy black eyes. Equipped with profound intelligence that, in the smartest specimen, could rival that of a dolphin, the birds become my pride, fright, obsession.

Gold dust was gathered at the tips of their wing feathers upon delivery. The dust has spread to the entirety of the wings, and now the body, of the birds. Each day, in the morning, I brush out the dust with a ceramic tool, as to not harm the delicate creatures, though have yet to do so with proper ventilation.

Claudia makes her way down the street, heels catching between cobblestones — stumbling, wincing, panting. She reaches the old warehouse where Forsa has been staying. Stumbling up the steps, the air becomes hot, unbearable. She knocks on the door loudly, her bracelets decorating the wood with a metallic, bell-like sound.

Forsa opens the door slightly, revealing only a sliver of himself through the crevice. She forces her way in, pushing the door open. The apartment is in complete disarray, covered in feces, dust, and feathers. Claudia, covering her mouth, speaks through her hand.

"Emiel..."

She examines him, noting the long tears in the grey fabric of his suit. Rolling coos sing out from above. She lifts her gaze to see the scarlet birds lingering above on the pipes, examining her with gentle longing and curiosity. She looks at Forsa again.

"I...I cannot account for them," Forsa whispers.

The sadness in his eyes overwhelms her senses. She drops her hand, moves forward, removes his tattered overcoat, and runs to his armoire in the back room. Searching through the drawers, she cannot find a single item of clothing that has not been destroyed by the birds. She walks back to him.

"You will be rid of them."

He shrugs. "No."

"Why the hell not?"

He turns his arms over to show that his veins have become white. Forsa lifts a finger to his lower eyelids, adjusting them so that she may see the deep, yellow hue of sclera.

She grabs his wrist. "Emiel."

"Leave!"

Claudia is overcome with a look of guilt. She breathes in deeply. "Tell me what Girard did, all those years ago."

"Huh!" Forsa grabs her by the arm and leads her to the door.

"Tell me!"

He closes the door in her face.

October 3rd, 1934

Weeks have passed. I grow lethargic. The ethereal beauty of the birds has mutated into an aberrant, demonic ferocity. They began to exhibit features more akin to vultures, though more menacing. Their gentle, curious personalities become dark. I notice that, in the hours of their recreation time outside of the cages, they play tricks on me by shutting off lights and hiding my tools, including the ceramic brushes. The last great change I noticed in the birds was the hue of their eyes. The pure glossy black became a sclera of yellow, with a red pupil. And the size of them! The size...

There are many poor souls who dabble in magic with dark intention, only to find that it will fail them. Emiel Forsa, hiding from the light of day behind shit-stained, moth-eaten curtains, cannot account for the labyrinth of confusion and disease that has come to him with the arrival of his treasured guests.

On the morning of the eighth of October, Forsa finds a concerning object in one of the golden nests the birds have woven into the apartment pipework. An egg as large as a melon, as light as a feather, held up to the light, revealing an interior city in glass, in pearl, in odd, cosmic illumination. Forsa thinks himself trapped in a dream-disease. The necrotic-REM of self-annihilation. He cannot think, he cannot breathe...

An ebb of pale light haunts the room, growing more red, more violent. The largest bird, Thesil, has grown to the heights of an elephant. It turns its enormous head around the corner, into the room, its long neck stretching through the lengths until its beak is inches from Forsa's face. There is an elegance to this defeat, perhaps. Forsa is unafraid. Their presence is an effortless haunt, and there is nothing that can be done to be rid of them. They vanish and appear at will, throw his voice through his own ears, torment him with rolling laughter, like a preternatural hyena. The face of the great one is lit by the last light of dusk creeping through the taped-up window. Forsa cannot stand this light anymore.

The night air will be dry. He breathes in and chokes, particles of gold dust trapped in his lungs. He is painted from within by this torment. Thesil leans in closer, the chill of his beak touching Forsa's forehead. He breathes heathen air, like black smoke, into his face. It has the smell of a thousand-year thing, alive despite the inklings of nature. Forsa has a fantasy, of his corpse encased in glass, untouchable due to the infection that lives within. He will not turn into one of them, not be eaten by them. He threads his fingers together and lifts them to separate his face from the beast. He does not want to look at it any longer.

October 13th, 1934

TEM micrograph from several weeks ago reveals atypical virions similar to the manifestation of rabies, but the symptoms do not align. They do, however, seep into me, in dreams and waking life. I awoke to two words scribbled in my bedside notebook. *"Nabryd-keind"* and *"Ulldythaer."* I can make no sense of them.

Claudia turns in the remnants of passion, Girard's quiet snores weaving through her cigarette smoke. She does not love him. Cannot love anymore. She remembers Roman. Thoughts rush in of the long stairwell, the space between steps, the fissure in the atmosphere between rain and great thunder. He had received the cloak she sent him. A wondrous thing. The door opened by itself, revealing Roman's silhouette on a far chair, lit by candlelight. His billowing form, expanded by the cloak, cast a cruel shadow on the wall.

"I was delayed a bit. The storm, you see," she said, trying to coax him out.

Roman, face obscured by shadow, turned in his seat, rising slowly. Walking in measured steps towards her, he did not speak. Claudia motioned for the nearby lamp, holding it up to him. Illuminated by this lamplight was the form of man eaten alive by fabric, folds of cloth clamping into flesh like a carnivorous plant. She ran down the stairway in the dark, each step lit by reflecting orange flame on floorboard gloss, a thousand screams sewn together behind her...

Forsa, in his rickety chair, sits with his legs positioned like a discarded marionette. He is still, without urgency. That which creeps, creeps slowly in the mind, in the body. The birds, having exited their cages, lurk on the overhead pipes, in the shadows. They are laughing at him. Forsa hears his own voice, his own pleading, bouncing from the walls. He thinks himself a companion of Alice, as tools and furniture change in size from one moment to the next. The horrid heat of the room blinds him to reason. The birds begin to circle overhead, their maddening caws ripping through his delirium like the last trumpet sounding over a forgotten earth. Forsa looks to his feet, unable to meet the eyes of the menacing creatures. On the floor is a mangled newspaper, Girard Augher marring the front page with his stolen glory.

Forsa tears himself from his predicament, stumbling out of the chair and to the door. The birds have vanished above him, as they often do in times of his surfacing resolve. He wanders down the hall, out into the street, to the village square, where the paper noted the scheduled appearance of Girard with his orange kettle birds.

Forsa spots Girard some distance away, embellished yellow sleeves glistening in the last light of dusk. His thoughts are without form, like an animal. There is instinct and intention, but no reason.

"Your birds!" Forsa cries out, frothing at the mouth.

Girard turns in awe of his former friend, who seems every bit the walking corpse. "Which do you speak of?"

Forsa stumbles toward Girard, taking the scarlet grip upon his neck, thrusting his nails into his throat. He whispers, "The Nabryd-keind…"

His jaw opens no wider than men without curses. He rips the flesh from Girard's face, as inhuman a gesture as the world will allow, collapsing the man against the cobblestones in a flash of blood and cartilage.

Forsa collapses upon him, the consumption of blood, a poison to his condition. Muddled cries escape Girard's mouth, frowned by the curdling emissions. He cannot breathe under Forsa's weight, increasing with each second as the man dies under his old friend. His last words are barely audible past the gurgling of saliva and blood.

"I…gave…you…no…birds!"

He takes an hour to die beneath Forsa, his cadaver spilling out in raven shades. No one on the street will approach them.

Claudia washes her face in a cracked mirror, the last layer of white powder falling away in rain from her sunken, elderly cheeks. She has never said much about Forsa or Girard, other than her last view of them was from the main room of the old warehouse in Manasseh, the gentle coos of precious scarlet birds singing out behind her.

in the way of eslan mendeghast

IT is the fourth time you have chased Eslan Mendeghast out into the Moors, and it will be your last.

The boy has made a spectacle of himself in more ways than one, always flitting about with his stories and peculiar reminiscences, quite unusual for a child of that age. The brawny types like you would use him for rock-target practice and other acts of force. *Stay away from Mendeghast,* you said. The children, and the mothers of the children, and the grandmothers of the children. The entire world seemed to have disdain for him. To you, he is stupid and superfluous. To you, he is nothing.

Since you struck him in the head, he keeps his ties in precise rows, organized by length and color. Even his grandmother cannot figure out the logic he uses to select his wears of the day. The little professor wears black button-ups, like a man ten times his age, secured up to the neck, soaked in sweat. Today he wears a yellow tie decorated with faint green thread.

Eslan has gone out to the moors for an investigation of *boegs,* a beast of fog and water language he drew upon a spare napkin during last night's dinner. You sought him out, hiding by the fence of his home, teetering on your obese legs towards him with that meditative, toad-like wheezing.

"Mende-GEEK! Mende-Geek!"

Eslan does not turn, but continues on towards the moorland, illustrated with grey-blue fog and the occasional light-dance of lantern bugs.

"What are you, DEAF now, too? Too AFRAID to turn and look at me, Mende-GEEK?"

You catch up to Eslan and begin poking him methodically in the back. Eslan's concentration breaks. He turns to you.

"Stop poking me!"

"Or what?"

You poke him again, and again, marking the small boy's shoulder. Years of anger brew up inside of Eslan. With force unimaginable for his size, he shoves you away and you plummet.

There has been little time for meditation, or contemplation, of any kind. You, child, undulate morbidly in slow motion, teetering backwards, ghastly gesticulations weaving in and out of the fog as fate becomes clear. That chalky froth foams up, as one would expect upon the death of a moth, but not of man. Not of boy. A wasp is latched to a burnt stalk, watching — obscured by the piercing light of dawn.

Little wisps of dead butterfly wings roll in from the valley. A great shape rises over you. Flocks of crows disperse over the scene, a silent choreography of dread. That which rises up croaks a single word, your name. The boegs appear, seeds of immortal death, flapping overhead with a glistening sound.

"*Eslan Mendeghast*," says the fog, the mist, the *boeg*, the boy, the nothing.

There is a face that sleeps inside of us — always aware, never awake. Eslan has reconciled himself to this face, as one does the inevitable death of a mother. It speaks to you with the cadence of mist.

"Help!" you yell, in despair of death. Your corpse bobs up and down, sickly pink foam pouring out of your mouth. It speaks to you in fog-tongue, the unholy language of the Moors.

"The help you ask, you must ask of *Eslan*," it says. Your eyes turn to the boy. He cradles his empty glass bottle, eyes dark, contemplating your fate. Is he willing? You cannot ask. You cannot breathe.

He speaks.

"With a withered wisp of black rope, threads adorned with beetle legs, lashed across their necks, I must walk these three out from the moors, into the town, *if* I am to help you."

Your attention is brought to three hideous animals rising up out of the wetlands. They have the heads of desiccated horses, the bodies of black toads. Your senses are screaming, caught in cold fire.

"If I am to help you," Eslan begins, slowly setting down his bottle, "I must bring them to the house of Archivist Igol. Not look into their eyes.

Not count their teeth. Mark the manner of his door, the opal handle, allow the croaking of the beasts to awaken him from sleep. Allow the door to open just a crack, the protoplasmic adornments of Christ ebbing out like candle smoke in blue. Allow myself to be invited in, among the blackwood floors and relics. Ascend the great staircase. Move nothing, touch nothing. Allow the hushed voices of spirits to flow through my ears, through my blood, let the vibrations form over my skin, bite my tongue, touch nothing, carry myself up up up to the roof of Archivist Igol's house."

You stiffen with every word, your surroundings transfiguring into dream-memory amid the indelicate rumbling of his speech.

"By the lamp of the moonlight, I will await a black and blue explosion like the sun, the ascent of sounds from the abyss, an immortal transparency of notes and golden songs from the darkness of matter from the petrified nights of nothingness. Pinkish veins will form over my face. I will know the earth. I will not sing with them — only listen with open eyes, a settled tongue, and the brief and bloody wisdom of a *Mendeghast*. Heathen sounds must wash over me like storm waves.

"Lulled to sleep by this heathen lullaby, in seven layers-deep of dreams, I will see faces eating out open drawers, find desiccated roots and fingernails chop't. *You* will walk out from the lid of dusk, up the great hill towards a wandering light. There is nothing there but a great tree, and from it comes black mumbles of confusion — of the absolute mystery of death. But let me speak as though it is *this* moment! The air is filled with dark spice. Lumbering up the hill is the luminous, the light, the scented, sleepless woman — a maiden of blood known as *mother*. She stumbles madly, breathless in the moonlight — panicking, but with her delicate obedience, the black murmur hesitates and wales and undulates — a volcanic explosion of language, never to be understood. The thing that sits and speaks stares out with red glares — as though its whispers kidnap her heart — speaking in listless language. She is helpless. Her dress slips off from her frail form. She dances in the limited light — in fascination, in ecstasy, in dark anxiety. Do not sob! Do not call for mother. Do not call for me.

"Generations of blood flow from her womb. A child will be born on the hilltop — its simple being bred from an unclear rhythm of passion. When mother looks out into the horizon for submission, express with the utmost brokenness and despair, your anguish. Take the child out from underneath her. Do not bundle him up or clear his eyes of slime. Ignore the weeping, and run down the hill. A great forest spreads out before you. Worry will flush across your face, your lips. Walk into the wood while shapes dance overhead, leaves obscuring the sky. Leave the child by the black tree, in gnarled hands from the deep hole in the ground before it. Question not the strangeness of these digits, of these limbs — do not ask if what is given will be returned or dissolved.

"You will turn and face the utmost cruelty — harridans, undisguised through astonished eyes and mournful croaking. Eight idiot beasts hand you an offering of eels — miraculous liquid, born authenticated by the coupling eyes of Olag Kengkhovra. This is a lottery ticket to the stars. Do not interrupt in false pride or fear! There are many inhabitants of the forest to see such things. Even being a *Mendeghast* cannot heal or protect one from such folly. One elongated finger sticks inside your ear and twists and turns! A helplessness of sensation — you are on the course of doom. Your heart beats out like a swarm of black flies, doubling-up against the sky, hanging aslant. Imagine writing down your faith as though the whole republic had been turned against you — as though the enormity of abandonment extends out into the utmost universe.

"One witch pulls you out from the others in the sky — a flight of circus flora, she escapes with enormous wings, shimmering and sugaring over the black river. She appears, her hand outstretched. You grasp it, callused skin ripping your delicate fingers apart. You succumb to this flight of harder life as you have understood shame and fear and reduction by adults. She has a tongue that drips acid like metal-on-limbs. Charging forward through the wood in an ominous flurry, alarmed by confusion and words and languages you cannot understand, a breeze brings through a chorus, faintly — of others. Other voices other tongues other worlds as the morning sky creeps.

"She brings you to a cavernous hole, shoulder-to-shoulder with great lengths of shelves. You answer loudly and you know nothing. All is composed in anger as black as your eyes. You seek out something familiar, something comforting, but this scene is an exact exaggeration of fetid knowledge, it is doom-intellect that you come to know through me! She bleeds it into you through slime, through touch, through heathen might! You smell a smell, the last chaos bleeding out. There are vases, there are vials, there are canisters and glass. Tendrils-worms and teeth, shrunken men and beasts, alike. Long-snouted, long-tailed, long-taloned, turnips with pupil-less eyes. That which lives in pale glass, no one ever understands.

"A procession of spectres walk backward with lowered heads, costumed in the armors of death and dismay. Some are dark and dreary. Some spill spleens, and some emit slime on the wind. Mile after mile, I will walk ahead of them, hands grazing cherry red blossoms, oleanders, and dead roses. *To the square of the city*, they say in silent language. Puffed-up chests bump against our backs. There is an irresistible wild here. The black cloth of eternity scrapes across your neck. There is no illusion left. This is the tiny spark of the absolute, of the violent, of the fluttering, sounding darkness that has lived within lilac bloom, black eyes, and blood spit onto you. There is no speech to be said that could wrap up such a plot. Pressed against us, the buzz of the underworld, cleaning and clanging, you are disembodied from yourself as you walk — once a child, now a man through endless space. The horizon blinks and blooms and blossoms and bends forth to your depths. I am a *Mendeghast*. I use circles within sacrifice and cynicism — the over-elaboration of grumbling against the neck with blood, with shame, with crowds of monstrosity. A yellow hue sinks deep into your eyes. Your suit is perfect. Your chin is high. I draw a semicircle ahead of us, ahead of the procession, from distilled liquors and limes. There are demons to be seen and beasts to be sought. Animals to be thrown afar and acrobatics to be taught. Distant voices bleed out into the absolute, into the nothing. A large, growing, fantastic, visceral circle of violence, this is your destiny! You devour this life! You devour your own mortality! And hesitate to descend — yet you do. Server in the mind, blind to the light. Blind to living in a dream! What you have if I save you is as much a dream of life as mine!

"There are certain superfluous influences that lean over life — prey upon it. You will find yourself a job against the normal aspects of living. Awaken from the lifeless monotony. It will be concealed, this energy. It will not be impressed upon your face. Something will be found from others — a parody of man, of nothingness. Severity screams out from your eyes. You have a spirit of another inside. All you need is a catastrophe of assistance — opportunity will open up like poison flowers. You must have a universal indifference to all things positive, to all things great and grand. Distant echoing through the air will be your reason. Your quiet, reflective nature, mocking good against all who seek decadent affairs. Your skin will be innocently discolored. Your nails will go unnoticed. Red flags wave for you when you walk down the street, settling into this new power, this new array of living. In a certain spring without friends, without laughter, over dinner you will fold the blue and brittle night against your chest — feel the oneness of this saga, tell crowd-stories of spring to no one and whispers of hours left beside cherry blossoms with your dead mother — the quiet serenity of autumn cracking against your walls.

"Should the day come let you take a wife, know that she is subject to the space I provide for you, like a glowing chrysalis yet to be shattered. Should a child be born of this union, among black stones and urns its tongue will be split, its ears manifesting slime. The eyes, unreal. You will await the hour of his death without words. Only stones piled against the breast that you have lain there. I know what it is to feel the stone of death against your heart. Open your face to me as I have yours, into the keenness of death, the origin of life spilling out of this mouth into you. I bring about the dawn, the room, disease, the breath of the mother. With hands pressed against the world, I will follow you forever, beyond time wrapped in dry seafoam. Do you wish for me to help you now?"

# of marble and mud

"Good sister, wrong me not nor wrong yourself."
—The Taming of the Shrew

THE windows will be the first to go. Then the walls, the bones of the walls, the ashes. Rotting skin touched by pale violet light, the scents, the birth of flowers from toxic soil. A great curtain from the sky will fall down, draping over the memory of the black tree. Instinct rises, the heat of the world, in mansions, in men. Today will be grey-dark, marble, and mud.

The place where the house stands was chosen with particular care, to avoid prior habitations and the potential for eerie nonsense, as Helen attracted such happenings wherever she went. At times, Vanessa questioned the strain in her relationship with her sister. The volatility. Then she remembered that blood would always be, and carried on with her preferred state of living.

The storm. With no television, no radio, no means of measurement, she can't know what time it will arrive. Only by the creeping darkness of the western sky can she imagine that it will be later tonight.

The great "Palace" Parsis, under the black globe. Not a palace at all, but her home, glowing faintly as a spectre of what was once a spectacle of libertine living. Imagine, the happenings in this strange town! In those days she would have found the neighboring haunts unmanageable, but in *this* age there is reason. In *this* age, there is rest!

The stairwell. Both doors, top and bottom, have been locked. A single candle lights the space, illuminating only her marsh-soaked shoes, and the occasional passing tail of her sister's mouse. That hideous creature, Mendelbaum. A dwarf shrew, flitting in filth about the house as though it were welcome.

All that remains in the house of Helen is her scent, though it is masked by the pungent gloss, newly painted on the staircase.

Disquieted by the moan of gusts, she sits, she breathes.

A theatre of pain it is, to dream without sleep. Images. Constant, assaulting images! Her fragile sister, now swamp wraith, hovering over the muck in eternal indecision over her predicament. She assumes this, caught in the tendency to assume when one has inflicted circumstance upon another in bad faith. She watches and listens, warmed by the ever-cooling rays. Vanessa sits in contemplation of Helen's body. She calls her sister, not Helen, fearing some supernatural stirring should her name ring out into the distant night.

Helen's eyes were bright and full of waiting. Her mythic glamour disgusted Vanessa. Her beauty, a shimmer of honesty in a house built by fiends. Helen too-often took to reckless wandering, getting lost in the tedium of the marshes, accompanied by an invisible court of creatures.

Engrossed in a singular reluctance, the labyrinth of the night, disbelief sets in. Met with supernatural claims alone, Vanessa listens, and misunderstands.

She didn't want to take care of Helen anymore. Her nightly jaunts into the wilderness had grown exceedingly tiresome. In the company of wolves, Helen was without weeping. So Vanessa allowed her to continue. But what of allowance, in sisterhood? Is it not obligation to watch over a younger sibling with the delicacy and attention of one's own child? Or is it duty to only warn, to nudge, to temper? Should one temper beasts, spirits, or wistful women?

After reasonable hours, the heaviness of walking through dense muck becomes a tiresome chore. At the moment of indifference and a swift turn back towards the house, a delicate globe of pale light lingered by Vanessa's left cheek, grazing slightly before shooting off into some uncharted distance.

The looming magnificence, painted by nature in black, sent pain through her heart. A raw, metallic scent disturbed her nostrils, as did a peppery haze that gathered on the surface of dense, bluish mud. She stood before the great black tree for the first time.

The orb circled overhead in a mockery of revelation. Exhaustion, the discharge of the evening, snaked through her, filling the empty space with deep aggravation. Still, she could not find Helen. The world disappeared in the omnipresence of the black tree.

Doubt filled her, wondering how she may find the area again. That doubt would soon be a distant memory. One look to the skies would reveal another natural abhorrence. All winged creatures, birds and bugs alike, would sway outward over a single patch of dense forest in the north, meeting again after traversing a semi-ellipse of strategic avoidance. All save for a single, coal-black owl that appeared out of the strained aether, shooting straight down into the mist with the age-old security of an expected familiar.

Are there witches in these wetlands? The spoils of their dark methods?

Vanessa slid a cold hand over an enormous root, protruding from the muck. How can it live? In wetlands like this, it should have drowned. The roots are exposed, though they must run deep. Logic cannot accommodate the existence of such a thing, but it lives, and ages beyond the comings and goings of the landscape.

I feel my life when I love, more so than when I'm loved
But this is not to say that the latter is not needed
It is a gift of excess
Rarely expected, cherished on high
As something I may not deserve
But wait for with the patience of the soul.
–H

In one instance of decorative chatter that left Vanessa humiliated in important company, Helen expounded upon wisps of light, lanterns of the supernatural lurking in bogs and swamps and all such soaked earth. A fire grew in her as she spoke of them, a rarity when she found herself among others. Each wave of exhaustion dipped Vanessa further into cynicism.

"Fireflies." She spat, tired of the esoteric nonsense.

Helen sat upright.

Vanessa shook her head.

"You'd be wiser to fear water snakes, my dear."

"I don't fear *them*."

Annoyed, Vanessa gathered herself and approached the old oak bookcase beside the great window overlooking the marsh. She continued listening, as Helen mentioned the orbs as being young boys doomed to haunt the marsh, or spirits of stillborns, or unbaptized children caught between heaven and hell.

"In Ipswich? Please." Vanessa spat. A dark look flashed across her sister's eyes as she continued. "I believe we have, at least, avoided the stain of sorcery."

Helen smiled faintly as a dim glow pulsed in the distant marsh, visible from the polished window.

"Have we?"

The faeries of nature know no lesser landscape than this. They crave the rainbow soil, rearing o'er the moonbeams. Not this muck, this gloom.

Without wings, they strut with a measure of grief, the Eternity worm gauging their anguish, weaving frenzied fortunes through mortal horns.

> They will have their ending, and I will have my peace.
> This is the way of things in the dark world.
> Blackness crowds failing eyes, and I
> See myself a memory
> Holding hands with the girl who shares my name
> Whistling in the darkness
> Sighing as I die
> And am born again, as water, through the hollow hills
> All is still in memories of wickedness
> I built myself there, in the well of shame
> Tasting life, as poison, to remember

How good it will be to be
Myself again.
–H

Vanessa can't put the dream out of her mind. It is living alongside her now, undeterred by reality. A sorceress of decrepitude, sinking inch by inch in the shadow of the black moon. She watches her, an elemental agony sinking into her long-dead bones, stirring up a new, virulent death. One that recognizes the conditions of her first expiration with an absence of earthly reason. She is not the sole wraith doused in the muck. A wind turns north and stirs a corpse of a different age. No — dozens of them. Fragmented. Dear lord... children. Infants! Mangled bones suggest deformity in every case. Long-dead bodies. Long-dead souls.

Dark deeds made porridge of sapphires and buried them here. Darker even are these deeds of menace and mayhem, a grotesquery of animals rising from the farthest untold reaches of the marsh. A heathen porridge of snakes, insects, and vague writhing creatures, amassing on the surface of the wetlands, a menagerie of warning... How can she see them? Sense them? These are not true senses! Vanessa is still in the stairwell. The pungent odor of the wood gloss makes her head ache. Mendelbaum continues to scurry past her feet.

I once stood as a beggar before the might of Autumn.
I walked into death's garden with the tenderness of the age.
Delirium struck – gold, purple, orange, yellow, blue!
Heaven hid from all when shown my teeth,
With ages sealed in red dust.
–H

Tiny carved hollows in the railing. The cascade of the steps — a delicate, wistful drop — a cryptic elegance that stood apart from the rest of the house. Nothing else, the wood, the marble, the furniture — nothing else was that black. Not even the dense darkness during a night of storms. The ornamental detail in the wood was immaculate. The golden fixtures at the top and bottom, striking, eerie, familiar...

Helen was distressed.

"Oh no, you couldn't, you shouldn't!" Angst soaked into her bones as her hand lifted from the black rail, a gesture seen only when one dips their hands unconsciously into the remains of the unjustly deceased. The tree now existed solely as the immaculate ornamental staircase in Parsis, a pretentious construction that didn't even fit in with the décor of the house.

"It's already been done, Helen." Practical reassurances. Helen's light dancer's body leapt unconsciously to escape the psychic odor of the tree's remains.

"All that is left is the gloss, and then, we will not speak of it again."

Her eyes grew wild with despair. Helen slowly stood upright and lifted her eyes to the space above Vanessa's head. Overcome by uncomfortable air, Vanessa succumbed to the bowels of her fury.

"You stupid girl, come to your senses! Your *true* senses!"

"This is evil!"

"I should tie your hand to the rail and whip you for saying such a thing!"

Tears of fury slipped down Helen's cheeks. Tread a worm on her tail, and she would turn again. Vanessa's fear of her sister was alive in her. Helen lifted her hand so strangely that Vanessa lost herself in that very fear. Her hands latched onto Helen's shoulders and thrust her down the staircase.

She didn't make a sound beyond a sharp inhale at the start of the fall.

Her body, with grace, plummeted down the steps. From Vanessa's vantage point overhead, her body seemed to float, a mangled heap of pale flesh and scarlet lace.

A luminous festivity it is, to die without attention. Without circumstance. To float off into an immediate darkness, the bells of a familiar street becoming warbled mumbles in the distance. If such dreams are to erode a hole in Vanessa, in the stomach, or farther down into the gut, she would not be offended. Such a retribution would be easier than all this waiting. Helen's scarlet dressing gown was removed carefully, burned without care. The silk ribbons in her wildly curled tresses, snipped away and cast off onto open flame.

With supernatural strength, Vanessa carried her sister deep into the tangled mess of the marsh. A dull, pressing instinct in her ribcage compelled her onward, towards the jagged remnants of the black tree.

Tired eyes wandered over the faces of punishment. Corpses, unobserved, over the fragile passage of time. The bliss of heaven glowed in some invisible high ground, beyond the sheath of screams in the quickening place. Weightless, invisible flesh crowds behind her. The Palace Parsis in the murky distance. The splendor of eternal night growing cold — cold in the depths of her bones. She placed her there, as quietly as in her crib. Rocking her gently, quiet-sick sister. Her figure, dimly lit and clothed in a billowing white gauze befitting the most delicate of angels, sank down into the murky depths of the marsh. Bodies, crisp and icy blue, stirred. Their frozen, mummified remains intertwined in some heathen embrace that knows no sound or memory but those of death.

The waking dream comes to Vanessa again.

The black tree stands still, in a desert of sound. A heathen wetness ebbs, feeding roots. The swamp wraiths gather, sprinkling dust over the blue muck. It begins to rise more rapidly.

An unfamiliar woman, in a long-forgotten kind of gown. Figures in black, holding books. Torches. Herbs. The tears, the helplessness! She is forced to swallow the yellow powder and pushed into the muck. Her face scrapes past one of the tree roots jutting out from the water. Blood pours down her neck, each gush of fluid timed perfectly with the croaking of hidden toads.

Bundles of cloth are unfolded to reveal deceased infants. A dozen other women are dragged to the muck at the base of the tree. The gouging of eyes, slashing of throats, disposing of all accursed flesh! Bodies, one by one, fall to the great, dense slop. There, the world trembles. There, the horror of the marsh becomes magnified. The great tree, once of an innocent color, grows blacker and blacker, fed by the flesh of the accused. The burden of history takes possession of Vanessa, in the stairwell, dream-awake.

Helen slips back into the accursed half-water and presses tired feet to the nothingness below. This is she — divinity marked by softness, and elemental whispers from the deep. Her mouth slightly open, tongue to terror, she trembles. The muck has come to her lips.

Stillborns, deformed children, mutated animals — a tree that was not black upon birth. A tree that changed course, as it soaked in the dense darkness of betrayal rooted beneath.

There have been witches here.

Might their very footsteps have passed over the land before the house was erected?

Half-swallowed by the scene at hand in Vanessa's waking dream, Helen grows earth-tired. Desperate and alone, she descends into the cosmic recklessness of hope. Her mouth pulls back against the wind. Vomit dribbles lightly down her chin. A blind eye sweeps over the dagger of eternity. Contained almost entirely in the depths of the muck, her head still hovers slightly above.

I am great and I am nothing.
The disease of eternity lives inside of me.
Blinding time, the dagger of intention
Wills me to move forward and move on
There is a seat to take above all movement
Seeing, breathing life as life again
I think of these brief moments at the end
When all has spun to spirit threads above me.
–H

She rips her face from the glistening lips of fiends and sees the dead world's dawn. This is the waiting place of fallen dreamers. The place of dismal recompense. Of slights. Vanessa fights. She will not succumb to the haunt of waking dreams. A solemn phosphorescence breaks out from the dying house. The storm grows. Helen, far from her, dissolves — a dream of meditation in alien light.

In the height of dreams, I want what is not meant to be. I have come again to the place of pure perception.

I forget the meaning of all things and bask in the eternity of not knowing.

I assign nothing with the vanity of consciousness I possess, only by some cosmic misstep.

With human eyes, I see nothing, know nothing. With the eyes of eternity, I no longer have to know.

–H

It is guilt! If not a pure and unquenchable masochism that led Vanessa's hands to hurt her own flesh and blood. She will beg Helen for forgiveness.

She will hear me!

She will forgive me!

She is mine and I am hers, and blood will be! Blood will always be!

The storm has not yet reached full malice.

That isn't wind! That is her gentle knocking on the door.

Here, Helen! I'm coming! I am opening the door!

The door opens.

Her body is torn to shreds by the swirling remnants of the decimated house, awash with broken wood and a sea of blood, strewn upward by a peculiar wind, decorating the grand staircase with the scarlet remnants of human life, bloody flesh and bone splinters and dust, lit by the single fading candle at the center step, the delicate patter of Mendelbaum felt by her unending consciousness for as long as the stairs may stand.

No one will tear them down.

For a moment, the faint sounds of a tired owl echo past the window. A flash of darkness speeds by and leaves with equal swiftness, off into the gloom of night and the great dark marrow of the marsh.

the visitor

"I'd rather be up there: around that stone
The fires blaze, they have begun;
The crowds throng to the Evil One
Where many riddles must be solved"
–Goethe's *Faust*

AIMEE loves "Rookie Swallows." The pounding of the opening riff. That melt-your-insides, wet-the-inner-sanctum drive. Every time she hears it, she tilts her head back and takes a swig of the rotting air. Blue veins in her neck pulse to the pounding of the drums *boom boom boom.* Miller watches a drop of sweat roll down her chest through the haze — liquid pink. One more puff, one more go around the turnstile...

Rook withdrew her primal instinct just in time. The clock, a mangled menagerie hosting crystals and creatures of a thousand tongues, sat atop the husk of the last living tree. Time stood still at an unknown number. The beast of dreams, drowning in the exquisite linens of the hypnagogic realm, swayed to and fro to the rhythm, strumming its abhorrent instrument with a sickly lust. Its unearthly materials were unknown to Rook, though it had the look of a bone harp, with delicate strings of forgotten flesh. Its long orange sleeves, lined in peculiar bronze-threaded loops and dangling blue beads — porcelain delicacies with mirrored shards betwixt the rim — scratched the strings of the archaic contraption, descending into a deeper growl — a tone doused in the desires of the depraved.

Rook worshiped the sound. "If only I could remember such sounds in my waking hours."

Her flesh sloughed off her bones, rolling through the sand in circles. Fragile sprouts shivered out of hiding as the flesh nourished the ground, collapsing back into nothingness as it squirmed its way back up her legs.

"We make only so many allowances for visitors." The beast's dreadful lament continued. Rook pressed on, as her eyes rolled up her spine and over her skull, securing themselves back into their sockets. Her pixie-like features restored, raven hair cascading in delicate waves.

Vegetation was a mere memory, save for the shriveled vines atop starved monuments, powdered pollen searching the air in desperation for soil to nest in, haunted husks of trees, wisps of life screaming out into the eternal dusk. Low-lying fires flapped silently. Sands cascaded down stone slopes, hissing quietly into the oblivion of the deep. The terrible valley called out to them, its frozen darkness wailing generously at the rippling edges of their hearing. This was the Afterworld in peril, wasted, rotting, reaching for the vitality of the waking world. The thickness of its thirst growing broader, more ferocious by the hour, though time had come to a standstill. Long-feared beasts lay withering under black pillars, newly docile, moaning alongside the rhythmic plucking in a different tune. One of desperation, of hunger. Rook ignored them, preoccupied with her own affairs.

"That song would change the face of Rock 'n' Roll."

The beast smiled, dreadful-odd features stretching, barely visible in the depths of its hood. Rook saw the reflection of the gilded haze on its fangs. That, and the troublesome gaze of eight entirely black eyes, darting back and forth between herself and the strings of the unearthly contraption.

"Have you not enjoyed your lessons?"

The last of Rook's flesh slithered back onto the bones of her left hand. She lifted her fingers in front of her eyes, examining them as one would a moth sipping its final air on the end of a toothpick.

"In dream transfiguration? I have."

The beast set down its bone harp and stood. With a height breaching fourteen feet, it cast a cruel shadow over Rook. The heavy fabric of its robe dragged in the violet sands.

"How might such a feat, in life, be received?"

Rook laughed and lifted her hand in protest.

"It couldn't be."

"No?"

Rook looked up into the hidden face of the strange life form. There was little to be deciphered there. Nothing but crooked shadows.

"Might I journey, as you have, to another realm, and find myself useful?"

"Not as you are."

"And if I were as *you* are?"

Rook hesitated, unsure of the now pulsating eagerness coming from the towering figure. She felt a threat rise up as if from the ashes of the firebird — ever present, oft' unseen.

"You would offer such a thing?"

"I would give you the song, Rook."

Her eyes lit up.

"For what?"

"For human life."

In the dream, Rook had taken pride in the melting. Every night in the throes of hypnagogia, her skin bubbled, sloughing onto the ground with a sickening *plop*.

"As masterful as any other," her host would declare.

The grounded flesh rose up, climbing the sinewy stalks; a dreamer's bones. It took form again, as clay would in the hands of an invisible sculptor.

"And this is what you call transfiguration?"

The creature, in shadow, nodded. That was the first time. But things had grown darker as the venture continued. In her waking hours, Rook found herself more fragmented than her prior Dreamland excursions had made her. Magic no longer yielded to feverish eyes. Not in this grotesquery — this mosaic of the elemental profane. There are spirits —

malignant worms seeking out the vanity of a dampened heart. This is where they lay their coils. She had not yet known such an anxiety. The perilous floating that breathes deeply from those earth-forsaking doors.

On the night of the dreaded proposal, Rook woke up on the floor of her trailer, soaked in sweat. She propped her elbows on the back of the mangled futon and raised her body up, kicking away empty beer cans. She looked over her right shoulder to see Miller passed out on the floor. Rook propped herself up, allowing the tingling in her lower legs to pass before hovering over to her clandestine lover. She could see only the faint highlight of his auburn hair cascading over his scruffy, elfin face. That, and the ebb and flow of his chest; a shallow sort of breath pattern one might expect from an aging junkie. Wasted talent, incarnate.

On Rook's bed sat the hateful tome he'd taken to in the preceding weeks. To say he'd become enamored with the old book was an understatement. He'd been utterly consumed by it, though she understood not a word and only took to her own imaginings in the study of the archaic illustrations. She wished herself a woman of wealth, and wondered if she may have had a chance at deciphering the material with the proper training, but this was a fantasy far from her grasp. She put the thought to the back of her mind and closed the book, taking it to the trunk in the nearby closet and locking it away.

Rook returned to the bedroom and reached down for the empty whiskey bottle under Miller's arm. She tilted her head back. One, two drops. Not enough to make it a mistake. Not enough to make her less guilty over what she was about to do.

Rook held the bottle over her head with both hands. She couldn't look. A lifetime of memories passed by her trembling eyelids. Years wandering without pause, striving for the dream. Trying to make the music they always wanted to make, and somehow never quite reaching those heights.

Miller would do the same, she thought. *He'd do the same.*

She closed her eyes, bringing the merciless weight of the empty bottle down on her lover's temple.

Apart from the brutal gash on the right side of his head, Miller's body was in fine condition. Rook kneeled over him, half delirious, soaking in the depths of her predicament. She'd been taken with this guilt for nearly half an hour when a coarse shiver ran through Miller's corpse.

Rook pulled Miller's blood-soaked clothes from his body and dragged his frail figure onto the bed. She was overcome by a clouded vision of a wind-swept mound, where temperance failed and all emotion burst forth in a rhythmic rocking. The wailing rolled on, unhinged. Her tears dropped into the gaping mouth of the slaughtered innocent. Then came the slightest quivering in the jaw. So subtle, that Rook didn't notice until a tremor made the corpse's head lift off of the sheets.

Rook stumbled back, falling over the futon. Miller's body stood erect, speckled in blood and the excesses of an intoxicated evening. He turned his head slowly to Rook, eyes flashing with a familiar, lingering gaze.

"How do I look?"

Its voice — his voice — alarmed her. A new musicality. A tone much deeper, more assured than that of the former flesh-holder. An operatic confidence that the real Miller never possessed. Rook blinked in succession to convince herself that she was, indeed, awake.

"Like a dead man."

The Visitor smiled. His teeth, so unlike Miller's originals, were whiter and more pronounced. A few of them even had the subtle hint of jaggedness Rook remembered from the Afterworld.

"What now?" Rook asked, staring at the gash on Miller's head.

"Now?" The Visitor pulled his hair back, examining the structure of his new face, an exercise in vanity quite fitting for his new incarnation. "Now, there is work to be done."

In the mirror, the Visitor lifted a finger to his eyelid and flipped it inside out. He laughed, marveling at his human form with various pricks and pulls to the lips and cheeks. Every stroke of his hand over human features was a victory. Lips, eyes, skin. So much skin. So much hiding beneath.

The Visitor rolled open the drawer underneath the sink and pulled out a pair of scissors with delicately carved handles. He lifted the blades to Miller's long ginger locks — his locks — and began to cut. Tufts of orange clumped together on the floor. He didn't stop until his hair stood only inches from his scalp. The cupboard, filled to the brim, became a wasteland of knocked-over tubes and emptied packets as the Visitor searched for a way to achieve his desired look. At last he came across a translucent gel. He poured the goo into his palm and ran it through his hands, enamored of the slimy sensation it produced. He swiped it through his hair until his head held a crown of orange spikes.

The Visitor had taken to Miller's carcass with glee. He wandered to a nearby parlor for a gold piercing in his right ear, complete with a single blue bead cascading down from the discount metal. His clothes he fashioned as a form of earth-bound convalescence, marrying the richness of his dream garb with the sleek, erotic decadence of 18th-century menswear.

Rook leaned back against the brick wall, a jagged edge of concrete filler scraping the shoulder of her leather jacket. She shifted, uncomfortable after the events of the previous night. The band loitered outside the studio, passing around a crumpled joint and kicking up pebbles with their beer-soiled heels. They were as reckless and unbecoming as children; laughing and picking moths from the brick wall.

"Where the fuck is Miller? Did he get up this morning?" Troy approached Rook.

"Yeah, he's coming."

"Maybe he OD'd again." Nomi brushed the long purple dreadlocks out of her face. Her slashed white leggings contrasted against her dark skin, drawing the eyes of all. She punched Nate on the shoulder. "Call him!"

"No need." Nate nodded his head down the street. The Visitor, in his new Miller suit, approached — carrying a guitar case.

"What the fuck happened to you, mate?"

"Holy shit..." Troy shouted.

"You're late."

The Visitor turned his head to Rook.

"Right, sorry, sorry. Shall we get to it?"

Troy held out the dwindling joint.

"Want some?"

A dark energy flashed through his features. The Visitor put a single hand on his chest and bowed slightly.

"I have no taste for grass. Only seas of flesh."

Everyone laughed, save for Rook. She remained as glassy-eyed and weary as she had ever been in the presence of the beast of dreams. Blown away by his temerity, but unable to lift a limb against him.

Rook hung behind as everyone filed into the studio. The Visitor looked to her before stepping inside.

"Might you go before and invite me in?" he asked.

"Is that some kind of protocol?"

"A courtesy. As offered many a time to you in the Afterworld."

Rook's instincts were screaming.

"And so I ask that you humbly accommodate me."

Rook pushed herself off the wall, staring into the eyes of her former host and teacher. She stepped beyond the threshold and turned around.

"Coming?"

"Miller."

"What?"

"You have to say my name."

"That isn't your name."

The Visitor's eyes flashed. Rook's stomach continued its violent churning. She paused, encumbered by the loss of power. Panic set in.

"Will you come in, Miller?"

The Visitor smiled.

"It would be my pleasure, my dear."

He entered the studio and walked past Rook. They brushed shoulders in passing, sending Rook into a state of hallucinatory anxiety. In her mind's eye, she could see a pink mist falling over the intrepid hillside she had known only in sleep. An impossible weather bleeding into the landscape, birthing new green coasts and a resurgence of vitality in the place of dark wonder.

Anguish was her predicament. And now she feasted on a broken treaty of the Afterworld, fluttering and writhing with these visions like the loathsome ghouls found beneath those ancient lands.

A dingy white pickup truck parked across the street in that moment. A woman got out, dressed in all black — stunning in the way some women are when they are centered in existential calm. Perhaps that is why Rook loved her so much.

The band, confounded by Miller's newfound swagger, continued to stare. In his prior incarnation, he'd barely been able to stand long enough to finish a set. They attributed this colorful resurrection to "some new-fangled pill concoction," looking him up and down and unable to fathom how such a transformation had taken place overnight.

Rook entered the recording space, soon followed by her partner, Aimee. Her excessively long copper hair, pulled back into a loose braid and swimming with black velvet ribbon, cascaded dramatically as she leaned on the doorframe. A knot formed in Rook's stomach as all eyes turned to Aimee. The Visitor, thus far subtle in his morally questionable aspects, grinned indelicately as she set down her purse in the far corner of the studio.

Rook looked from Aimee to the beast in its charade, panicking at the pulsing light in his eyes. The Visitor jumped over Nate's amplifier to stand behind her. She leaned down to Rook's ear and whispered.

"Are you feeling okay?"

Rook looked up, shaking herself out of a momentary trance, but could not answer. Not in front of *it*. Aimee looked up and across the room, getting her first full glance at Miller since entering the space. He had since shut his mouth, but still examined every inch of her without censure.

"Miller?"

Nate and Troy laughed.

"Miller lite, no longer!"

Aimee walked over to him, a laugh of disbelief escaping her. She put a hand on his shoulder. The Visitor looked down slowly, examining her fingers with the same erotic tension he had so often emitted in the Afterworld. Rook shivered in terror.

"Moving up in the world, are we?" Aimee asked, weary of his newfound confidence.

"We would try our best."

The Visitor peered into her eyes, intensity brewing. Aimee stepped back, suddenly overcome. Nate broke the awkward moment, crossing the room to grab his drumsticks from the counter.

"So, you said on the phone you guys had something?" Nate asked.

"I did," Rook answered, resting his head against the wall.

"And you like the shit?"

"I do, indeed."

The Visitor grinned and opened his hard case.

Aimee leaned beside Rook, resting her hand on her shoulder. Rook couldn't stand, overwhelmed by what she was about to hear. Her memory of the song had been muddled. Many a morning she had beaten herself up over not being able to remember the subtle nuances of the melody. Rook wondered if she would feel the same sense of awe in the living realm, being exposed to such a thing. She would not have to wonder much longer.

The Visitor took out his new guitar. It was an elaborately carved masterwork, with an appearance more like a decadent utensil than an instrument. Familiar, but only to Rook. It had unique features as an earthly object. Purple, with flecks of orange, a black neck, and curious gray pickups. Their eyes widened.

The Visitor took the gold wires under his fingers, sliding them through with a sensual fluency. He plugged in. Rook froze, preparing for the onslaught. Then came the first chord.

The overture was a quiet orchestration. One of abysmal melancholy, growing ever stronger with each passing whir of the strange, ethereal guitar. It grew, shriller, louder, until the rapturous pounding of rhythmic muscle overcame the subtleties of the beginning. It had theatre, poise — an erotic tension so powerful that one would feel as if a serrated wheel ran back and forth over the genitals, ever-satisfied with a cosmic teasing. Every second thrust the listeners into a seemingly eternal orgasmic fury. A lustful thirst unquenchable in the land of men.

The outro commenced. An exhaustive depression hovered over Rook — an omnipresent cloud. The others struggled to recover, overcome by the mad genius of the composition. As the last whirs of the denouement spun away from their ears, Nate spoke.

"What do you call it?"

"The Flesh..."

The Visitor looked over at Rook before continuing.

"...of Rookie Swallows."

"Haha! Fuck. I like it, man."

"You got yourself a hit," Troy added.

"*We* got ourselves a hit."

The Visitor looked to Rook, who glanced at a far corner of the studio, unable to meet the eyes of the abomination. He played through the first chord progressions again, allowing the resonance of the foundation to speak for itself. Rook heard strange sounds emitting from the amplifier. Prone to dithering, she talked herself out of her fractured senses.

"Well, fuck, man, let's get that track down!"

They scrambled to set up the recording. The Visitor stared at Rook, smiling. Aimee rushed to her bag and swung the beaded handle over her shoulder.

"Aim?"

Rook stood up, pulling her aside. The Visitor made an effort to eavesdrop, despite Rook's pursuit of privacy.

A cloud passed over her consciousness, forcing her into a state of melancholy. Rook had his answer, without even a word. He'd known her long enough to know she wasn't ready to discuss it.

"I have to get a sculpture to the gallery by seven."

"I'll see you tonight though?"

Her hand was shaking as she held the handle of the door.

"Yes, I'll be over."

She glanced quickly to the Visitor again, who had retained his inelegant smirk – though this time, without baring his teeth. Aimee left the studio.

Rook stood and stumbled over to the Visitor, keeping her voice to a whisper.

"That wasn't the song," she started.

"Rook, of course it is. You're not remembering properly."

"You cut parts of it. Changed it."

"I assure you, it is intact. Recalling dreams in full is a difficult business, you know!"

Nausea overtook her. Rook left the room quickly, fearing her condition would intensify. She found solace in the filth of the studio bathroom. Slamming the stall door behind her, she sank to the floor beside the toilet and held her head in her blistering hands.

Light is scarce on paths of frost. Rook embodied this dimming of the mind as her limbs trembled in the liminal torment between man and corpse. Her energy had been stripped away as her soul rocked in the arms of the Visitor. The weeks had failed to go by without the maddening creep of some new and radical pathology. Her legs were bloated and carried the gruesome hue of a swamp's untreated muck. The muscles in her neck all but disappeared, giving her skin the premature shriveling one might only see in an insect left to die on heated pavement. The fevers alone were monstrous, leaving her with the sense that she was being cooked from the inside.

Desperation crawled across her bones. Through silent investigation, many a time Rook found herself outside the door of Aimee's bedroom, taking in the sounds of erotic entanglement. Rook knew who was in there.

Her senses suffered. Her tongue found no pleasures, her vision blurred. Only Rook's hearing experienced a peculiar increase in astuteness, sending her into a frenzy of fear whenever the slightest fly lifted its leg on the nearby windowsill, or when a quiet worm rolled nine feet beneath.

The first time the song played on the radio, Aimee and Rook were driving down the highway. Rook pulled over to call Miller, ecstatic. Rook got out of the car and vomited down the embankment. The blisters on her arms and legs opened up with a release of translucent plasma. The growing rashes on her head screamed in the faint heat of the October sun.

The song was released as a stand-alone single locally, experiencing one of those momentous bursts of popularity reserved only for the most synchronicitous of recordings streamed through alternative channels.

Then came the album, and the success therein, all centered around what was the band's new image — a Miller-centric postmodern Gothic, bursting with the sexually charged art sensibilities of long-dead rock stars and Expressionistic artists. It was what Rook had always dreamt of, though now she wished it had remained elusive — and untouchable — as she also wished of the mysteries of the Afterworld.

"Seeing faces in crystals? Monsters on high, are we?"

The clanging of bracelets and the creaking of leather made Rook's ears pound. The noises grew louder and louder. She squirmed at the ever-present grip of the Visitor's hand on her shoulder, even when she stood far across the room. In flesh or in spirit, it was always there. An eerie sensation lingered — skin melting under his grip — but there was no such thing as dream transfiguration in the earthly realm. She had been assured. The Visitor cast his leg over the damask stool, resting the ornamental heel of his bizarre golden boot on the fringe. Flanked by four young women in various degrees of undress, he raised his hand to the sky, beckoning a drink from one of the new studio attendants. Rook crouched in a corner, overcome by the sickly nausea that rose up every time a scourge of memories was cast down upon her.

"Rook and her fantastical mind!"

Aimee rolled her eyes. With a wet cloth in hand and bag of ice in the other, she kneeled beside her.

"Give it a rest," Aimee said.

She ran the cloth over Rook's forehead. She held her wrist gently and took a deep breath, taking in the sight of her girlfriend for the first time in months. Aimee looked like a completely different person. Her long copper hair had been cropped in a boyish faux-hawk and bleached platinum. There was barely a spot on her that wasn't tattooed with some nameless archaic symbol. Even her clothes were different, no doubt chosen by the Visitor in his strange fascination with the intersection of modernity and menace.

"So, what was it that you wanted to tell me?" the Visitor shot at Rook, unimpressed with her deterioration — and jealous of Aimee's attentiveness.

Rook finally looked into the Visitor's eyes and was overwhelmed with the deep-seated fear of a woman who stands before those to which she is forever indebted. There would be no equality there. No chance for resolution. Aimee thought Miller had taken to wearing reptilian contacts, but the new, diabolical slits were something of a reaction to being in the living world. He hadn't the luxury of excess that eight eyes gave him in Dreamscape.

"The official tour schedule came through today," Rook mumbled.

"Oh, how wonderful! Where will the opener be?"

Rook's head pounded with each syllable. She couldn't remember what she had read only moments earlier.

"Boston, Providence... Somewhere north."

The Visitor walked over to her and pulled her head to his mouth, kissing her temple fiercely. Rook wanted to vomit, but held it in.

"Tell us about 'Rookie Swallows!'" a nearby groupie chimed in.

Miller straightened his collar and smiled, preparing to expound.

"It's about a man who finds himself a wanderer between doomed worlds. He indulges in one, and saves the other. Temptation leads him to make quite the mess! If that doesn't have the making of a tragic masterpiece, I don't know what does."

Rook imagined digging her fingers under the lower ridges of the Visitor's skull. A breathless pause, and violent yanking — blowing threads of flesh in crimson spouts. This was the bitterness boiling over. The resentment and shame, that she had not a name of glory. She had nothing to call her own in this world. Fame meant nothing. Aimee was lost to him. She faded from view as harshly as she had entered into it.

All I can see is death, upon the arid hills of the Afterworld, Rook thought. *Will they see it someday, too?*

The uneven shadow cast on the opposing wall horrified Rook, who took to closing her eyes as the Visitor whispered something unintelligible. The cadenced pounding in her head overtook her. Rook listened to the devious language slither in and out of her ears until her head tilted back against the wall. She lost consciousness.

Pink mist, pink mist...

Rook's eyes jerked back into focus, knocking her out of her dissociative daze.

"What is it, Rook? Speak up! We're on!" Nomi yelled.

"Don't play the fucking song..."

Her mumbling had grown tiresome to all of them.

"Not that song... Not the song..."

"She's trashed, let's get on before she blacks out." Troy went onstage. Nomi followed.

"You..."

Rook bent over, retching. The Visitor walked over, cupping Rook's chin in his hand and lifting her face to his. He said nothing.

"Leave her, she'll come out on her own."

The Visitor released Rook's face from his grip. The screams poured in from the other side of the curtain. The Visitor went out onto the stage with the rest of the band. Nate hung behind, reaching out his hand and placing it on Rook's back.

"You're a little old for stage fright, sister."

He handed her a cloth to wipe her mouth.

"Come on."

The blinding lights increased the sensation of being cooked alive. She approached the microphone. The Visitor stared at her with a strange elation, but she could not meet his eye. The whirring began. Rook couldn't bring herself to focus on the overture. She hummed, an inaudible hiss to break the deep horror of the approaching rhythmic onslaught. The audience, a pool of rebellious youth and has-been rockers, punks and Goths, artists and angels, were falling victim to the melodic ecstasy. Rook could see it through glazed eyes.

The Visitor's pink button-down shirt, soaked in sweat, stuck to his gaunt form, wrinkled beneath glittered suspenders holding up black pants. His coat, an immaculately distressed velvet masterpiece in delicate orange, was quickly removed and thrown offstage, the shredded tail and high collar folding under as it hit the speaker beside him. A glint of light reflected off his earring. Rook looked away, her senses overcome by the frenzied happenings accosting her from every angle.

Glory days in golden haze
Down the slumbering steps I creep
Skin and bones and flesh they raise
Rains of death, the spell we keep
and time forgets me as I sleep...
and time forgets me as I weep...

The swaying of limbs, the flashes of flesh. Women and men alike removed their clothes and took to pressing their bodies together in a hypnotic rhythm; a new and obscene ritual that only the sound of "Rookie Swallows" could incite. The thrashing of arms, the waggling of tongues, the clattering of genitals. And then, a single face was illuminated — a harbinger to a devil's denouement. A melted face of flesh, indecipherable amidst the muck and mortar. A frozen form so like Rook in the land of dreams, in the throes of flesh-melt; the highest form of dream transfiguration.

Rook turned to the Visitor, who continued his bestial playing. The penetration of souls, so unnatural in its delight, continued. The glittering of unknowing eyes brought Rook to regretful tears. Then, everything stopped.

A thousand faces, gone. Frozen in time, as glitter and ash rained down. Their flesh sloughed off onto the floor — their bones crumbled like the remnants of rotten books. Rook's mouth opened to scream, but no sound would escape her. The song was not playing. The twiddling feet of flies could not be heard. Not even the turning of worms.

The knot in the bottom of her throat choked her voice away. Rook shifted her eyes. All else was drowned out in the darkness, one of the spotlights — moving seemingly on its own — illuminating the Visitor. He sang the last chorus in Rook's place, in an octave he had not used before during his earthly incarnation.

A deep shiver ran through Rook, intensifying the choking sensation. The Visitor smiled. Without warning, Rook was accosted by visions of the Afterworld.

The hills were born again. Green swept over the landscape, blowing sands into the sky and toppling the remnants of the ailing age. This organic expansion spread with a great, shining might across the Afterworld.

Unnatural ruins, as sliced veins, bled vegetation into the distance. Great temples beamed the light of the new, nourished moon. Every beast once hailed as horrible stood again in this assessment, from the penalty of slumber, reborn under the pink mist.

The violet sands were gone, the ancient clock, ticking again. The green illumination of the bone harp, held in the hands of some darkly magnificent host, welcoming another friend, another fool into the Afterworld. She had come to know and abhor this place. One last

glimpse of the audience let her know that they were living. Their faces —
no longer marred by the horror of dream transfiguration — were still
intact. What she had been afforded was a glimpse into the future world.
Of the fate that the song would condemn them to, as it had done to her
over time. Rook knew at last what would become of all things.

This was the song in its proper form — an indelicate means of
melting man into feast, into fertilizer. It was terrible. It was magnificent.
It was...over.

Rook collapsed where she stood, holding her chest. The guilt of her
predicament overwhelmed the last sliver of her dying mind. Rook's heart
pounded out of sync with her breath — louder, harder — every beat
falling out of pace with reality. A piercing pain shot from her chest to
her right arm, then to her back, then her gut. She lay down slowly on the
stage, closing her eyes.

The crowd looked on in shock. The Visitor set down his guitar and
walked over, leaning in to examine his crippled band mate. He ran his
middle finger down her mutilated face, accumulating the fetid grime on
the tip of his long green fingernail. A few of the patrons in the first row
climbed over the barrier as the Visitor backed away and returned to his
microphone. He switched it off. Nate yelled at the roadies to call for
help. The band crowded around Rook, astonished at her lifeless form —
the unrecognizable mess that was her features in exodus. They had
become a puddle of nothing, sloshing back through her eye sockets and
onto the stage floor.

The Visitor took a swig from the flask he had tucked into his pants
and looked on with indifference. An unkempt roadie, upset and
shaking, approached him as emergency personnel moved past the
distressed fans. The Visitor held his gaunt hand up to the light.

"What's that?" the roadie asked, watching a single drop of
discolored blood roll down the finger of a dead and long-starving Miller.
The Visitor's eyes flashed, the image of a lush, moonlit hillside visible in
his shrinking pupil.

"The new face of Rock 'n' Roll."

the land of other

IT began with a pull of the heart into lands unknown. After a period of unrest, when a flickering of muscles descended into a tiring ache, I awoke to find my higher self staring at me from across a distant plain. An imprint of an earlier life, reflected in form and function beyond the veil of some perilous Afterworld. I took in sights through sunken eyes, where senses scattered like so many pebbles on the breathing shore. There was no dignity in this, though it came with a sense of awareness, often reserved for newly fragmented minds. Delights descended into the cold illuminated waters. I succumbed to the peril of the gale overhead. The floating glory opened up to me in that moment and dissolved, like morning mist. One really can venture out too early before sunrise. In that way, I hold a never-ending regret. There are no sights free from the garnish of torment. Not anymore. No sweetness free from the grip of the ice, choking me with the burden of these remembrances.

The doctor serves as earthly foil in this labyrinth of mourning. I tell him to take my blood and he resists, like the other clever emissaries of his profession, so attuned to modernity that they forget the methods of their predecessors. When blood drips from my arm, I feel my son floating in the distance. Would they drain me of all, I may even see him breathe. He didn't understand that this room was not a place of healing. That there are no such places — for fish, or men, or the worms beneath...or me. That there was little hope, in any fashion, of returning to that precious former life.

The aging doctor has flown from the tarnished pages of elder collections. He has that look of playful deceit in him. He isn't without humor, though I scarcely listen. If I dare to, I will surely turn to a deeper madness. When in an exile in the mind, essential learning often includes the muting of voices in that way. To avoid the onslaught of some sick and grinding anger, that others may live around me in a lesser horror. That blindness, shaken from me by the pitfalls of a dreadful life, does not go unmissed.

I tried to explain to them the meaning of it all, but only murmurs fell out. My nostrils flared, taking in the sweet but useless fragrance of spring. "There," they said. "Her senses are in order." Not knowing how pronounced they had become. Not knowing the torment of their persistence. I hate the smells. The sounds. Everything that touches my eyes and mind in this oppression.

Something lit up the trees. I can see it from my place by the window. An electric pulse, flashing over the leaves, igniting them – flickering embers of ivory and grey spitting out over the road. These are the living things, neglected by my former mind. How I long for their absence.

I remember nothing of the slide. Nothing of screaming wheels, or broken glass. Nothing of the coldness in the water. There were no sirens, or seraph songs. Only blackness from the bitter corners of my mind. Some would be thankful for the absence of thought in such a place. It became only another pain for me. I am without him now, and without the memory of his loss. Not permitted to see his body, as he had been interred by the time of my waking. These are the misfortunes woven for me in a life without warmth in equal measure.

It had been an age since I'd last seen the horse. A crooked white stallion with wavering legs, long dead and buried on the island off the coast. They'd shipped him off after retirement, as they did with all tiring beasts. My morning thoughts wandered to the old shore. Memories are rarely provoked without reason, and this was no different. The upstairs hallway was thick with the smell of him. Hay, hair, and dirt from the stable hit my nostrils as soon as the bedroom door opened.

The old beast was making his spirit rounds, I was sure of it. Images swam through my head, decorating the hall with the length and breadth of the great stallion. He would have been a snug fit in the narrow space, with hooves clopping on the tarnished wood and either eyelid grazing the golden walls. I thought it fair to yearn for the shore we found together. Perhaps it might have been a novelty for Oliver to see the waves from that place. The smell came as a comfort. One in a silent row of moments we sometimes long for. Those that arrive before or after some great upheaval, like a calling card from lands beyond logic. I never believed in such things. Not with my old mind.

Oliver despised beaches. His only memory had been the dreadful scurrying of bugs in the granules between his toes. They set off a creeping panic that he had not yet forgotten. It took a great deal of convincing for him to accompany me to the old shore that morning. Ice cream and the attendance of several toys strewn about the back seat. That, and the repetitive telling of his favorite rhymes, though I sensed he still couldn't understand them.

In retrospect, I could have examined the odorous hallucination with reason. Logic is latent in the early hours for some, and I'd had a night devoid of rest. I might have noticed the window left open a crack and wondered if an unkempt vehicle had gone by. Or street sweepers – the most likely scenario – though I didn't hear the hammering of those engines at any hour. Did the damned horse matter so much that I had to wake him?

Few venture out to take in the sights of a winter ocean, though these were the times I found myself, in earlier years, galloping atop the old stallion from cove to cove. Oliver hesitated, watching winds blow sand off the dunes. I picked him up and carried him onto the beach. Soft gray granules, unusually large when one thinks of sand. Like cane sugar, tinted by the reflection of the overcast sky. The water shared this hue, without the ebb and flow of waves to break the palette. This was decidedly not the way I'd remembered it.

What are oceans without waves, but canvases of defeat? I didn't see it in such a way then. Oliver looked out to the horizon. Discomfort surged through him. He held on tighter to my chest as I shifted. I thought of the old horse again as the expanse of the shore came into view. I'd imagined the beast roaming there, and of his life on the island several times over the years. The white coat of his youth faded into ivory, at home in the high grass and salty air. I'd known a rider or two who paid visits to their steeds after retirement, but never felt compelled myself. Why? I figured the old horse was sick of me. I'd taken him by one too many hornets' nests and snake pits in my day. The old beast seemed relieved, the day they loaded him up into the truck and hauled him down the street to the ferry. I knew I'd miss him, but it wasn't as though they were shipping him down to the butcher for stew meat. He'd have a good life out there. In a place, deep down, I knew I'd never see.

The waters were so still. Unsettling to the point of birthing an uncanny rumbling in the gut. I held my son in my arms, taking in the smell of salt. It had the look of a storm's premeditation. Dark grey clouds loomed on high over the farthest reaches of the sea. Oliver turned his head stiffly, looking out to the horizon. His heart pumped heavily and I felt it through mine.

I'd had my tastes of floating shadows over harbors in that town. Those of the heart and the mind. Seeing was another thing entirely. My eyes were once watchers of sterile valleys and subtle cries. Not the twisted abhorrence of a primordial earth.

Oliver gripped my neck, not remembering the wound of worlds pulsating there. I dropped him in the sand. Sea foam flowed through his boots. Gloom churned inside of me. He wailed – more so than in any season of retribution that had come to him. He shuddered. I bent down to lift him up, cradling him close to my chest.

"Will you take me home now?" His eyes were wide, like one who has seen something untimely and rotten in an ill-fated distance. The nostalgia had been enough for me. I carried him away without glancing back at the sea, or the darkening skies above.

Mother, Father, aunts and uncles hover over me like a vat of flies, always aching. A breathing pustule, living, without life. I struggle to sit up, to the dismay of seeing every hand held up against me. They don't want me to try. "There is no honor here," they are saying. "No dignity in this defeat."

I sit weakly, warring with my brain in a loathsome time-after-matter. My mind sits on an elevated platter, above the somber plain. This is the first stop towards the Land of Other. The gift of the senses to that unknown, endless realm. It watches on, even now.

That gentle stirring of a familiar world lives on in me, but I am betrayed by these wistful images. I knew them once, though long has passed. Of water-bleeding skies and scarcely hidden rays. Of differences which made us all ashamed. I could sing a song of passing to the light, but there are no ghosts here. Only cruel shapes, draped in blackness, mingling at the edges of my eyes. They've been around since sanity's fall. Since the error that ripped me back into this detachment. I call out into my own oblivion, a vault of tired silences. Might these shadows make a meal of me and sweep my hands from ground to sky?

It'll never make sense to my mind. Not the way it sees now. Not the way it remembers. The pit of blackness remains, as dense and unyielding as it was the first time I tried to think back. But, there is something. A thick, penetrating whir — the sound of the raging deep.

The greater fear, living outside of the shame of this, is the idea that I will someday remember. That like the flight of birds from some crippled birch, there will be everything, strewn out before my eyes. A canvas of horror, untimely in its arrival and altogether maddening. I can see myself there, consumed by the final breaking of the lucid plane. Words will come out in dribbles of spit, mopped up by whichever poor soul is tending to me at the time.

His father hadn't the stomach for insular burdens. He called me Asphodel, like Bronte, only for the pain of knowing. The child was mine in blood and in duty. In this, there was no regret. Only a silent sadness for a boy without a father to hold dear. This is not a world for such a loss. I would have thought the man better than all that. On the morning of the accident, my neck still bore the hollows of his hands. There are fears hidden in the hearts of aging men, more unstable in their dreams than the young. There were no vows, no declarations between us. Only careless passion in unconsecrated beds. There are shameful acts in this age of glass, but these acts leave only a faint imprint on my heart. They gave me the gift of eternity, and the strength of knowing when one must leave. In this, regret was an unnecessary expense.

I miss him in the thoughtless hours of aching, but it is the most subtle of my pains. He'd remembered the trinkets of my desire. Gentle potions of lemon and ice, blue roses, black orchids, timeless books, and gentle touches to those ugly places inside that birthed a long-sought stillness. I will only have the memory of that passion. Only one kind of love lasts on earth, and it doesn't manifest in brutal marks upon the body.

How does one describe a state of longing for the world in which they live, as though it were eons past the final desecration? When toes are jammed in sands of the present-day and the sun burns on overhead? The first sensation of the Afterworld was the onslaught of a side-swept gravity. Unable to stand or step by earthly measures, collapse took the place of wobbling.

I began to see the world as he had seen it. Senses gave way to a glitch-laden abhorrence in the eyes, ears, nose, and mouth. Light rays swooped down like falcons over a shadow of the deepest shade. The formless chaos, watching from the Land of Other. This world after death, after destruction of the mind. In these days of retirement, I hope to find the door above to other kinds of silence. A gateway. A place entirely different from the abhorrent wash of tragic life. The Afterworld is here, not there. This must be understood. These visions of torment rely on the burdens of earthly eyes. On the dreadful cadences of a ruined brain. The Land of Other is another world entire — exalted and eternal.

I remember hills of gray on the horizon. The call of tyrants young and old, descending. We think of a division of placement after the dark pull. Directions, held in polarity, as we think of good and evil. I think rather of a captain's wheel, steering through a boundless sea. There is no direction in which there is no destination. No place bound by duality. A betrayal of omens shocks them, on the brittle earth. They know not the Land of Other. A land that is no land at all. A oneness that is a multitude.

In the dawning hours of my predicament, I looked for my son. In the shadows of the distant plain, I felt him wandering. How I fear these unknown worlds. In those times of watching and wondering, a creeping revilement caught inside of me. Shame has wings that fly out to the darkened skies, telling dwellers of our black and earthly gales. There is no love like love with doom above us. I would penetrate the sky with arrows, bleeding the guardians of the Afterworld. Lifting the veil from rock to rock, or cloud to cloud if only to know that he does not linger there alone.

I sat with him in circles, on the porch, bleeding yellow jackets from the rickety banister. Rocking him on my knee, singing songs of cheer in the dying season. This would be my strongest memory of him, had I not learned the unpleasantness of the addled mind. The post-apocalypse in bloom; my organs, shutting into a rotting phase of limitation. Something he had known all his life, but I had no idea of it. He had received the rejections inherent to such a being. The stares and taunts. The sickening judgments of man, given only to those unfit for lives of tradition and conformity. I protected him the best I could from all of that. There is no horror like hateful eyes upon that which is yours.

I look around my bedroom and all I see is rupture. Decay put on hold for me, waiting until I get out of bed to collapse in a pile of dust. My swollen feet stick out from beneath the lining of the comforter in yellow lace. The bureaus are a similar muted yellow, delicate and ornamental in their design. Not unlike the décor of affluent girls, chosen by their mothers in preparation for their inevitable arrival on society. We were no such family. Every piece was inherited from the street, though we made no note of it.

They've removed the photos of him from the bureau. The closet is shut, so I know nothing of the contents. If they remain, or were sold to afford my convalescence. My sore attempt at rising resulted in a comical stumbling. A humiliating feat for anyone at this age. I am not as I was in the womb – human, or altogether assimilated. My brain grips the eons of a strange, infirm ever after. I will not be without it now.

The perilous Afterworld becomes me. I am its fate and it is mine. The whistling whirs, the purity of time falls to ash. I am the bringer of such brokenness. I am the deceiver of such days, godless in this sea of static. No enchantment leaves my lips without severity. I would fling insults at the skies, should I not fear the locking of the door. I would surrender myself, bodiless, to the wars of a thousand worlds. The gaping wound, my heart, enveloped in a gossamer glow. The pains began to leave me, and I knew I loved them. They were all I had of my son within my grasp.

Is there enough of him in me for them to let me through? If I am as he is, vulnerable, gentle, willing? Thrust before the door to be taken or left? Would I see him reeling in the distance? Would I see myself in his eyes ever again?

The first steps are the heaviest, and as ungainly as in youth. I wonder if the shadow watches as I pull myself up from the ground. I had the strength to hold a book today. To turn three pages without help. This is a new luxury.

With healing comes clearer memories of these bleak days. On the first day of my waking, I was carried into the house by two. Bodies shuffled around me, tending to my every need, though none had been asked. I was voiceless for a time. In those first hours in the protection of what had once been sanctuary, I cowered under a floating blackness, hovering over the window facing the road. When I dared to look at it directly, a blinding light flashed. With a shrill crackling, the shadow was absorbed by the world, as one might see a tissue slide off a table. I am not without the feeling of these watchers now.

If flames were to ignite the distant sea, would this torment fall to the eternal blackness? Might I wander aimlessly in the horror between worlds? Permit me to the Land of Other, in pieces. The part of me beyond the veil lives on. I see it there, beside him, in the shadows.

There, where toothy blossoms grow, and blue trees bow to touch the earth in secret places. Where hearts grow as soft as flowers inside every breeze. Where spirits kiss to kill the wounds of earth. Heal his wretched ailment there, before myself. Cleanse the spray of poison from his veins.

A thousand visions fill my bones with aching. A thousand voices breathe into my mind. Here I stand petrified before the twisting gorge, torch in hand and held to spirits, without means to measure time or torment.

If it is guilt that brings us to the door, then what might open it, but the hope of absolution? We are such creatures, still. Warring in mind and body, thirsting for the drink of eternal forgiveness. There are those who would seek nonconformity, or abnormality, as a decorative veil. It is these I wholeheartedly wish to avoid. They don't know the grip of the Afterworld, or the manner in which the parallels sway. In the twilight hours of my ruin, shadows grew in rooms beyond living vision. The majesty of the ethereal footman. The mysteries of men without flesh. This new and abhorrent earth after loss. With arms outstretched to skies of red, out to the higher world. The place where these hands, these eyes, this mind may come to a living rest. This is the song I will sing as I fly out of the shadow place.

I find myself endlessly afflicted. Of domestic duties done and accounted, I am the failing mother. I could not digest toadstools like honey. I did not want to live in the shadow of his exit, but even in this, there is a frail rebirth at hand.

"You can throw a pearl ten fathoms deep," the doctor said. "It will not return to the mouth of its mother. Down, down it will be cast, into the crevice, illuminated only by the angler's lamp."

I lean back in the agony of hearing, in the glow of the northern window. My deep red hair falls to my sides. Seemingly unnatural in shade, but the shade of my birth, nonetheless. Stray sands glow copper in the faint light bleeding through. This doesn't bother my eyes. It is subtle enough – a delicate glow, reminding me of the onslaught of days. In these cruel months, I found my only hope in the strange shapes of light dancing on the windowsill. Doubts as to my healing melted there, like so many waves left behind lessening storms. The doctor, satisfied with my progress, packs his bag for the final time.

"You will heal completely, young lady. Whether you want to or not."

Today was made for walking, and the silent crawl. I can shuffle my way around now, and thusly have led myself down the slope of the garden to the patch of tiger lilies. All have shriveled to nothing in the August heat, save for one in brilliant bloom. With eyes struggling to adjust and my scalp beating from the rays, I touch the petals as though they are the first of earth.

Fighting the urge to pull off each finger, planting them in the soil so that one, through flesh extended, may he grow back to live as he lived. The sun on my head is death. Death, unbridled, unhinged, beating. I stand tall in the onslaught of the rays. The dark pull to the endless night carries on. I return wearily to my confinement, without defeat. I have seen and I have felt the rays again without succumbing, and this was glory enough. Tonight I will sleep, and I will sleep in peace for the first time.

It's here now, gliding towards me in the gilded pre-dawn. The world at the stage of breaking — underwater, frigid, and real. That is the most gripping part. The authenticity, as though I had lived and breathed it all in full awareness, never having forgotten a detail. Logic plays with me in this, I know. There are regrets interwoven in this realization. An aggravation that only I will ever truly understand.

My hands still gripped the steering wheel. The bones of my fingers jutted out like the metal armatures of those too-tall buildings that leave us without light. The fragments locked my hands in place. Scarlet waters mixed with the eternal blue, surging forward amid glass through the shattered windows. In part, from wherever my head had been torn open by the crumpled metal. The greater portion of blood - that of a body, entire — came from the back seat.

Survivors of great horror often speak of the angst, the apprehension, the instinct within that warned them of their impending experience. They wade into the story with descriptions about the sights and sounds, and with maddening optimism spin it in some way so maybe even they can handle reliving it all. Am I guilty of this? Without question. But of this moment that was hidden from me for a time, of the progression of horror within seconds in a descending tomb, I have neither the will nor energy to describe. I will say only this: that in the twilight of your doom, when that apprehension kicks in and the tolling bells bear down upon your senses, I hope that you will be spared the remembrance. I will not speak of him as he was in that moment. I will not speak of that moment in time ever again.

I grip the white fence, flakes of aging paint crackling in my palms. The sun is bright; an oppression, still. Even in this, there is a seed of becoming.

The Land of Other beckons. I am not ready. I'll stand in the light until then, in wait of a distant shadow. It is all more bearable now. In a simple dream of quiet oceans in the sky, I will wash ashore. To each hand drawn upward in refusal of my way in, demanding I fall back, I will bury a laugh beneath my breast. There may be no honor here — but there will be.

as unbreakable as the world

[East of Bohemia, October 27^{*th*}*, 1919]*

THERE is something amiss in this paradise. Something rotten. Such things don't do well with subtlety, do they? That which is wrong erupts — a loathsome pus, as waves — over the usual.

I can think of no fair way to describe them. The people, that is. Being too polite to mark them as mutants and too stupid to break them down to a science. I would rather evade them in the dark corners of the village streets, not taking into account the compliments thrown my way. Admiration built on sand. Praise for something I have not done. Have never done. Will never do!

You feel yourself walking into it. Like the last time, though there were lesser horrors then. Lesser burdens sitting at the rim of the conscious mind.

"What a performance!" a woman said to me, throwing auburn hair around, unnerving in the wind. What the hell was she talking about? What performance? I had done no such thing. I watched her face and saw only a shriveled garden. Dandelions growing out of crumbling granite. Weeds aplenty from the toppled tombstones. A graveyard, then.

"I think you've mistaken me for someone else, madam." I backed into her cart of lemons, sending them rolling in every direction. Oh, the embarrassment!

"Pardon me!"

"What of the lowly lemons! They mean so little. So little compared!"

I tipped my hat and left. As I crossed under the sign, heading north, I heard her yelling,"...as unbreakable as the world!"

I am in dread of life, though perhaps wiser for it. I think myself worthy of this mess, my dear, and therein lies the true predicament. My work in other realms of living, now worthless, in this huff — this thoughtless departure. I could not live in such a way any longer. Could not bear the weight of worlds upon me, not being enough for myself, let alone you — you! Oh, if the affliction of thoughts had not been so damning, I may have stayed. But one life of failure is enough. To inflict my losses upon two would have been absurd.

Love pain — a thousand deaths on a silver morning. Where the place of birds holds still, and I discard a nighttime of fear. Your face will be indifferent to my death. My will is like that of a fly, broken by the hours trapped in a covered window. My anxious imaginings lead me to a crippling notion — that all of my eccentric leanings have amassed on my skin in some grotesque art of a disease, only visible to these outsiders. A whimper escapes me here and there at the very thought. So I've been dissolving my health in bottles, as the devil dares.

I feel corrupted in the hour after your letter's arrival. It means I am to be as I am, eternally. I ran to unmapped places — burrowed in the rime beyond your reach. And here you reach me, all the same! I can blame only Mother, who has her way with all things. She knew of my passing through the mountains and of the little villages sprinkled through. This explains the overwritten postage and despairing aroma of the envelope. Obsession brought me to the letter opener, and I gripped the thing with the gloom of ages. I imagined a long memo, word-for-word, announcing my significance. My worthiness! Surely you could not refuse me then. Not with such praise...

I watched the flames die out amid that fantasy. I could not open it. To the inferno it went. Which is perhaps why, with guilt, I sit and write to you now. I am too angry, still, to wish you well. Despite my reproaches... Oh, what of them! There is not enough paper to speak of them now. Only enough to say what must be said. I think the pen more honorable than the knife, but ten times as useless.

I met the first of them before sunrise three months ago. A barrel-gutted woman, pockmarked and haggard as any village rat. She smelled even worse, and from five meters, I gather. Her left eye bulged a mound of dulcet blue, a sweetness endearing in a creature of such disease. I continued walking after the first vision of her — a reflection in the bakery glass-front. She followed, muttering under her breath, "*As unbreakable as the world!*" A river of drool flowed down her neck. I quickened my pace and left her to her nonsense.

How might I have seen this town in passing? Far differently than in residency, that is for certain. Keepers of black corn, festering farms, rotten gourds, dead hens, hostile specters, landlords of gloom! That which is peculiar lives and breathes around me. In this way, I recognize the foulness — the familiarity in myself. It is a comfort to them — and to me, at home at last among the mangled. There are no distinguished gods in this delirium. I sleep in my chair like a slab of granite. I spin in this world — my senses limited by the air. The greatest ocean is there, you know. I grieve not of heaven, but of the travel to.

Many a time have I choked back a cry. In this condition, I surrender to the urge. The sound is swallowed by the thickness of the air. I look out the window at the fog, the constant mass of undulating green, watching as though the song of my sorrows has been carried beyond these walls.

I know I am a menace. Not for lack of grace, but lack of trying. I would do nothing on an evening of beauty, and you despise my slowness. I am not ashamed, in this slowness. Not in the same way, here. In a dream, you held a globe of white to me, and I cried what would conceal a mountain in gold.

What use have I, in an idle universe? I think myself the most loathsome insect. So loathsome, that it cannot be seen as itself. That it must be seen as human, to hide the depths of repulsion. But perhaps this is an insult to insects? Might I look down upon them so harshly, as I do in the mirror? The insult is a perfunctory one. I think, rather, that I should liken myself to excrement, seeping from the dead. The putrefying muck of organic atrophy. I see myself in this, clearer than any living thing.

I am repulsed by my existence, to be sure. The face, the limbs, the long, droning sounds and midnight murmurs. I would end this dismal existence, if not for the parallel attribute — cowardice — which keeps me preserved as this humanoid filth, wandering to and fro among the adjusted masses. It is not only cowardice, but a growing indifference to all things. The pain lives, but the cloud of living has reached a density of delirium so thick, that I cannot see two moments ahead, or behind.

Is this the precursor to the stage of rot? The final bow before succumbing to one's own abhorrence? I wanted only to be touched. To feel myself vital in the arms of some foolish girl, too strange in her own way to notice that she cradled monstrosity in her arms. You were not fool enough for me. This ugliness of the body and mind, this body of ill health — deserving of death more even than the most horrid of healthy sinners. What might be changed in this cage of capture? I sit in contemplation of the eternal sleep, not in rage or melancholy, but in reason. If there is no life beyond the halls of hell, then I am spent already in this grievance.

If I had known myself unafraid for but a moment, I could find some beggar's hope amid this ruin. The repulsion creeps and crawls. It dominates over all, and I can't be rid of it. I can't be rid of it! Not until I am touched, even in defilement. Not until I am seen in the depths of repulsion and loved there, all the same. But I have been. I have been...

The hallmark of my stupor — discontent — boils up as rot within this flesh. This much was expected, as it is in any other place. Why should it be different here? There are no fumes of fancy wafting through the alleys. No bodies of temptation swaying there. The bell tower clocks the hour in and I am haunted by the passage. So little is accomplished, day after day, sitting in contemplation of one's uselessness.

There is an elemental tedium buried in this. No — a mechanical one. The motions of a day have come to that dreaded consistency, though only in the confines of the house. On the street, I may as well be wandering the corridors of another distasteful world. The market boasts the flavors of the nation, but in it, I find only mold and misery. In another life, I would think something of the scene at hand. Rickety carts of strange fruits and vegetables, twisting flowers in unnatural colors, the decadent shine of ribbons in every crevice and corner. In this new way of living, I can think of nothing deeply.

This old town would make no declaration upon my vanity, or contempt for former places. It would make no effort to gut me with words of my ineptitude. They are unsuspecting of my lovelessness, perhaps. I still wear the ring on my finger, to keep the dear girls away. Not of vanity or pride, but of precaution. I cannot bear the loss of our togetherness. Not yet.

A spell of youth visits me in these broken hours. A memory of moons glowing white on tall grass — and you.

It seemed to me always that in schools where children were allowed to play, there was a neglectful anguish regarding their education. With age, I know my younger self to be a fool. It is, rather, those that play who find the absolute in existence. Who are privy to the sightless sights and soundless sounds of life. I know this now, living among these people.

The second who made a mark upon my condition ambled forward a month after the first. A dwarf of sorts, with no limbs to speak of — naught but severed humps. He had a joy in him, despite these ills. Or perhaps because of them? There is no way to tell the burdens or bemusements of the afflicted by expressions of the face alone. I am at least not fool enough to believe in that kind of nonsense. He echoed the phantom sentiments of the young lemon-seller, and more.

"What a performance, indeed! Your presence, your passion, your power... It was as unbreakable as the world!"

Performance? What is this rubbish? My last performance was at the village fair showcase back home, where I played a silent leaf falling from an oak. I was six! As unbreakable as the world? What did that mean? Is the world not breakable? Are we not wanderers on a fractured globe? Are we to believe in eternity on a rock? Am I to believe all of this praise? Is it not frivolity? Is it not...false? I haven't done anything! One should not be made to contemplate philosophy in the streets!

My tragedy is that I have done nothing worthwhile in this life. Have I measured your disappointment properly? Or is it my own discontent, projected onto you? Though even that which I have done — in it lives a piece of me that may blossom, after death. To someone, I may be a sort of something, someday.

The gilded halls of horror, they call heaven. Places that would press an ugly face, a tormented body against the world and leave. The deformed are divine displeasure, manifest. This is my assumption today. But might I say the same thing tomorrow?

I know of no thing as horrible as this — features in perfect symmetry, concealing a mass of agony. Would I pour the acid down and geld the face of this deceit? Might they think me less glorious, less threatening? But they do not see me that way at all! They are, rather, welcomed by the charade. This is the proof of my presumption. They know me. They know me as one of them! Can see the rot inside. Feel the heart that bleeds a thousand lies, the gut that bleats in anguish, blackest blood!

It is some phantom genetics to blame, to be certain. That which conceals the abhorrence within was written quite some time ago. A comedy of horror from unmeasured time. Is this all there is to it?

There is always the belief that opinion is the right of the home-born, not the traveler seeking sanctuary from his failings. Who am I to be, to speak, to breathe? Here, of all places, where I expose my wretchedness to those who have not asked for it? I pity them, for their exposure. But they take it as no insult. This is infuriating. I would rather hear the honest confirmation of such wretchedness, not this mockery of admiration! They even have to devise some splendid event to thrust worthiness upon me. In the land of good Samaritans! Perhaps we should displace them, littering them about the world to uplift the spirits of the deserving. Leave the town barren, broken, alone. As I need it to be — my mirror.

These are not the afflicted, those cursed with divine displeasure. These twisted bodies are the blessed among us. Let us be truthful about it now! In this very moment! Concealing themselves from the able monotony, left to devise a theory of living alien to all, familiar to me. How might this be, that they hold a luxury of living, because they are betrayed by the lighter lives? I would not say it aloud, though the heart knows they would understand.

Horror is the freedom-soaked condition. You said to me once, "Do not be safe, be happy," knowing that true freedom of genuine living brought torches to our door. Another dream, my dear. You hold a fragile egg in your left hand, sliding those dazzling fingers over a lavender ribbon. *As unbreakable as the world...*

It is easiest to imagine the dark world in the brightness of a clear day. Where might a world be that hides from us the horrors of this organized wilderness? Poison runs as blood through my chest. Brought to tears in the vulgar act of describing, I would rather imagine us as art that walks on earth.

To those who excel in their pain, I marvel. I can only bring myself to stare at these ruinous fingers, the mice on the hearth, the creaking door...

You know me well enough to suppose that my first visit in town was to the small, unkempt library. There weren't many books, but piled pages, scrambled in such a way that I could nigh make sense of the mess. But this is the agony of the fringe, perhaps. Care is mistaken for gathering, but not in organization. What purpose might that serve, anyway? I mean to return to the old place and make something of the chaos, if only for amusement, or the nourishment of dreams.

I pair my vexations with lust, to my own demise. It occurs to me only now that I ask questions I may never see the answers to. Even should this letter reach you there, it takes a wayside mule, several trains, and all manner of motion to reach you from this hollow countryside. The journey forward will take patience and time. The journey back, nothing short of magic.

My cries are flares into a listless darkness. The dream returns to me — that of the weighted skin. Heavy, pulling horror in the form of phantom organs. I took to my scribbling earlier than usual. The heat of the fireplace pulsed into the parlor, the mice taking their place under the warm glow. The fireplace mutters to the tiny creatures on the hearth. I reach for my quill and find that my arm cannot take the weight of the gesture. It flops down on the desk with an alarming *glumph.*

I lift the arm with considerable difficulty, examining it for discoloration, bleeding, signs of decay. Nothing. I feel the air underneath, and hit something of a mass in dimensional exodus. Periled by this vile manifestation, I lift my letter opener to the winds and *slice.* Grey sludge appears in a line and gushes out of the air from the invisible nothingness. The faint outline of a fleshy pouch can be seen in the air as the falling sludge clots to a stop.

What am I to make of this seminal grotesquery? I awaken every night from this horror and am sick to my stomach. I flail my arms overhead with decided ease, to be sure that such things are held in the favor of dreams alone. They must be! But there was an oddity even in waking. With a single touch, I found a riddle of gold drops on my head.

Why might it be that when I am in no condition for folklore, such eccentricities are thrust upon me? I am completely alarmed by myself in moments, convinced that I hear the echoes of countless wicked throats. Then the silence comes again, and I am weary of the nothingness even more. Exhilaration is the vanished state of dreams.

Disclosures are plentiful before nightfall in these streets. The third encounter occurred during the first flakes of winter. I found my immortality one glistening evening, in the mouth of a mutant. He pressed his mangled lips to mine and I saw the fallen world. Fluttering tongues were interrupted by the flow of spew. The mass of this passion was spit on the opposite wall. It sprouted gossamer wings and, floating back to his formless hand, began the tale in whispers.

The cloud-capped valley, overrun with steam. Every globe set down atop a ridge of rock by birds, and she – a veil of smoke, a dress of red and yellow – leaves the world with arms set to the wind. A turquoise glove, etched with golden thread. A collar so vast it would not conceal a human neck, but a neck all the same. And these...strands of orange hair, like shredded silk, basking in the underglow of a waning world. One hundred dead faces in bronze, around the governing mirror. A glimpse of calm – blue oceans. Blue skies. Clouds of white – purest white. No screaming on the wind. An ebb and flow of eternal living. And the horns begin to sound...

"Horns?" I interrupt the fluttering mass. The man takes over the tale as it evaporates in the growing storm of ice.

"Echoing over the river, over the mountain..."

"Mountain?"

"The buzzing, the growing of the bells! The glittering womb burst open! Red smoke! Red smoke, everywhere! They shot smoke into the sky that numbed the wings of angels! Glowing tendrils, levitating! Bodies huddled over the water. Red smoke turns to orange. Closer to the end! The bodies! The womb! Thousands of them! Thousands and their horns, calling out! Calling out to you!"

"To me?"

"You awaken from your liquid sleep, walking from the womb! As unbreakable as the world! The glaze drips, a garb of invisible cloth. We know not your face, not then, but now!"

I am in the shock of contemplation, unable to follow his tale in real time. A slurring of the senses causes me to lean on his lump of a shoulder.

"As unbreakable as the world? What does that mean?!"

He leans back against the brick wall. I stumble, brushing my face against his chest. He thinks nothing of it, running a ghastly limb across my forehead. Gold drops. Gold drops.

"The wind was water in the other godless place. We sipped the air as sustenance, and then..."

Silence, for a moment.

"And then?"

"The sky split in two."

"And all were..."

"But we were not afraid, you see. Not afraid! It was as we are. As you are!"

"As unbreakable as the world?"

Thoughts of everlasting consciousness sit well with the Godhead, but ever more with the Devil. As I thought upon the earth and our timeless travel, he disappeared as paste into the cobblestones.

D

Is a veil cast over other lives? Are other worlds bursting with life in the firmament, hidden from me? Imagine! I do marvel at the thoughts of these extraordinary people. Why this torture, then? Why this grief?

Time is not a diamond, but a worm. These are not warlocks, but fateful souls, lost in their imaginings, as I am in the late hours. Might I condemn them for a dream delivered in the daylight?

I indulge them in their revelry. It is only a kindness to a wandering stranger. To a man who knows no home but the quiet depths within, perilous in their weight and worthless to this world. The utterly flattering and the foolish, I will keep for myself.

I can tell without being near you, and with no manner of seeing, that you are overwhelmed once again. Do not fret, lovely one. These groping tongues fall as shadows may, halfway back to the land of ghosts.

There is something to be said of me after all... A letter left in ashes, another on my desk. I will send this to you in the evening and that will be it. A quiet walk, then, on these cold, quiet streets. The faintest gaze of eyes on skies of black. They follow, chanting their words — a glimmer of a ghostly confession in their eyes. I will not hear them. I have done nothing in this life. Nothing worthy of such praise. Nothing, I believe, at all.

—Yrs

an account above burnside park

It is not with haste that I travel to the new residence of my onetime mentor. Something in the air is wanting, no — prying. Some devilry is abounding in these parts, I am sure of it; though I have not seen Burnside Park since I was a boy of eleven. Even the sky is a sickly green. Why he has chosen such a shambles to live in, I am oblivious. Perhaps he can enlighten me over tea, or a glass of wine. If the circumstances of his life have changed so drastically that he must live here, then something tells me I will need more than one drink to get through the evening.

—A. Marchand

I remember the lights of Eden, and the blinds that never fell. I recall the hearts of hours and the castles of black stone. Alone on rooftops, spotting silhouettes in open windows, watching for the water sounds to break. Sleepless on a night of death and shame; the happenings of my demented town. Forgive me, my old friend. My mind is not what it once was. I have taken to delicate pronunciations in the dark to account for my solitude. Elaborate, poetic phrases such as these — to make rounds at midnight was no sin, but beggars, never early, know the game. They know the dance of eyes that marks their deaths.

To watch such wheeling, turns, and terrors, Marchand, was a warning of such hellish tidings. The swaying flesh of harridans, unsightly, always naked at hours never slept upon...and children's filth so thick, their form is indecipherable. Everywhere these low and lilac-scented devils attempt to steal my light, but they won't have it. Not on this day, when I will tell you who came to see me after so many years.

I remember love. I remember it as something peaceful, and yet the wanting pain never left. That constant resistance of my mind — met with the insistence of my form. Towards her, what attempts might there ever be? This vision festers. Will I ever be at peace again? There is the clock...that echoing chime. One might think upon the gilded halls of yore and ask themselves in my house, "What age is this I have fallen into?" I fancy someday a passerby will ask, and I imagine I might respond with, "Oh, such an age of mice and men, sir. An age I brought about with my mind, which you may enter at your will." Then they would run, Marchand. They would run.

You remember her, don't you? I could see it. I could tell. You dropped the matchstick a tad too quickly on the iron set. Your wrist flicked with angst, your eyes shifted. You thought of her eyes, did you not? Yes, I daresay they were majestic. She stood by that very fire, you know. The embers lit up the violet in one iris, the other remained blue. Some faerie of the netherworld stood by my fire, and she smiled with the sense of light and darkness held only by such holy things of nether realms. I thought it queer, myself, to make such associations.

I gave her the kiss of death years before our last encounter. She tried so hard, poor child, to navigate her way out of my life. I told the child 'Good luck' and sent her on her way. Her eyes were the parting shots of daggers and I lay victim to their cuts. I knew it would not be the last time.

Just a moment, Marchand. It is painful, these recollections. The hurt is one of centuries, boiling up inside me. I cannot reconcile such a manner that I have fallen into. I cannot try to do so without much false expectation. What is it, after all, that darkens one's inner self, and leaves naught but hardened ash betwixt one's heart and veins? I am a fool of numbers, not of nights. How did I come to such ramblings of persuasion? Why do such tainted whispers journey up the stairwell to this place? I do not speak of the screams of Burnside... They are of the territory and shall forever remain. There is an understanding that we have of all that occurs beyond the lower gate. But the whispers from within...they hold the key to my gruesome secret.

If ever you cross a flailing dog in the street, I advise you to let it die. Such an encounter was the marker of my misfortunes, and I will never forgive myself for kneeling down and caressing its head as it perished. Sometimes, in the confines of my room after nightfall, I wonder if some demonic specificity haunts the airs of ailing creatures, waiting for some helpless Neanderthal to show concern. Perhaps such entities claw into our very souls as we observe martyrdom in wonderment.

Will it be tears of black or green? Just the liqueur, my friend. The order of the day, Marchand. We were swept beneath the rug, I think, long past midnight as the revelry commenced outside my window. Perhaps they heard the crackling of the juniper candle and thought it best to leave us. Perhaps they thought my guest was one of delicacy...that childlike form of beauty from the garrison...my heart. Yes, even I deign to laugh at such imaginings. Why, by heaven or earth, might she return, when the last image in her mind is of ash and blood?

I have not told you of that day, Marchand. I daresay I find myself caught between two worlds. One of candid chatter and delights of daybreak. The other, the twisted ramblings of a mind in hell. A dismal darkness of the night. This is what I am, sir. It is the causer of that untimely ruin they speak of on the streets. I am sinner, I am savage. I am the last to see the horror in these eyes. The mirrors, Marchand. They have lied to me. What once was a reflection of glowing white is now a sullen grey. Tell me, friend, what do you see in these eyes?

No, sir, do not rest now. Do not shut your eyes. It is not safe for such things. Not in this house. Allow me to continue the dance, Marchand. Remember my passing at the gates. As black as the gates of Hades were, or so I would imagine. As black as onyx, charred in that charlatan's sunken city. When I first touched her... Now don't get embarrassed, Marchand. She was quite ageless in the mind, and not a tad anxious. I had hoped she would be flattered, that one such as myself might deign to touch her form, to stroke her hair and feel her breathe a sharpened breath. Her heart beat through her chest and into mine. One heart, Marchand. One mind.

Thoughts upon thoughts raced through me. Indecipherable, at best. Words become hieroglyphs to a mind in passion, my friend. There is no vintage like that of the lustful soul. Man may never hope to consume something so tasteful, so elegant. It is the breath of the living that keeps my veins at ease. That pulsing from the chest denotes my pleasure, her pain. All things start and end with the beating. To be king of evolution must be a charming spot, indeed, to witness the birth of such rhythmic practices.

SIT DOWN, Marchand! Sit down. Be at ease, my friend. My revelation should come of no surprise to you, you are no fool. Out of thousands you were chosen by me, and though an unlikely disciple you have been, I did not expect you to act so rashly. I taught you better than that. I was about to say, "Good God," but then I realized, what a foolish remark to make. There is no god of earth that is good. It is but chaos upon chaos under that wheel of stars. Fathers killing daughters. Friends cursing friends. What is it but chaos that propels us into the world? I have seen things. Markings, signs of a presence. Sounds in the darkness. They are but passing cues of a dark dream in motion. I am led on by such enticements. Such blistering cadences through dim candlelight. I thank you for your ear, Marchand.

I hate that dismal look from eyes of toads; a staring wonderment begrudged by swamp-like growth. A carrion vein, it has, that wall to the North. That pulsating nonconformity that spews the blood of ages every night upon the hour of the wolf. Forgive me. I fall into fanciful imaginings so often these days. But the remembrance hearkens back to this — I may not have her. And such a tearing has fallen betwixt my forehead and my neck. One might think a drop of acid had taken refuge there. Markings of black and green have set into this skin of pallor, and night owls harp on it from the sill, in that detestable cooing. Nights of ominous rambling, and they are spent alone. But this cold air is fit for devils, and I walk with the patter of an iron hoof. These streets were made for wanderers of the storm. Wanderers beyond some forsaken realm of light. I am the night, Marchand.

I discovered something, deep in the confines of my despair. Something that in my wildest dreams I had not hoped. That is, the girl did not love me. I declare it to be true. And men in my position are in no fit state for false declarations. I should have known it, with her resistance of my curious limbs. The way she turned her gaze. The anger she felt when I reached out to touch her.

I would have had her, my old friend. I would have had her in my arms, and in one swift motion, had my way with her. I imagined it many a time, after hours. Don't think it vulgar. I daresay you had such fantasies, at your age. She knew nothing of my heartache. The death of Rosa, or the fires beyond Calibrasi. I told her nothing of the untold wards behind these doors of oak. Would she have come if she had known? For she did arrive, long after I affirmed my resolution of leaving her behind. Long after I had seen her last. Her hair was vastly longer...flaxen and shimmering like some doll in a seat of sunlight. Some forest nymph with eyes of blue. She sees me. She saw me. She saw me, Marchand.

Might we return to our conversation? Your distraction is unwarranted, and frankly, I am surprised to see such heavy lids upon that fat face of yours. Is it not enough that I might hear the screech of fornicating cats outside my window; I have to look across the foyer and see that face, too? Does my tale not dispel the woe of your own life? Look at me! This face, this torso, these hands! My mother remarked quite often upon them, citing the heavenly brush strokes of Magnasco. Might I have lived up to such classic form? Had not my mind twisted and followed forth my body, perhaps. Instead, the heavenly form migrated past me in the form of woman, and by god, it has done me in.

She said, "I can only imagine the worst possible reason that you would behave this way. I'm not here to save you." To save me. Imagine. Oh, she saved me. From that fiend they call life after death. What was purged on the floor of this frigid hole...was the very thing that lets one in that magnificent door of angels and men. I am banished now, Marchand. They will not let me in.

What I have yet to grasp is the manner in which the conversation turned. Her eyes were intense upon me. I continued my lament. As I pulled her deeper into that space that is the honesty of my predicament, I thought her eyes flickered in the manner of a wounded animal. Perhaps that is what drove my senses away... Something awakened that inner blight.

It did not happen so swiftly, mind you. As the nerves came running through my veins like volcanic beetles, I shifted... I asked her to leave. She was amenable to the suggestion. She had assumed my discomfort was some unquiet leading to my intimate approach. She was not wrong, not completely. Every fiber fought to keep my hands from her. It was sticking out from underneath her skirt, wrapped in mockery of black fabric...some slashed lace and thread that can only be described as a fish hook to the accoutrements of men. But it was not lust that drove me forward. No — despite all errors of expression, I was compelled by a very different intrinsic force. You see, it is not enough to consume by means of love. Don't be confused, my old friend. There is much left to touch upon.

Burnside is no longer what it used to be. In those days, upon a hallowed evening, one could pass the revelry at the corner where the iris plants flailed under winds of north. The chimes from Mame Lokken exceeded the rhyming of those dragging jesters, and what now falls to whispers was once loud exultation of man's triumph over evil. What new devilry is this, which has hushed the tones of angels under bells of dire gates? The pride of the city, Burnside was. The gathering spot of all that was holy in a place of tried ambition. It has led to this, Marchand. It has led to this.

With one sweeping motion, I may miss the mark and proceed into a tale untold by any other in this house. The room I rent, this limited space...it is the domain of rats. The sanctuary of beasts intemperate. I might have known it when I took the original tour and marked an odor of petrichor by the northern window. A scent pleasing to the masses, but a persistent haunt to me. It is the odor of thieves, Marchand. The scent of the blood sovereign, unchained from that heaving mass protruding from the infinite lake and boiling up into the very soil beneath our feet. Such fumes are found in this house. Fumes and fires... They have met this face.

What is it that has fraught your eyes with green? Is it my robe, Marchand? Forgive me, it is but a mockery of an outfit. A fool's attempt at looking like I have something to say. The lavishness of velvet and brocade. The darkness of the seam, hidden underneath the fold of ivory silk. The robes of a crocodile king.

Have you ever thought about what it is to exceed evil? Not to overcome it, but to embrace its dire avenue and somehow overthrow its dominant suggestion? Do you think it strange that I ask such things? I have thoughts upon the matter. Thoughts, because speech in times of great disorder is drowned by the horrors of activity. Just the screams that jolly up from the park demand so much of me. These wars of man in depravity conduct the orchestra... My mind is uneasy. It is as though the screams are a new silence; a new tradition. Any tenant over Burnside would say the same. If they dispute it, then they are one of that sickly order of men who cannot reconcile the coming of a new age. With the coming of steam, there must be bubbling in the cauldron. Am I right, Marchand? Might I refill your glass?

There is no tide worth turning like that of unrequited love. It is a worthy oppression, to say the least. The passion incited in one's veins, as potent as the most cryptic of Renaissance medicines, leaves one breathless. The tingling of the legs is my personal favorite. The manner in which they faint, and float as feathers in a sea of ecstasy; one can only imagine what it would be like to fulfill such desirable notions in the flesh. For the body may be a result of the mind, but what is felt in the physical circles right back to us. All things of love and passion act in such ways. It is the ungainly truth that such things also destroy us, and it is this truth that has brought me to the window. I call out not to any heavenly lord, for they have done so much for me already. I do not need recollection, or redemption. I have not thought upon miracles. These veins are of glass, since she left me in the street. This heart, as black as ash. No, this is no conversation for the Lord and myself. I went to the window in the wine cellar, and dug out the bricks that covered the ancient iron. Beneath the foundation of the house lies a forgotten room, untraceable and derelict. The old window looks out into some unfathomable darkness, but if one deigns to wait until the witching hour and tap three times on the broken glass, a small flame will grow some great distance beyond the pane.

I wonder what it is that the devil devours? Is it the eyes of charlatans, or the blood of virgins? Is there a feast of the foes of man, or a toast to the corruption of the innocent? Such oppositions keep me up nights, Marchand, ever since my arrival at the lower gate. Who would welcome filth to such a place? My body is for rot, beyond the mud of tongues and feces.

We first met years ago, you know. Only for a brief time. A few weeks of casual encounters in the park, and nothing more. That was before my excursion to London for the new position I secured under Lord Archer. You remember. You saw me to the carriage on Benefit Street that March, after the great snowstorm. The snowbanks were up to our chests, Marchand. I remember because I thought to myself, if the torrent of ice should reach my heart, might it be frozen forever? There were trivial thoughts of romanticism after my spare moments with her. Something was awake inside for the first time in years. But it was soon replaced by that strange, primordial desire.

Every once in a while in the solitude of my London home I thought upon her, but the thoughts faded. When I returned, I came across her in the oddest of places. In the Balfour Gallery, down a long, silent hall. I saw her hair first. That long, blonde hair that was just as unkempt as our long-lost days in the park. That drew me to her for obvious reasons.

Have you ever been with a woman in her prime, Marchand? That is to say, the very first time. It is not a stroke of vanity that leads me to such fervent desirable delicacies. They do, after all, shiver quite often in a manner of deer under ornament. What a sight it is, to see a young girl tire. To feel her fragile flesh beneath the weight. Such ventures are made for floating diamonds, my friend. Such creatures are oft vulnerable to the endowments of men. I was once of this hungry persuasion, but I look back upon it with apathy. There are greater things, Marchand. Much greater things.

For shame, sir, for shame, the priesthood would say. The rabble would dismiss it. Those urchins carry out more heinous crimes under the sheath of night. I hear them on occasion beneath my window. The screams of helpless souls wandering too far into the dark. Fools. Can one not feel the climate falter when entering the vicinity of a monster? I have heard such nonsense more on these roads than ever. Need I leave my home to taste the world? I think not. I need only sit by the sill and become lost in the wonderment of a deviant circle of men, whose voices carry up and through the glass like devil's vine on a stonework temple. It poisons the air, Marchand. Sweet, sickly poison. And it has gotten into me.

"What do you want of me?" That was what she asked. Darkness flickered o'er her majestic iris. I swear the violet turned to ruby in that despisement. I did not mean it as it was received. She took my words to mean some hard declaration upon her worth...a suggestion of a perverse pursuit. What I meant was that I wanted so much from her, that there was no way she could ever give it to me. Beyond bounds my wishes wept, and no day upon this earth would she be equipped to accommodate them.

You ask me why I wander so late into witches' hours, laughing at dark deeds and remarking on fate. There is a clock in the corner. A clock of the deviant angel, and with one broad stroke unto the midnight hour, an eye appears in the center. An eye! What a terrible manifestation of my horror. But it is a timely one. A well-thought-out accoutrement of the master. I am thankful. I am thankful.

There is a sliver of mockery in that smile, sir. Wipe it from your face, lest you hasten the denouement, and there is much to be accomplished before then. I have counted the many letters we have exchanged over the years, and found myself to possess seventy-nine correspondences with you. Imagine the fated correlation of lust and longing, and all the time I was distracted by ink pushed to paper over you!

Might I touch your lips, I said to her. She declined. As soft as daisy polyps, love. As fresh as flesh could be. That haunter of the dark, that smell of petrichor rushed me into excitement. She panicked. Dear child, I thought. Must ye make the final fray so piercing? So untimely? So rotten? Lay down like whistles on the stroke of twelve. Fall asleep. Sleep forever in this guilt.

I never had an affinity for old blood. It stings the senses. Youth dazzles the mind in more ways than one. And the body? The body... It arrests in its entirety. I am not immune to the charms of young women, friend. Nor, I daresay, are you. Do not think such happenings are exclusive to an ailing cynic like myself. No, no. There are things that come at night that few men are privy to meet, and like me, you are a man of heart. Of feeling. Of susceptibility.

Please tell me it's over, Marchand, even though I know it can't be undone. This haunting is of darkest hue, and my shadow has become one with my shame. Do not think me wicked, for I am a man who shifts by hours. Upon the clock hand, I am right today. There is no such horror to fear in these eyes. In these hands, there is but a faint echo of the tremor that shook with such dark vigor. Just a touch of weakness in my jaw from what occurred. Do you think me sinister?

I didn't see the mess until it was finished. I was caked in her. Her blood, her fumes. I pulled hair out of my teeth and nails out of my collar. She held on so tightly, to be but dust in a dream. Wouldn't you know, the music box she knocked over on the mantle...it started chiming that very minute? Just as I looked down to see the pile of flesh. I had no recollection of it... Not a clue what had transpired. Not until I saw my reflection across the room in that damned rococo mirror, and lifted one finger to the dangling carnage betwixt my mouth and forehead.

Now you know, Marchand, what I have done. I am the creator of such hellish strokes. Tell me, friend, that you are not wily. Tell me you are not afraid, but do not offer forgiveness. That, I have not asked for.

Good, because the account above Burnside Park does not end here.

I would advise you to shut your windows at night. And god forbid, Marchand, do not go through Burnside after dark. Do not even pass through during the day, if you can manage. The sounds... the sounds are horror in its purest form. Look at me. Such sights are untenable. You deserve the company of better men, my friend. Sometimes I wonder what could have been, had I not moved to Burnside. If I had stayed in the elder city, or traveled abroad and found the homes of my ancestors. Of course, one might think it strange that I chose to come to such doldrums, but my inner heart has always been humble. My inner being a clock by which the decency of men is measured.

as with alem

THEY were heavy days, when I knew him. Dark blue eyes, the warmth of his mouth, the tightness of his skin against me. Simple breath, simple movement. The dead parts of me bursting out — no longer painful.

He had come to my husband's studio in a frenzy of anxiety, the dark glamour of his eyes piercing into me. A portrait, he requested, for the paper. Our dear friend Marid, having recommended me to him, after sharing tea over solemn volumes and the new fragmentary oblivion of my husband's nearest breakdown.

I positioned him before a broken mirror, the shards splitting up his face into a thousand persons. He liked the surreality, the suggestiveness. "Like a panther," he said, as I climbed the stool, the couch, the ladder to find him in the most appealing light. I knew him beneath this mess to be handsome and alone. The fullness of expression was in the spirit. I absorbed every bit of this man. A feathery, familiar feeling.

"Closer," I said, directing him towards the mirror. He stepped in, his pale face becoming wider, less obliterated, among the shards. His gaze took to floating in a dream of velvet. I stepped in with him.

"Closer," I said again, his being almost one entirety, split only in half at that proximity. I stepped in. His hand moved atop the camera, lowering it away from my face, my features.

"Closer," he whispered, pressing his lips against mine.

I could see the reflection of my husband's beach landscape on the far wall, through the mirror. My eyes closed, fathoms of passion flowing into me, his dark blue gaze cradling a broken boyhood. He would come again in these abandoned hours, seven or eight times that year. Upon the ninth, his shadow lurking outside the door, I would not let him in. I never said goodbye.

"When did you last speak to him?" My expression dips, a concealment of wonder, phantom scents of Alem's black coat, his solemn notebook, slipping under my nose.

"He wrote me a letter, to say he'd taken up lodging here, at the estate."

Marid walks with me on the shore, looking of another age in his black corduroy suit and cane. His spirit still hums with the melancholic wit of our former acquaintance. What he knows of my dealings, there is no surety. Only speculation, and the microsmile upon witnessing my unease. He insisted that I come here.

The water is sickly grey, like watered-down gasoline. It ebbs with an elderly hesitation. The earth has swallowed my heart, but it has not been fatal. Not yet. I raise a hand to my temple and wince.

"Forgive me, the headaches have returned." Marid nods, and continues.

"So tell me of this woman he has taken in." I twitch at the eye, the mouth, wrists twisting towards the ground...a dancerly defiance.

"She looks exactly like me." A fit of laughter breaks out of him.

"Fear of similarity is a desperate humor, my dear."

I track the dying sunlight with beats of the heart. The house is white, sullen. The cupola is blue-green. I did not mean for such a thing to come up. All that he says, signaling to the sky with his book, is that some people have forever dancing about them. Perhaps she was one of these miraculous creatures. He won't admit to me that he introduced my husband to the girl, as with Alem.

"But she looked like me," I say.

"You will come to enjoy your privacy here, I think, my dear," Marid says, dismissing my brooding with a sweep of the hand against the sea, the bulk of his coat billowing behind him.

"Far away from all that nonsense."

"What did Alem make of his time here?"

"Oh, a bit of writing, a bit of reading, as was in his character."

"I'm surprised that he would seek out your company, after all."

"It was penance, the offer. But even a favor cannot save one from being consumed from within."

"What became of him?"

My tone is feverish, but he is not thrown by it. A curious grin curls left, then right, measuring madness.

"He drowned. Swept out by some misfortune. Drunkenness, perhaps. Or a lack of will to begin with."

A blue beetle spits on my left-most hand. I am the beneficiary of buzzing and bleeding in this dreaded house. There is a large colored portrait in the lower room. Gentle limbs painted by gnarled hands. I pull old books from the shelves without titles. They are written in languages that are unknown to me. There is a certain sense of fullness in the house. Something that comes to me in the absence of a crowd. Cold rooms, creaking doors, the stink of the sea hangs in the air. There are no birds but bugs, salt, and memory. One must imagine themselves immobile at the end of the world — miserable, as miserable as I have become.

It is not without merit, this horror of mine. His words and thoughts were my tender companions once, against a tide of violent paint. One might hear infinity in the language of beasts, should they put aside their designs and listen. Each a stranger, among another's oppression. The senses become inflamed in the widest throes of guilt. What can it be, this blue spell of anguish? He wept in my hair, still erect, streaming out new life into me. His body was beautiful and violent.

My husband never discovered us. But like the familiar wilting of my passion years before, his eyes and heart turned elsewhere. He became accustomed to a particular pretension, a vulgarity of the mind, that undoubtedly would have set him against me, no matter who wandered in or out of his arms. But why must it be her? She, who looks so like I did, all those years ago?

I turn down the moth-eaten covers, take off my clothes, slide my nude form into the musty sheets. I have not strength to change. My black hair has grown back, as tough as wire. I don't wear makeup anymore. My cheeks are sunken, eyes rimmed with thinning skin. I run a wooden brush through when sitting. Dust falls. I tremble and watch my long fingernails — red, gold, white. Page after page of this life, I encounter deep dark things. My capacity for wonder has exceeded reason and the essence of myself. I will be a shut-in for many days and nights.

For months, perhaps, listening to the trickling tide coming closer — ever closer.

He left me for her. I slow my tears, mock the hope within my chest, come to in the arms of sleep.

The light coming through the windows is green. Ungodly color spins over the bed sheets. It beats like a beacon for me. I do not know whether to feel threatened or at home. I am immobile — rich with the bodily responses of fear. A form approaches from the infinite night — a form of man blurred out at the sides, in a long shiny black coat. The mask of green is cobbled together by broken wood and weeds. This person towers over me, setting in the deep urgency — a dream in the waking world. These are the touches of ancient things.

What is a worm but a nightmare of passion in small form? I have had dreams before of water. Streams of whispers. Spindles of black smoke. Alem. The outburst of memory sets me against the world again. Irritated with an excess of heat creeping up my spine, I glare to the absence of life through the window, a willful mysticism lingering. There is no governing body to this madness. There is something to the eyes...a familiar look. Painful, and fiercely engaged.

Suddenly, what lies outside the window is quite different. Signs are here of a tropical phantasm. The red eclipse crosses the ocean and a sky as delicate as the old world. I feel myself before this dark element, walking up and down in confusion, my heart tight with the pulsations of passion, of regret. I get up, step as lightly as a bird to the edge of the floor, heart racing. Do I know this man? Have I known him, or do I recognize the emptiness, a spectral projection of my most fragile self? In the disenchanted evening, I will collect these dream projections, but not write of them. If I write, turning page to page of these horrors, this impure poetry, I will bring to myself only travel into time, unbearable — time that towers over me in the heart.

At the center of all things, silence pops. There are no bright rooms in the house. All the lanterns have gone out. I walk into the hallway, down the staircase, towards the parlor. Every step is matched by this figure — black bird of night. The endless, empty worry breathes into me.

I feel him behind me. I feel him within me. On the shore, I reach down. My hands are weak, unable to grasp the sand.

I see from here all of the changes of the landscape. The grey of the water is now green. The richness of color, the clarity of the sea, the cliff rock, sharply lit by the pale yellow light of dawn. One can discover new avenues of frenzy, of regret. Dreaming torment under cobalt skies, drunk with the reality of my human heart. Vitality plucked away with the permission of God. Dead birds fill the beach. Shadows stand still, rocking at times, effortless in their indifference. They are not a manifestation of worried dreams. They are, in fact, quite real. All look at me, silently. I would not entrust my guilt to such images. The faces are shapeless. As dark as Vantablack on canvas. And then I see the machine.

It is a great metallic thing, like a giant screw *in situ*, bearing down on a nearby cove from the zenith of the cliff rock. Its shadow obscures the beach. Energy pulses from there to here. I'm a spectator to the rot, the horror hidden by shadows on the beach, but I will not hold my lantern up to their faces. Not yet.

I go back into the house without respite, hands twisting madly against myself. Days will pass now, longer than before. Evenings of hours trying their part with shame. I cannot remove this trickery of time, eyes half-closed. I remember his suffering after the last time. Had I known the pain of it, I may not have done such things.

I tremble, in expectation of madness, consumed by this compulsion to chase, to abandon. I would rather stretch out, sleepless and alone, than gaze into the infinite light beams of the past.

I look out the window, wrapped in a blue sweater, cup in hand, phone in the other. Waking life. The shore has returned to its original form.

Minx is on the line. She tells me the girl is a cunt, a usurper. I don't use these words. Among the stories that took root in the mouth was that she was like me. It was not until I saw her that I knew this to be true. Have I not earned this horror through a fatal mistake of my own? The irony is inconceivable. It is in the worst of things that I recognize in myself. I write this down, but later in the morning, the pages will be stale. Green and indescribable, and I will remember nothing of them.

Marid returns to deliver the papers. I sign away my partner, my life. I free him up for his pleasure, for my discontent. But was I not unhappy with him, always?

"Without rest, I take it?"

"A troublesome dream."

"Oh?"

I tell Marid of the light, the man, the great machine in the cliff rock. I tell him of the shadows. He is struck, though his expression maintains its rascality, its reserve.

"Your visions are worrisome, Samirah. But did you not mention having a terror of a headache upon entry to the house?"

"I did, yes."

"My uncle had similar aberrations of the head, not unlike yourself upon entry. I imagine the stress of coming overseas under such circumstances has driven your dream world outward."

There is something of an understanding in him, behind these words.

"You sacrifice sleep for an army of dream spirits. Damn them, curse them, get them out, that's what I say. But tell me... Did it feel as though it were an evil thing?"

"No. Familiar."

He stands, gathering the papers, grabbing his cane from the nearby wall.

"Such things are a child's concern."

Her beauty struck a victory against my intelligence. It is all not as simple as that. We only become what we have acted towards. I have had my perverse enjoyments. My glimmers of happiness in a body that was not mine. It is the doom of natural life, to see your eyes on another face.

He left me for her.

I reach a hand to my sagging breasts. A clumsy, failing gesture to grasp, to understand. It is absurd, this spasm of hatred. Granted, one may protest violently, loudly, but Marid had offered his home as sanctuary. I must be grateful. Maybe it was the thought of Alem here that brought me on. He was stealthy in his decomposition, wasn't he? He had always known that he wanted to soar above the indignities of men, in the silent spheres of waiting art. How can one cherish such moments of deceit against another? Is this not the definition of evil? I take what I deserve, as one is inclined to do on occasion, with only slight remembrances. I hate her, and cannot hate her. There will be something of my trials in her fate, something of hers in mine.

But did Alem not look like some dark angel's illustration of my husband?

The upper halls gleam, a cavity of silent sound. The night has come again, and this wave of green light. A shiver in my spine guides me out of the bed. My heart beats to a universal clock. Wind rustles my hair. I become flushed, lips dry from the salt of the air. I am alive in a song of great magic. Wind blows over the beach, through the cliff rock. The strange machine twists down, a permanent shape among the stars. The great booming sound lives through the senses.

He stands with me, this man of night, concealed by metallic cloth and fractured nature. A chill strikes my cheek, and I know myself to be inches from him. In this proximity is the fear of everything. Of death, of discovery. I ask without thinking, "Why does Marid bring us to the house?"

Alem rests his hands on my shoulders before pointing a hand to the shore. Froth and loam flow up closer to the porch. The shapes are undisturbed. They watch gently in the darkness of borrowed nighttime. An urgency boils up into me — the vastness of my guilt. I walk down to the beach, towards the shadows, the distinctive edge of madness brewing. I suddenly feel bolder, cluttered up, degenerate. Quiet tides of silence build in me. I take to running towards the shape, the person. I see on the far side of anguish, all of them. Through a deep laugh, the tones of Marid in his collective genius, I am pulled into the infinite contemplation of passion and regret, into these apparitions of myself.

sorcerer machine

Wickford. 17 September 1939.
"*I can no longer regard you as a Doctor of Science, Dubrovsky. Your grasp has succeeded that of physics; that of time. What might I say to you now? Must I believe in the very things I buried in my adolescence because you tell me we tore something more than light out of the sky that night?*"

—K.E. Malleavich

i.

I am not my sister's keeper. Not anymore. And yet, in some distant corner of my memory, I can recall a time when I felt burdened forever by that very eventuality. I carried that burden for some time; with honor, with pride. With a sense that I could shelter her from the perils of her own mind. So little did I know then. So little do I know of her now.

The letters. Eighteen in total, written in some curious amalgamation of Polish and ancient Hurrian. There they sat in an unmarked envelope on my desk, underneath a copy of my resignation notice.

"You exaggerate your character, sir." The department chair was furious.

"No. You underestimate it."

Some doors must be closed without a storm of passion. An international education long lent me towards a career in academia.

Pouring over ancient tomes and decoding lost languages, I had become a slave to the past and a victim of the future. I had to escape it.

The department will miss me. I'll miss the long nights locked away in the cathedral library, writing down the phrases that swam through my head in the precious few hours where I could find sleep. I was well on my way to creating a language isolate, or so it seemed at the time.

Haunted. That is the only fitting word. Or perhaps the Ervelian phrase, "*aradosia*." Yes. In that, I can hear the sound of my predicament. When I received word that the letters did exist, after years of speculation and dead ends regarding his correspondences, I felt that I had been overcome by a new purpose. How dark it is to consider that journey's beginning now.

Must one feel shame over the intensity of one's internal world? Achieving a long-sought seat at a table of doctors, scientists, philosophers, and historians had done nothing. I had imagined some sort of relief. A rebirth in the realm of the accomplished that would quench my thirst and settle my obsessions. Instead I sat down to a table of decided ignorance, and came to realize that all I lauded was, in fact, decorated deceit. These were not the men of honor I longed to know. They were not like he was. My grandfather, Dr. Nazar Conrad Dubrovsky. He was the man I truly sought, to no avail. He had been buried for over seventy years.

My resignation came as no surprise to the students. For that, I am to blame. My dissociative ramblings on theories of Sumerian syntax had often put them to sleep. Sometimes I would look out at them and wonder why such indifference had never existed within me. Who else is there on this Earth that mourns forgotten worlds? There were those that claimed to, but only to get close to me. The letters — they were dubiously regarded as my salvation, and I took their appearance as a sign. I declared that I had made the right decision and that delving into the forgotten world of the unsung hero, Dr. Dubrovsky, was my calling. As I sat down to untie the string that held the letters together, my descent was set in motion. It was furthered by the harsh tone of the telephone as it began to ring in the parlor. The phone hung on the far end of the wall where that blasted cabinet used to sit. I hesitated to walk over there. Out of the corner of my eye, I sensed a large shadow over that accursed spot. But I convinced myself of fanciful imaginings and answered the phone.

ii.

Misanthropy had a chokehold on Allenspark, Colorado. I'd never seen anything like it. The world felt rather small, as though it ended just beyond the veil of mist and shadow. I thought the isolation of the town was the source of their depressive affliction. But there are deep, infernal roots to such woes. I know that now.

I traveled to Colorado as soon as I could after receiving the call. I put myself on the line for no one — except Gina. Although her name was Katarzyna, we took to calling her Gina once we hit school age. Though her Americanized name did not quite have the mythic ring that fit her manner, we thought it best to convince the girl of her own normality. She didn't take too kindly to the notion.

The call came as a shock. Gina's husband was one brand of awful, but not once did I suspect him of suicidal tendencies. She had found him in the bedroom, hanging from the light fixture. Or Charlie did. I couldn't quite piece together what she told me on the phone. I don't envy the kid, growing up without a father. Maybe that's what made me go out there.

Escaping Boston was necessary, after all. The noise — how can anyone do anything with that noise? I was faced with the task of decoding the elaborate language developed for the letters, and the West seemed like the perfect place to dissect it. The mountains, the trees. The fresh air. It all became part of the plan.

I arrived in town nearing the outer limits of May. The town itself was majestic, but I remained unsuccessful in finding someone to tell me where the Linley farm was. I'd done my best to downplay the city look, but the Coke bottle glasses and expensive watch probably marked me as an outsider. I understand their apprehension. I wasn't at ease, either.

I ended up passing by the town library and stopped in to look up the address. The only computers available were three PC desktops straight out of the mid-90s. Scanning through the recent obituaries, I found Paul Linley's address. The farm was out on the western edge of town. I grabbed my bags and began the hour-long hike.

The landscape — a breathtaking expanse of mountains, forests, fields, and unpaved roads — was not in any way relaxing as I navigated its splendor in pursuit of the aging farmhouse. I feared the condition I would find my sister in. I feared the condition of her son, whom I had never met. And I feared the peripheral shadows; the sense that I was being marched by unseen spirits down the road to my eventual demise. I looked behind me constantly, to no avail. I was alone on the road to the disaster. It took two hours to reach the cornfield that marked the edge of the property. I could see the faint outline of the house in the distance and turned onto the grassy path.

The house was in shambles. Chipped paint, dislodged gutters, and cracked windows were the accents of that condemnable hut. It was the last place I would ever hope to see her living in. She deserved better than that. I walked up to the shabby oak door. Three knocks and it creaked open. I looked down and two wide eyes were staring back at me under a mop of red hair.

"Charles Linley?"

The boy had turned seven before his father died. Charlie opened the door and held out his little hand. His handshake was firm. I liked the kid right away.

"I'm your Uncle Conrad. You can call me Connie if you want."

The kid nodded slightly.

"Is your mother home?"

"Yes."

"May I see her?"

He nodded again, and started to walk through the kitchen and down the hall. I walked into the house and followed him, despite the ominous absence of light. He led me to a closed door. Steam poured from underneath. I knocked.

"Gina?"

I looked at Charlie. The kid looked scared.

"Gina, it's Connie."

Still nothing.

"I'm coming in. Stand back, Charlie."

I turned the knob. It was unlocked. As I opened the door, steam poured out. The heat was unbearable. I had to wait for the steam to thin before I could see anything. Water thrashed. As I began to see limbs, I reached and pulled my sister out of the bathtub and laid her down on the floor. Her eyes were rolling back in her head. Then I saw Charlie in the door.

"Kid, call 9-1-1."

He nodded.

"Go! Fast!"

The tremors subsided as I picked her up and carried her to the hall. I held her face gently in my hands as she passed in and out of consciousness. Then she woke up. Her brow lowered and she pushed away my hands.

"Don't touch me."

"It's me, Gina."

"Where is Charlie?"

"I sent him to call for help."

"No."

She stood up and returned to the bathroom, grabbing a towel from the rack and wrapping it around herself. She yelled out for her son.

"He's already called them."

"Well, we'll tell them it's a misunderstanding."

"You had a seizure."

"Mind your own damn business."

"Well, have you been checked out yet?"

She gave me a scathing look as Charlie ran into the room.

"Charles, go on the front porch with your uncle while I change. Go on."

I walked out first. The kid followed.

We sat on the rickety iron bench on the front porch, waiting for any sign of flashing lights or even the faint sound of sirens in the distance. They never came.

"Did you give them the right address?"

Charlie nodded. I wondered if the kid had been beaten. He could barely look me in the eyes. I looked at him. After a few moments, he spoke.

"People don't come here."

I shifted on the bench to face him. He didn't move. I looked out over the massive fields. The crops were mangled and overgrown.

"They don't? What about the farmhands? The people who work the crops?"

Charlie stood up and started to walk inside.

"They stopped coming."

"After your father died?"

The kid tilted his head down.

"Before that."

He went inside. The sun began to set over the distant mountains. Just as I'd felt no peace when I traversed the pale sands of the dirt road, I felt no harmonious peace with the natural majestic. These lands were cursed. I didn't know what the townspeople knew that kept them away from the farm. I only knew the instinct — the feeling — that something was not right in this old world I had entered. It was a feeling I knew all too well. And the source of everything was sitting in a quiet, empty room of that house where it would not be disturbed.

iii.

Gina was in the living room when we came back inside. Charlie ran off to what I could only presume was his bedroom. I sat across from my sister on the aging pinstripe couch.

"How are you holding up?"

I regretted the inquiry immediately.

"Have you brought your precious letters?"

I hadn't recalled telling her of them, but in the heated thrashing of our phone conversation, I daresay I could have and merely forgotten.

"I have them."

"They will take an enormous length of time to decipher, I expect."

"It can wait."

Her gaze softened.

"Can it?"

Gina rose from her seat and wandered over to a portrait of herself, her late husband, and her young son. She turned to me again.

"It's better to occupy yourself in this house. I don't recommend wandering the fields or going into town."

"Has something happened to alienate the neighbors?"

She let out a derisive laugh and raised her eyebrow.

"Paul killed himself."

"Well, yes. I know that. But that's no reason for them to shun you, or not send medical help in an emergency."

"Conrad, keep to your letters and leave fools to their indifference."

"Rejection is not indifference."

I watched her face. She looked so changed from when I had last seen her. It was just after her college graduation. Gina had met some fool and had fanciful plans of moving out west. We had laughed at her. It was the last time any of us ever did so.

"Gina, where are the farmhands?"

Suddenly her wistful contemplations had vanished.

"They aren't here."

"Did you fire them?"

"They left and won't set foot back on the property."

"Why?"

She swept her raven hair out of her face and walked out of the room.

"See to your letters, Conrad Dubrovsky."

I stayed still for a few moments before following her into the kitchen.

"Where did my bags go?"

"In your room. Up the stairs, second door on the left."

I ascended the rotting staircase and stood outside the door. I anticipated a quarters in vast disarray, but when I opened the door, I found a room that would not be out of place in a hotel. There was even an old cedar writing desk in the corner, where I could translate in peace. It sat right beside the window that overlooked the cornfield. I smiled for the first time in ages, but it didn't last. I looked on the desk to find that the letters had already been placed there, with fresh ink and a pen laid out for me.

iv.

I'd done a good deal of deciphering in my day, and piecing out the Polish and Hurrian was much easier than I had anticipated. In fact, I had already begun the work of translating on the plane to Colorado. I sat down and finished the initial excerpt.

Bialystok. 7 July 1939.

Kramer stopped by yesterday to make his demands. Which seem to me as though they were desperate pleadings, and so my apprehension has lessened. There is no monster here. *Just a boy. A boy misled by promises of a new world. Who among us has ever been immune to such promises? And the Veil has a way with words that is far greater than you or I could ever have.*

Of course, the terms were laid out before you took leave, so you well know what is at stake. To save this boy's...friend will be a tremendous challenge. His disease is not unknown to me. I have seen it on occasion among his kind, and it is a vicious, multi-faceted affliction. With a 100% fatality rate, mind you. This is not child's play, Malleavich. I have a chance here to right some wrongs. But will it be enough? It's never enough, is it? Never.

—N.C.D.

Kersham Malleavich had been my grandfather's scientific research partner for decades before these letters were written. That much I knew from family stories. I was suddenly overcome with the reality at hand. Their last correspondence was laid out before me, and there was no telling what could be revealed as I continued the translation. I left the desk and decided to walk around the rest of the house. I needed to breathe before I jumped into history that heavy.

I found Charlie in the next room, writing with chalk on the floorboards. He was drawing what looked like rotating portals, with little cartoon hands. I sat down on the floor with him.

"Is school out for the summer?"

The kid nodded. It was his go-to response for everything.

"Do you want to go outside and explore with me? This room is kind of cramped."

He put the chalk down.

"Mom won't let me go in the field."

"Because you might get lost in the tall grass?"

Charlie took a breath and looked up at me. He didn't answer.

"Charlie, where are the people who worked the crops?"

A frightened look overcame his tiny face.

"They disappeared."

He swept his hand over the chalk drawings and erased them.

"Is that why no one comes here?"

Charlie gathered his chalk and stood up. He put it in a little chest of drawers beside his bed and left the room. I looked at what was left of the chalk drawing and noticed the faint outline of the field, with vast circles of white floating over it.

V.

Wickford. 18 July 1939.

 I'm glad to hear the young soldier isn't giving you much trouble. Although I will admit I had doubt that he would. With a devil's badge and a boy's heart, there is always room for compromise. And you, of course, could not have refused him. Not after the...unfortunate mishap weeks before my departure. Which I would not like to speak of under any circumstance. Nazar, I know that you are looking for answers. You won't find them. And I won't find them here in the States. Some books are meant to be sealed.

 —K.E.M.

Bialystok. 29 July 1939.

 My friend, how you do not know me. No book will ever be sealed in my vicinity. No thought closed off in my mind if there is something to be derived from it. You may refuse to reflect upon the ordeal, but I will not turn my back on the research and field work and back-breaking study it took to conduct what was one of the most innovative and confusing experiments on this earth. Have a heart, Malleavich. This is what I live for.

 —N.C.D.

I barely saw my sister in the days following my arrival. She wasn't ever in the house when I woke up. After a few days I had settled into a routine that ended up revolving around taking care of Charlie. I didn't mind it. The kid lightened up when I showed him some of the old books I had brought with me from the University. He couldn't read a word of it, but it was the art of the calligraphy that he loved. It took less than a week for me to feel that the kid was a son to me. For that, I will always be grateful.

 He took me out to the barns and taught me how to feed the horses and cattle. The animals were gaunt, but friendly. All save one prickly black goat that wouldn't let me near his pen. I set the nights aside for translating. The admissions continued to be vague, but I pressed on in hopes of substance. They were written in an isolate for a reason, and I was hell-bent on finding out why.

Katarzyna took to reappearing at night, after Charlie had gone to bed. On occasion I would hear the door creak behind me as she poked her head in to watch me at the desk. Sometimes, I swear I could feel an elation coming from her as my pen swept across the pages. But she never said anything. She would close the door again and make her way down to the farthest door on the right; the room where Paul had died.

On the first Sunday after my arrival, I ventured out into the field to get fresh air. Superstition had never been a concern for me, and I had chalked up the workers' "disappearances" to some cowards who were too afraid to tell Paul Linley that they wouldn't work for him anymore. I couldn't blame them. The man was a menace.

When I went out into the tall grass I was followed by a tabby cat. It was one of the strays that Charlie and I had come across that were living under the back porch. This one took a liking to me, and trailed behind if ever I wandered around the property. I had been walking around for half an hour when I looked back and saw that the cat wasn't there. I called out to her, but heard nothing. Nothing until a loud, horrific screech sounded through the grass, followed by a flash of light.

I ran towards the spot, but found nothing except for scorched grass and slightly disturbed sediment. Shadows of darkness ebbed and flowed from the farthest corners of my vision, but when I turned to look, nothing was there. A sense of dread transformed me into a passenger in my own body as I automatically turned and started to run back to the house. I was about halfway there when I found Gina, with her hands over her eyes. I stopped and walked over to her, pulling her hands away from her face. Blood was pouring out of her eyes, nose, and mouth. I grabbed her hand and rushed towards the house.

vi.

It took a lot of yelling and threats of litigation to get the EMTs out to the Linley farm. They got there within half an hour. They stopped the bleeding, but decided to take her to the hospital to get checked out.

Charlie and I jumped in Paul's old Ford pickup truck and followed behind the ambulance.

After all the typical routine tests that find nothing but cost a fortune, Gina was cleared to go home. I pressed the doctor for answers, but they said it was a nosebleed and hay fever. I questioned them as long as I could, but Charlie was getting tired, and Gina, increasingly irritated. We drove home in silence.

Wickford. 3 August 1939.

The kids are well. Antonin has almost fully recovered from what his mother called "permanent sea legs." Although I daresay the boy continues to act peculiar and disobedient with remarkable ease. I hope that your wife and son are doing well.

—K.E.M.

Bialystok. 10 August 1939.

Don't be an imbecile, Malleavich. We perfected the language isolate in my home and no one outside of the family will be able to decipher it. You can speak with me without fear of interception. I'm glad to hear of your family's well-being. I've been holed up in the lab and not spoken to Ingrid for a few days. My son is remarkably well. Thank you.

Now on to pressing matters. I have done all of the preliminary blood tests and biopsies on Heinrich Luther. I was right; his affliction is one that is known to me. Kramer stopped by with flowers before reporting for duty. I must say, the boy has remarkably changed. He is not as I first thought. He is of tremendous character, lost in a storm greater than you or I could ever reconcile. I just hope it ends before it spreads beyond our walls.

—N.C.D.

Katarzyna spent more time in the house after the incident in the field. She rarely spoke, and when she did, she was terse and abusive. I maintained my schedule with Charlie and attempted to accelerate my translations. Though the house had a depressing effect on me, it was nonetheless perfect for translating in peace. I hoped to return to Boston once I finished, but my sister's condition was erratic. Charlie deserved better than being alone with her. I love my sister, but she had descended down some terrible path that I could not decipher. Her life is a language to which I have never been attuned. I wish I had been.

One day soon after the hospital visit, I found her on the floor of the bathroom, in tears and shivering. I helped her stand. I stood behind her and held her up by her shoulders. She struggled to lean forward, examining her face in the mirror as though it were the first time. Her right hand slowly rose to her chest and rested over her forehead. Tears rolled down her cheeks. Red tears.

"Katarzyna, you have to come back to Boston. We need to find out what's wrong."

She shook and went limp. I picked her up in my arms and carried her to her bedroom. I laid her down on the bed and sat beside her. When I looked up, standing before me was something I had wished never to venture upon again.

In the room where Paul Linley died and Katarzyna slept in every night, stood the detestable Black Cabinet.

vii.

Bialystok. 13 August 1939.

I have been experimenting with derivatives of the tonic I have been giving Heinrich Luther. It strengthens the body in preparation for biochemical changes. It is also excellent solely as an immune booster in a new environment. I told Kramer that developing a cure could take years, but he persisted. His hope inspired me. It inspired me to push beyond the limits of my own mind. I daresay that within days, Heinrich may be on his feet again.

—N.C.D.

The next few days were better. Gina stayed in bed and Charlie and I took turns cooking for her. She ate nothing, but something in her expression suggested that she appreciated the gesture. I saw a look in her from her youth; that look she only gave when she felt safe. But it would soon fade away when she glanced over my shoulder and over to the blasted Black Cabinet. I tried to ignore its silent fury. The sense of pulsing melancholy that it projected. I told Charlie to stay away from it.

On the following Saturday night, my sister disappeared. I tried to remain calm, remembering that she had done this very thing routinely since I arrived. Thoughts came in waves as to her whereabouts. Drugs remained the most logical eventuality, but something told me that wasn't it. She didn't come home for three days. I checked the property every night, hoping that I would come across a set of footsteps. I didn't. On Tuesday night, I grabbed my flashlight and headed out the door, with my eyes on the horizon and the edge of the forest.

Bialystok. 16 August 1939.
He has been cured. They are both elated. Kramer even brought me a gift that he managed to salvage from one of the raids. An old cabinet carved from dark wood that he says belonged to an old Jewish alchemist.

–N.C.D.

viii.

I entered the high grass knowing that it would be a fruitless venture. If she was there, she could be anywhere, and unless she made noise, I would not see her in the dark. I spent two hours there before exiting from the northern edge. A hundred feet away, the great forest lurched in the wind. I entered.

I lost count of the time that I spent searching the forest. I walked in circles and acquired scrapes from jagged branches that tried to block me out. When I reached a rather steep embankment that led to a much darker section of the forest, I hesitated. A quiet wind crept up and shifted the branches of a tree just enough for me to see a figure at the bottom of the embankment. The figure was surrounded by rune-like symbols drawn in the dirt. I did my best to ignore them, but something in the back of my mind insisted upon a familiarity with their jagged, mythic form. As I approached, I could see that it was a person, naked, lying in the fetal position. The individual's skin was steeped in pallor, and soaked in a thick pink slime that looked like amniotic fluid. I approached slowly, hearing labored breathing. I reached my hand out to turn the form toward me. There she was. Gina.

I rolled her over gently to see that her face had changed; not so entirely that she was unrecognizable, but enough to make me doubt my sanity. My once glamorous and feminine sister was now bald and her features took on a vastly androgynous overtone. The slime was beginning to dry, and took on a darker pink hue. A circular hole bled from her forehead. I looked down to see similar holes on her neck, chest, stomach, and genitals. I took her in my arms and carried her back to the house.

Bialystok. 7 September 1939.

My dear friend Malleavich, today that veil was cast over my house and I daresay cannot be lifted. I received that dreaded company of our age, not five minutes past eleven on the morning of the 5th. Suddenly my grief over the departure of my family gave way to long-sought relief. They left just in time.

Heinrich and Kramer are dead. Murdered. Slaughtered for the very thing that so many of us seek so ardently. I've reflected upon the sequence of events. I've tried to imagine some alternative history that may have spared them. Perhaps if we had allowed Kramer to arrest us in the field that night. Or if we had deigned to run, and been shot. Although that is not a fate I would ever have wished for you, my friend. You tried to stop me, and fiercely, from conducting that experiment. I wish I had listened. The pursuit of knowledge, power, achievement – it has brought a curse upon my house, and yours. I am so sorry.

In that way, I am no different than the Fuhrer. I have destroyed something so pure, so innocent. You tell me we displaced unknown matter from a passing cosmic light source. I tell you, Kersham Malleavich, that I have killed God, and there is no turning back for any of us now.

Unless this new experiment works.

–N.C.D.

"Are you telling me my sister is insane?"

"I'm telling you your sister needs serious help, that you are not able to give her."

The doctors would not let her out this time. They said that she had done all of those terrible things to herself. That no drugs had been found in her system. That some form of a psychotic break had occurred and that she needed to be committed for her own protection.

Something about all of it didn't seem right to me, but I had no more options. I rushed home, remembering Charlie was there alone. A storm churned in the open sky as I drove the Ford pickup down the old dirt road.

The lights had gone out in the storm. Thankfully, when I looked in Charlie's room, he was sound asleep. I took one of the candelabras from the hall and took out my lighter. The flames were small, but I could see enough to make my way down the hallway. I had to check on it. Something was wrong in her room and I couldn't turn away from the door. Not on that night.

The Cabinet was a source of torment. Being in its presence again was a curse; a curse that could not be lifted. Something indefinable emanated from it — perhaps I am convinced that the troubles in this house are tied to that monstrosity. An old curator friend of mine once spoke of a very similar item. A clock, manufactured from some unknown black substance. He said that it looked like tar, but with human forms sculpted within the mess, reaching for the stars. Reaching to escape. He came across it in the collection of some eccentric German artist that often delved into the sinister. The clock, he claimed, had often been found in the houses of men who had been driven insane by cosmic delusions. Part of me wonders if the Cabinet and the clock have a similar origin.

I would never have given it to my sister, had I known that my thoughts were not madness. Had I known that my fears were, in fact, legitimate. I had thought I was losing my mind the entire time it resided within my apartment. Not to mention the unease of not being able to open the damn thing. I had to get rid of it, but being the last thing that connected me to my grandfather, I couldn't bring myself to dispose of it. I had buried the warnings but now, after all that time, I faced the offender again. I reached out to the handle and twenty years after I first set eyes on it...

The Black Cabinet opened.

If I came to consciousness immediately, it was not known to me. I was there, on my feet, but not in my mind. I didn't fall. But I was lost in what I felt was the resurrection of some isolated element; some accursed steam or mist or fog that lived in that bound construction. When my eyes were my own again, I lifted the candelabra to see what the Cabinet held. Some indistinguishable language was etched into the inner walls. All the shelves were empty, except for the second. There I found some sort of ancient metal contraption. I set down the candelabra and reached for the machine.

What I held, upon first examination, seemed to be some curious composite of a medical device and cosmic compass. Even the metal was of an origin unknown to me. I grazed my fingers over the edges and found dried blood at the tips of the five jagged rods. Upon further examination, I found that the contraption did, indeed, unfold to create a much longer device, reaching almost five feet in length. The lightning storm picked up outside. I re-folded the contraption and set my eyes back on the inside of the cabinet. The flashes of light illuminated the rune-like letters and I was immediately struck by a phrase. One that I knew all too well. I only knew how to pronounce the strange markings from my dream ramblings.

"*Uzul raga aja kul*"

There. There lies the answer to the affliction. Hers, mine — everything in this house and our family that had been so insidiously challenged by those things that go so recklessly against nature. This phrase had echoed through my dreams for months. No, years. And I was so selfish to have assumed it was my own brilliance that had devised it. Cognitive deceptions are profound, are they not? I set the contraption back on the second shelf and leaned in closer to examine the letters. The phrase did not end here. It continued.

"*Vishnul zerith agna vun*
Coon coom raga amkhim har
Lagka vey yusul"

I rushed back to my room. I had forgotten the candelabra on the floor, so I took out my lighter to illuminate my unpacked bags in the corner. I set it on the desk and began to rifle through stacks and stacks of papers. At the bottom was my folder labeled "CD-LI." Conrad Dubrovsky — Language Isolate. Thinking back on it makes me cringe.

I took the folder with me to the Cabinet, along with a stack of blank paper and a pencil. I began the long process of tracing the lettering, inch by inch, from every shelf of the Cabinet. The process took over two hours, and included labeling and sorting according to location. I set the scribblings at my desk and pondered beginning the new translation, but my instincts told me otherwise. The Dubrovsky-Malleavich correspondence was not finished. I reached for them instead and continued the translation.

Bialystok. 14 September 1939.

They tried, Malleavich. The tried to coerce me. Then they threatened to kill me if I didn't agree to make the salvation serum for their superior officers. I refused. And there may be only hours until they claim me.

Long gone is my curiosity for humanity's corruption. Now that there may be no consequences. Now that...the eternal indifference is upon us. What I previously regarded as hideous alchemy, I now see as a means to resurrection. Maybe not of physical strength or the trials of the body. But of that very disputed element that we once insisted was a fragment of an elaborate fiction. I know that we are men of science, Kersham. I know. But there is not one fiber of my being that can forget that moment of the descending light, and how much it made me want to die. Damn you, Malleavich, why can you not see? That what happened that night was not some trivial accident or failed experiment? It was the worst possible outcome of the most irresponsible, egotistical, and reckless experiment ever conducted!

I have been given a gift, Kersham. The Black Cabinet. Within it lies the salvation of us all. In elaborate script there is a warning. A warning and a solution. See to it that the Cabinet reaches my son in the States. In it lies my last and final contribution to this world, constructed from the elaborate equations of a brilliant man. A man who knew more of Earth and the afterworlds than we could ever fathom believing or denying.

There is no denial left to be had.

The language of the Black Cabinet can be translated, but not in full without a key phrase. That phrase, which sounds phonetically as 'Uzul raga aja kul,' and the continuation, 'Vishnul zerith agna vun Coon coom raga amkhim har Lagka vey yusul,' is to be written in the enclosed manner after the machine of the sorcerer has met human flesh. It must be spoken aloud. Only then will the cycle be completed. With the merging of these sacred elements – the murdered sorcerer's machine and the serum, pursued by the hand of one brave enough to ascend the limits of human reality – only then may a new light ascend. We must make this right.

–N.C.D.

Wickford. 17 September 1939.

Show me the machine that will make God and I will show you his tombstone in a field of ash. Nazar Dubrovsky, you were a man of profound learning. Why did you not come to America when you were given the chance? Why must you insist on this morbid martyrdom? It is my utmost hope that this letter reaches living hands, and that you will have calmed your senses long enough to admit your own folly. My friend, our experiments were regrettable. Our friendship, irrefutable. But I cannot accommodate your madness any longer. Life is a miraculous accumulation of finite nothings. A mirror facing another mirror. The answers that you seek were not ever there. With the way the world has gone, I'd say if God ever existed, he has been dead long before you killed him. I can no longer regard you as a Doctor of Science, Dubrovsky. Your grasp has succeeded that of physics; that of time. What might I say to you now? Must I believe in the very things I buried in my adolescence because you tell me we tore something more than light out of the sky that night?

—K.E.M.

I heard a crashing noise. Within seconds I was at the door of Charlie's room. I found him huddled in the corner with his hands over his eyes. He was terrified. The storm outside was becoming violent.

"Charlie, where did the noise come from?"

He pointed to Katarzyna's bedroom.

"Of course it did."

Bialystok. 19 September 1939.

Might there be freedom from this catastrophe? I think not. The ailment possessed in my body is one of a tyrant's. Even now the heat of my disturbance festers on my face... A boiling sensation fit only for snakes in a stew. I could eviscerate myself for my own compassion. It is that very thing, that sickly weakness, which has led me to such deeds of demonic vulgarity. I am not sorry, no. I cannot be, for the acts were not mine. They were of some unseen force; a trait foreign to the totality of my base condition. Perhaps we are not so alike after all.

I am not a man of prose. I remained rather silent for years, but I am compelled to change this. I worry about what festers in the mind of ancients, despite the coming of new light and the promise of redemption. I am not a man of words, but of acts. And oh, the acts have fallen with such fury to some resentful pit. The whispers. All committed by this body, these eyes, these hands...

It is a privilege of the possessors of such whispering tongues, but not mine. Never mine.

Those deemed children by some are born of times unaccounted for. She will have the eyes of a thousand-year-old mystic, and they will bore through all like a burnished dime.

—N.C.D.

The light continued to flash. My gut told me to check the Cabinet again. I crept slowly down the hall and opened the door to my sister's bedroom. All three windows were wide open. The harsh wind and rain shook the curtains violently. I turned my head to where I should have seen the Cabinet. It was there that I found a mound of black ash. I kneeled down and touched it gently as the vast pile gently lifted and flew out the open windows, leaving not a speck behind.

Instinct drove me back to my room, where I found that the letters had disappeared. I looked out the window in the event that they had been disturbed by the wind, but saw nothing. Panic struck. I ran back to Charlie's room, but he wasn't there.

The light continued to flash. I rushed down the stairs and found Charlie in the kitchen.

"I heard it again." he said.

"What did you hear?"

Charlie's arms spread out and quickly swung back with a loud clap. A flash of light ripped through the dining room from the front window. I walked to the door. Charlie stood behind me, hiding behind my legs. I walked outside and he followed closely behind.

As I stepped forward, I noticed grooves had been marked in the ground before us. I kept walking, and they became more elaborate. I realized what we were passing over was Dubrovsky's drawing. It was then that the sky before us lit up.

Nine orbs of light hovered about two hundred feet away over the field. They were no bigger than a pinprick at that distance, until they shivered. In pairs, from the outside in, the orbs burst into large, ovular portals of swirling light. They looked to be seven feet tall. All except the last...the ninth portal in the center. The others slid to the side as it began to grow, reaching at least eighty feet. It was then that I saw Gina, standing beneath the ninth, draped in shadow.

I yelled her name. She didn't move. I turned to Charlie and told him to stay put. After running a few yards, I stopped at the sight of things falling out of the eight smaller portals.

One by one, human bones poured out of the vortices. The pace quickened until full human skeletons seemed to drop out of midair. Dozens of them.

I was closer to my sister now. She held the bundle of letters in one arm, and the small machine in the other. A vicious wind blew out of the ninth portal. It was then that I saw two giant, gaunt hands the size of cars reach out and linger in mid-air. I yelled to her again. This time she turned to me. The pure white skin, the dark eyes that looked down to her shivering son, who had crept up behind me. She turned back to the portal. The hands began to lower and rush towards each other. The impact was so loud that we fell to the ground. I could no longer hear. The smaller portals disappeared, but the ninth had churned into a large, brilliant ball of white light. We looked on as it stopped spinning and began to rise.

We watched it climb to the heights of the stratosphere and continue on into space, where it grew as faint as the dimmest stars before disappearing. When I lowered my eyes, I did not see the world that had been before me only moments ago. The fields fell to ruin; piles of dust as far as the eye could see. And it was quiet. As quiet as dawn in the age of iron seas. I could still feel Charlie's grip on the back of my legs. I turned to look and found only his bones.

I wonder how many miles I will walk before the dust ends. If there will be rain, or fire beyond this. Or just lives lived in pleasant ignorance of all that occurs beyond unspoken realms of space and time. But those are questions for those accustomed to dark skies. I could say as much in the final chapter of this story, if I can bring myself to finish it. I'm not a master of words. Not anymore.

dark ocean

IF there is a discomfort in writing, it is because death is in these waters. Not the death of life entire, but the death of life as is. Coughing up a mist of marrow, I imagine my bones have turned to soup within me. I can bend my toe back like rubber. My ankles ache — ball-jointed rot, I fear. It is as it will be — this predicament.

I am, in the boat, as I am in any other place. Gliding without purpose over the surfaces of life. There could be stillness without pain. I tell myself this, to believe something — that there may be more to experience in sweeter places than the wounds of wartime exile and their repeated torment in my mind.

Clouds, like curtains, shield me from the crimes on high. Broken vessels floating in a fractured haze, blurred by the burden of heavy eyelids. I can see very little, that is the truth of it. In these nights of liquid languor, menace brewing in my bones — wheezing, viperous venom. I soak in it. I soak in the terror of being nothing — surrounded by nothing, seen by nothing.

The sun hardly rises anymore. A green streak will peek out over the steam ridge for an hour, maybe two. Mischief catches fire in my mind. A yelping, gyrating banquet of untoward dreams. I am not opposed to them, any more than the myth of matter splashing over me in this rickety excuse of a ship.

There is a great door to the ocean depths, and above it sits Munjavi. I can see very little of his sand-scathed cloak, or the tiny bristles of fiber cascading down the length of his spine; those that once glistened in the desert sun amidst the pouring sweat of merchant skins and soldiers' coins. I see only dawn-tinted waves, singing songs as omens to the brittle depths, warning whales and deeper flesh of a drifting darkness.

If I were ever to return to the old world, they would ask me to speak of his face. There are no words within worth speaking, though I comfort myself with their design. As sea foam spreads into these veins, seaweed strangles my ribcage, now delicate from the soreness of being lost at sea.

I have never felt discomfort run quite as deep. His eyes have the deep-set anxiety of the oldest, most tired of horses, until they flash towards me with the gruesome hue. I look away, marking the disturbance in the air in this moment. The peculiar frost, as though swimming ghosts — in their immortal absurdity — have marked me with some inconceivable design. He glances at me with eyes harboring the deepest of disease. Or contempt? I doubt that I will ever know which.

Nobody asked me about the offer of poison. A chance to avoid this dismal affair altogether. Apparently I misheard the council, or wandered to a far corner of the room in my despair without ears, or some such nonsense. They didn't ask about my personal brands of torment. Soaking myself in darkling odors. Drawing despair with fists over my own vanity. I was like the beast with no tongue in those old places. Racing to the glory of honest people and failing — falling here.

Ruby red sails. War-tossed oak splintering into midnight waves. I have seen such things, on what ocean I no longer know. One ought not to look into the eyes of the withered. There are too many things there to be absorbed. To cross over without consent or consideration. I, myself, have wandered too far into the eyes of mutilated men and found myself a carrier of a wayward pain, here, right above the stomach.

I could drink up the poison of endless cosmic oceans and never be so drawn and derelict as I am on the waves beneath him. I would wait for a brighter dawn to unveil this wreckage, but in this I have no say. We sail to vile shore, beyond the reaches of guiltless foam. I whistle to a passing throng, unaware of my own mindless imaginings. Those ports of splendor are absent in such regions of desertion. They are the resting quarters of sunken souls. What hurricane could bring down greater gales of shame than these — shadows from beneath the waves?

Sailing to the vile shore. It is a ways away, though with squinting eyes, I see the haunt of the rim. A scream gathers in the pit of my throat, but is strangled by the soreness.

Munjavi, the collector. Delighting in tormented notes as we wade through the darkest waters. I can think of no other currency for his great game. There is more to this pleasure of sea and sand than mere vengeance upon me and mine. Or is he merely that merciless, that evil? Perhaps he waits for me to shriek in regret. No doubt these have golden weight in his trade. I will not allow him the luxury, or the collection. My voice will remain confined.

Caution sinks to the realm of folkloric wonderment, but not of warning. I heard such protestations against mythic figures in the old world, each growing more passionate. I likened them to the religious doctrines I had long-since rejected.

If there is glory to be had in this mess, let it be fleeting. I don't want it anymore. Or anything that isn't meant for me. There could be nothing underneath the sheet of black. Or everything. The dark ocean itself could be my own soul, laid out before me as the ultimate punishment. My thoughts are as black as aging gaunts, in laughter, under the shadow of Androvac Munjavi. His soul can be nothing more than a fragmentary snow, blasted from its core and dribbling out towards the sipping haunters of the deep. I reach up into the sky and out falls the pale light of stars, slowly milked by the touch of living flesh. My chest burns, but this is welcome. This is living.

We close in on dawn — tired, but alive. I hear the faint sound of a whisper on wind, let out from the saving place. If I could find it, perhaps I would escape. This cosmic confounder of which I find myself imprisoned — how did I ever let myself become lost in such a way? There is little hope for me, so detached from the riddles and rhymes of someone so diabolical, so profound. I think no less of him. Rather, I must think less of myself. Of ignorance, I was a guiding light. I so wish I'd harbored protection over deeper things. Deeper thoughts, deeper times. I may have escaped this torment.

By the foul pungency of strange, dark liquid, I fall to my knees — cracking my head on the railing's edge. I drift in the dark pull of dreams. The eerie glide of notes travels up and around every sense I possess in this unknown world. The needle of time has moved into place by itself, spewing out the elemental atrocities that would let me live — and suffer — forever. Here comes the chill of dead water again.

The question now becomes, what will happen after this? When the vile shore is on the horizon and the current locks my course into its grasp? In a daze I imagine a horrible thing. My soul turns dark and rips through my mouth in swirling particles. My body cracks like land under the enormous weight of a volcanic blast. The place is a festering Hades. My melancholy is so profound that even the orchestra in my mind's eye plays only songs of bitterness and suffering. I wish I had something else to think about. Somewhere else to go. Some dreams of fancy that far outweigh past grievances or current aggressions, but I do not.

He could summon some sky hell's progeny in one fell swoop! The uneasy pulsing of the ship towards the vile shore meets with an unlikely current. An age passed before I came to understand these as a shifting in this dark and unparalleled universe. The very skies catch fire as haunted moans and bloodied raindrops pour down into this hellscape. I look upward at a stab wound in the bleeding sky.

My hands grasp to the broken boards, sending me — salt-soaked, splintered — into the deep. A shriveled mass. An excuse of a thing. The vile shore is ever closer, and there can be no hope left to lift my spirits there. The ship itself can't stand the unseen onslaught of malice. My squinting eyes can barely make out the faintest mark of a sheath-like barrier between the vile shore and myself. Reaching up to the heavens, if such a place could even be conceived of in his presence. Every misstep in life was a seedling in this forgotten ocean. If I had known of what occurs beyond the indulgences of mortal travel, I may have never lost myself to such a place.

The waves overtake the bow. My grip is lost in the onslaught of foam. I grab onto one last twisting rail as the vessel rips in half, being sucked in by the ominous power of the burnished sands. Only now, after so many ages, I let out that guttural scream reserved for the last of conscious moments. As the power of the body leaves my arms and barrels into my throat, I let go of the rail and fall into dead water — unspeakable, rotten, and wondrous dark.

ash in the pocket

THE gleam in his eyes betrays his unhappy genius. Her father, your father, the father of all. The girl in the bed stares outside of herself, despising the green monotony of the earth. That which is unfamiliar brings the sickness, so she seeks sanctuary beyond dark sleep, in spirit. There he hovers over her, continuing to dread the wakefulness of his ancestors, because this is all just too comfortable — too intimate — to risk.

Father is of the opinion that his rivals, those red-winged wielders of dread from the firmament, fling themselves toward him in a pendulous telepathic rocking. Their elongated heads, like rams stretched by ghastly cosmic force, gnashing baleen teeth against the wind. He sees them in dread-sleep. Unhinged clockwork of the mind, begging an adventure that he simply isn't up to at the moment. He must know their whereabouts. Stay alive. Find a way to evade them, though ever-haunted by their final mystic muttering: "*He who is without a face will lean over the lake, tasting disgrace and empty dreams.*"

"I am happy," he says. "Not in the way they are, but in the way I *am*. And I *am* because I stay away from all of *that!*"

Nine of her cousins have tasted psychic death. Succumbed to the best of his intentions, drunk with the lifeless flowering of heathen instinct. Each of them buried in their beds with flowers, lured into submission, destroyed. These white linens are weighed down by deep blue orchids. The smell will bring her calm, he says. Lull her into sweet fantasy.

She can see the great king from the window. A statue of no mortal life, looming over the distant fields by the lake, a playground of gentle beasts. Generations passed under this sky without birds. *I am dying*, she thinks with relief, petrified as the floor of the upper room vibrates. Now the mesmerist calls her spirit to him. She has not sweat her weight in fright, and there is simply no excuse. No excuse! For this retreat into tranquility.

He stings her skin with liquid glaze and climbs on top of her, fully dressed, a hand on each cheek, his forehead pressed against hers. All is lost in the cage of capture. From time to time, she reaches a hand to her crumpled thoughts — painted like icing at the eyes and mouth. The night demands a white dress. Clean hands. Gentle strokes from the invisible places, and the quiet, breathless wish for sanctuary in the sky.

Arms spread out over the rolling blue. Golden blossoms grow beneath her skirt, and the sun beams bright in the deep pool of her dreams. The only place a girl's eyes sink into without blood, without theatre.

Black roots twist around her ankles, tying her down to the bed. Healed by gentle chirrups, scents, and balms of the afterlife. Whispers from the depths of darkness slide over her skin. Old confusion. A familiar wandering.

In the soft, mute language of the endless night, serpents fly with disembodied heads. Black bulbs with wings, gnats from the underbrush, crowd on invisible bodies. A white wraith with nine eyes stands guard in the mist, knowing all, hearing all. She holds her breath. Hesitates to move. Keeps living.

Standing out beyond the door of reason lives the red tomb. Violence, rebellion. Indulgences of the imagination, only. In this mess. In this cage of capture. In quiet sleep, deep enchantment watches over deepest despair. Exhausting, and irrational, this familiar night. A deep buzz, self-accusation blinding her to the door. It is open...

Father tastes her lips. Terror notwithstanding, he revels in the ethereal warmth. The temptation passes as a curse into the dreary vale. In a rock, a lake, a cavern, the shadow of death — no pain but contemplation. She holds back a stream of vomit as his shriveled lips lift away.

"Nature breeds perversion because boredom is the atlas of the universe," he goes on. "Here there is tedium, let us stir. Let us stir it up with nonsense! Fear! Disgust! From this there may come some kind of meaningful vexation." Fables speak of repulsive things that know evil as good and good as evil. He makes this admission, levels with himself.

"I will meet the darkness with deadly aim," he says, staring at her. "Stroke the frown from the faces of hell and let them see. Let them see! I still live!"

The brightness of her heart glows black. Her hand rips through his chest with a phantom suddenness. The lights dim, and he is swimming in the excrement of his deepest mind — words and worlds. Words and worlds. All around him, all within him. In a trance of peculiar origin, she speaks.

"You would silence worlds as you feed on grim death," she says. "Never to see or speak in ways expected."

"Might I bother with ways expected!" he throws back, protesting the scolding as he had from mother to patron saint.

A deeper vision knocks him to the floor. The cerebral door opens, and it is deepest fire. Heat rippling forward, stinging pulses on his head. Sweet burns for sweet brilliance. A furnace-frost for the soon-dead.

"Was it God, woke me up to life as art and unease? I have every mind to shut the door on *him*."

Gut-red wings flutter in wait beyond a dark cloud. Talons of glass curl forward, pausing in false time. In her eyes, he sees himself in earnest — old, approaching death. He recoils, but not in weakness. Only with the twisted apathy of a long-sitter.

"Enough!" He breaks the trance, pushing her back down on the bed. Every image dissolves into exhaustive dullness. In one swift motion her wrist breaks free of the bond, thrashing against his face, her nails dripping with acid. He pins her to the bed, beating her chest and face, dark froth bubbling from her lips, chaotic wheezing singing out the frail, funereal horror of her place.

"What is going on in there?"

A servant pounds on the door. Father climbs off the bed, adjusting his silver robe before answering. Tears stream down her face, onto the orchids. She cannot move.

"She is frightfully unwell. Go and fetch some water," Father tells the servant.

"She must eat, sir. Her blood weakens. We wish to slay one of the goats."

"Any goat but the white!"

"Yes, Father."

Magic seeps through the weakling roots of wilderness. The girl's soul sails out to the fields and slips in among the white weeds. In the company of simple beasts, rabbits and gentle goats. Eight brown, and the white.

What a journey it would be, to be abducted by spirit senses for a day. To roam the untouched lands. Derelict, abandoned, alone. In sickness, perhaps, one might venture to cherish such trivialities. There are the watchers in the mist. One must heed the call of such creatures, Father says. Praise the beasts, for they are honest. Mark the manner of the others, and eat them on golden plates!

Among many dark associates and murmuring of nature, the shimmer of horror lurks beyond the leaves. Believing little in the light of day, frightened by her wax-like hands, her winter skin, her sickly spirit watches from the white weeds. She trembles, lost in the trance again. Hands of unseen order reach down from the firmament with sightless strength, pushing stones down on the goats, mashing them into the mud. Feasters from the sky, knotted hands reaching, tattered robes dancing, baleen teeth bare, swoop down into the fields, drinking the mass of matter that was once animal life. The uncanny manifestation of their feast — whale-goat fiends from the cosmic abyss. Their great red wings flap so fiercely that she is thrust into deafness. The sun has become something else — a beast that feasts on itself. Blood rains down from the devourer, over the corpses, over her.

These dangers of night are known on the calendar. Washed-out skies and great winds wail. Father, invisible magnetism pulsing through his wooden eyes, dips her fingers in the green acid, preparing her again. Orchid petals shiver, wither, fall. At an unexpected point of suffering, she smiles, knowing a thousand other senses lie beyond his access. Wandering through an incestuous dusk, warm drops of saliva running over her breasts. The ritual is executed with silent gestures. Spirit and body alike lean into the horizon, absorbed by the departure, in heart and in mind. Once amethystine eyes are now pale pink, blinded by the sucking, the saliva. Phosphorescence sweeps through the blackness.

She comes to in the belly of a sight unseen. Awash in the pink valley — blood and mist — odorous, with ash and dust climbing up her legs. A quiet murmur from the blackness makes the rocks shiver. She is in her own mouth and lost in horror. Stripped of her clothing, devoured by demon orchids in a petal-cocoon. Giant worms writhe in the stellar haze. She is covered in pink rot, green rot, black weeds from the sea as she is spit out into the lake. Deafened further by the onslaught of her own screams, she flails. Father covers his ears. Her life force vibrates against his chest. His wooden eyes fall out, infected sockets absorbing the psychic filth.

He demands this feast of the senses through trickery, through deceit. His life-force liberated only by encroaching death. He has the look of darker worlds hidden in the treasure of his consciousness.

Her limbs are now useless. Her eyes are painted glass. There is no season more visceral or more reeling than her anguish. The house, disengaged from the town at the end of the valley, keeps pace only with the black magic of our father. He reaches into his robe and discovers ash in the pocket. Hot stones sewn deep into his body break apart, poisoning the blood. Bones jut out of his palms. With his back turned against the moon, he cries.

"On the first day, God said *the abyss*, and flooded the cosmos with the dregs of time."

A great vibration hurdles through the atmosphere, as horrid swooping pales the senses against what has become. Father falls unconscious, his body limp against hers on the bed. The girl gains color in her flesh — the pink hue of new blood, new life. She finds within herself the will to blink, to breathe, to move, and forces his body away, pushing it onto the floor. Her eyes fall upon him and find no features, no face.

The field, soaked in pink mist, sings out the sorrow of an uncanny feast. In time, the girl finds the strength to walk, to leave the house, to wander back into this natural world. As body and spirit walk as one into the fields for the first time in ages, she stumbles to the edge of the lake. The white goat, drowned in the emerald wash, comes into view. Its rotting carcass floats up and turns without grace, face forward and frozen. It no longer has the face of a goat, but of the man himself.

Her father, your father, the father of all.

folie à plusieurs

J ESSICA Dara sits down with the object at hand, and takes it in. She
sees the sculpture, the image of a poltergeist, dancing. Her mother
was a dancer, and so this means something to her. Only one limb is
hovering off the ground, and yet it is entirely stable, suggesting even
more power when stabilized by both limbs. One set of monstrous hands
is turned upward and out front in a dance articulation. The other two
are closer to the sphere surrounding his figure. His headdress fans out in
small limbs which evoke the thought of sun rays. The sculpture itself is
clearly deteriorating, with an aqua tint that evokes the thought of lichen
on tree bark. A typical metallurgical reaction she knows of as the
oxidation of copper metal. She leaves the sculpture, unable to assimilate
its contents into meaning. What it speaks of is something very different
– very sick. She feels the heat stir up in her body.

Turning light, like foam contained inside a human glass ornament
– her skin becomes pale and bloated. Her legs turn into a great orange
boulder. She is surrounded by half-phantoms and all manner of devilish
things. They dance around her in the brown excrement of hallucination.
Art evokes such sordid remembrances.

This is humanity painted in wax. She reaches down, touches herself,
remembers again.

Fiery red and grey-cloaked, fading into the blackness of the horizon.
His feet were painted black. He removes his wooden eyes and she sees
un-love in them. Leading on, laughing intoxicatingly, walking down into
this abyss of incomprehension. She was followed by white flies that fell
into ash.

There are more beautiful things in the gallery than glass globes and
the preserved bells. One might close their eyes and think of a multitude

of universal gardens of the mind, like wine spilling onto black hills. In the supreme depth of this thinking, she remembers herself floating aside some bony thing, her lower half fading into an ecstasy of green tendrils, gray light — a face comes upon her like a sponge. Its eyelids shot waves of warmth. Her head lowers as the roman candles flicker. Bottles fall, spilling moss and cherries and the disgusting bacteria of rotting time. There were many stories spoken about the people she saw that day — of larvae and worms and phantoms from the sky. Wandering, she transcended herself without blood, without mind — in the possibility of the firmament's cherry pink odor. Like an enormous rose picked up by the heathens of the sky, she had an inclination to watch the men and women fondling each other in the bright light of dawn — sucking at limbs and faces and breasts. Cocks sob over dead mouths. She cannot escape this parade. She referred herself back to the old broken books and remembered the smell of her own body as she sought that one forbidden pleasure. Strange desperation wriggles through her heart like a serpent captured on the ground. She sobs on her knees, a shadow passing over. There is no study to be done of this day. All that were there blew a kiss and passed into the great abyss of death — melting into the ground, an ecstasy of warm wind, blood, and pain.

She looks away from this mess and sees a pale lavender butterfly painted with copper and gold. Its metallic sense is eaten by a finch with red eyes, devouring it as though it were a worm instead of the glory of its blossoming form. An ell-horse watches as her body turns white in blood-milk. Her nipples are red. Her lips are red. Her eyes are black. She cannot know herself among such things — among these multitudes of madness.

She is afraid to reveal her fear. Embarrassed by this devouring of the mind, an extremely important thing. She sees smoking candles sleeping in the corner of the room, distinguished by a red glowing light, preserved as poorly as the paintings on the walls. She wants those heated ideas that were burned up — reassurances in the form of whispers. Her breath labors, and the memory is no longer a poor glimmer — boundless feeling. Rising up, she feels a deep stabbing fire in her heart — something she acquires with great calm. Her arms cross over her breasts and full light flares. Columns rot, images fade into the distant darkness. There is no protection from this rain of reminiscence. There is no veil to shield her from eternity. The firmament glows like raspberry syrup. A ghost-thumb reached deep inside of her and the noise is abolished. Her heart hurts, like it has been beaten by a hammer. Her pussy throbs like it has been touched by the gods. She snatches the painting with her hands and it burns her. She cannot drop it, but stares at the paint. The air sucks in her gaze like a sleepless drunk. The painting in brown and tan and black — a woman being strangled by some unimaginable bony horror. She looks into the painting, shimmering underneath the pale globe lights. Her hand still burns.

There will be no roses on her grave. She slides across the paint, transfixed and deeply moved. The air becomes nothing — black stars scatter in her mind, in her eyes. Dead silence shames the room for its indifference. She is obliterated by this darkness. Her hands disappear, then her arms, breasts, torso, her eyes — all sucked into the deep, demented landscape of the painting that floats back onto the wall. A third figure crouches in the background, in the agony of eternity as though it has always been there.

The painting becomes simpler — deep lines become thin colors, become bloody. Forms become faint against the canvas. What can be seen is only an image of a woman facing down — great brown hair blown out like fire, a hand reaching deep inside of her from beneath.

rithenslofer [the corpses of mer]

IT *was the sea*, she said, black froth rising on the waves. Spirits dance on the deck — glowing white shadows, painting the would-be winter with regret. I swallow, covered in weeds and black slime. The banner rips apart, falling to the waves. Bathed in the dead-sea glamour, she stares blankly out into the horizon, towards the darkness of war — dark ships sink with horrifying speed.

Swells soar like the laughing of harridans. Red blood rises up, turning to black foam. A cyclone rises, then ten, then a thousand, circling the great mouth of the sea.

Rithenslofer has destroyed the sea kingdom, she chokes out. *This war, he has won.*

The final ray of sun hits her. In many lives she has fought, in many forms. Now as merfolk, whale, and water. The waves stir up more blood, more bodies. I'm blue in a lament for the deceased I have yet to bring aboard. There is no land, there is no air, there is no breath free from the bitter taste of salt. One could not fall asleep during such a wild night without a dream of injury or substance. Oh, how silent it is, the face of earth when surrounded by water! How the creatures of death float up as though they are all evidence towards the truth that God is dead! The hostile forces of life are coming. There is destiny and there is guilt. There is a silent vision that thrills the thought of salvation. The black barge leans forward into the deep.

A child, no more than thirteen, rises up from the water, quite alive amid the procession of flesh. Her skin glows white, contrasting with the hideous deep.

"Mother!" she cries. "Mother!"

Her mother will not look. She cries again before her voice turns to a croak. The girl lifts her hands to her ears, weeds dangling forth from every finger, her eyes dimmed by bloodshot. A great boom haunts the expanse of the ocean. Her mother is catatonic. Cannot hear her. Will not hear her. Her hands are held high, over her ears. Her eyes will not blink. Her daughter turns to foam among her sisters. Her body falls to dust in a flash of green — oh god, I cannot avoid counting the horrors on the open sea any longer, but be it my inclination to explain! I saw the death of a daughter that even her mother could not watch. There are moments when the waves crash violently on the deck, full of a silent heat. I rise up, looking out into space, admiring falling hours which in hindsight I had not realized would be the last of pleasure in life. That's why, as one might dance, I rise under the weight of all destruction.

On a high throne of black slime — among other objects — I see splintered wood and water crashing against us. A great black wave as long as the world stands still, blocking out sun and moon. The same takes place before my eyes — an illusion of death. One gives up everything in such predicaments. One must wonder how they have come to such horror through the most feeble of actions. The corpses of Mer ride in on the black foam, dead in the fatal thrush. I'd bypass this phenomenon with my eyes closed if I could. I cannot hear the waves. I hear her scream and then choke on the memory of Christ, discharging sanity with one final sound.

Her face — disfigured by sorrow — knows the end has come. She knew the quiet blue and white of water — soft waves gleaming under moonlit skies. The ghostly silence of traversing the ocean, unhindered by such bleak demonic force. Little red fish fly up and are eaten by the air. Her eyes sparkle in pain and then horror — in the gloom of ending life. I wrap her in my blue uniform coat, however tattered it may be now. Her skin feels as hard as a shell. This creature is on the precipice of death. Melancholy seeps into me. Long have I avoided the slog of eternity. I have seen the strange and dramatic rise up and fall from the waves. I have despaired in the mind, holding lamps high over tides to see what may have been.

Was false hope of a god above me as I sailed the seas in youth? The illusion of power and passion never was. There is no security in the glamour of the ocean. It sinks its victims as easily as a drop falls to a great body of water. Corrupted by the endless horizon and old despair, I raise my red lamp to the last night and see a shape in front of me. My eyes burn in the solemn distress. I'll wait in the gloom of night. Sadness deepens overhead. I will remember the tides of golden hue. The seas of my childhood.

It's what I have done, she says.

I almost feel at home on the sea again. I almost feel dead. Sense is nowhere to be found. I hear the voices responding to everything — responding to me. My screams blind me — a hammer from the deep arms raises up in want of land. Her eyes are still. I see, lost in a haunted dream — sea anemones, flies, coral, broken limbs, fins, and flesh of fish. The will of ghosts rises over the bones of whales. This is a new underworld. This is the remnants of war. Speechless passion cannot tackle the darkness of the sea. We witness every death — the fall of every living thing. The forced birth of evil over the infinite waves. The ocean is a tomb of torment. The black flood seeps onto the deck. Other beings will meet doom in their own time...those on land and in the air. We hear a voice stir, or I hear it alone. She is catatonic in contemplation of herself. Power lost to the mistake of half sleep. There are no lamps of faith over these waters. I have dreamed at night of ocean birds flying over, flying past, flying out into the horizon, leading the way towards the end, towards dirt, towards former life.

In the morning, she says, *end me as you will. This has been blessing and curse.* She knows herself as womb and winter.

There are sicker souls and colder eyes than these. The sounds come in on the waves — murmuring prayers and choked languages of the deep. I fancy myself a witness of the absolute annihilation of fathoms. I lift her nude form from the deck, phantom voices crying o'er. Do they send love or doom or sleep to me? An infection from the infinite night? She swallows her fear, or is it regret? I grow mad as I come through the water, as I came through the dawn after battle, murmuring to myself of the glamour of the sea. Of a beauty who might enter here under certitude of death. The ruins of the barge hold me still.

She falls from my arms into eternity. I wait for a silhouette on the horizon. My eyes glow in this betrayal of the self. I have not escaped the tomb of the world. For one final moment, my eyelids grow heavy. I clench. I see her sink down, forever lost — surrounded by the corpses of her daughters. There is no veil to be lifted. This is a war of endless night. She sinks down to the ruins of the fallen kingdom, eyes wide in recollection of guilt, a wound of black opened up with the best of intentions. My eyelids close to the last thrashing sound. I sink into the crimson dream of night and dread the rise of Rithenslofer.

in the room of red night

BODIES. Delicate, with a dying breath, caught in the stillness of the world.

Bodies. Bloodless and betrayed. Art as death, death as desire under the northern flame.

Bodies. Lovers entangled by bones. The womb of the mother — infected, dribbling. A gentle sway without reason other than to welcome us through — our procession.

There were too many good days before this — and now, there is a price to pay for them, in the room of red night.

We come over the dune like cattle — a long dried-out species in these plains. Forms are muddled in the fog, appearing as bundles of blackness beneath tattered passage coats. Fur drapes over the body entire, most notably at the crown of the head. Long scarves of black mesh cover our mouths to keep the bitter sting at bay. One would not look upon a sky so red and think of winter. In this way, our souls hold some seed of exception in the universe.

Colton, on the leash, is like the hyena. Dragged in his derangement alongside us because he cannot bear the chamber that calls him back. Dalton, the bear among men, taking the front. Busiris and Bostro, the brutes, and the quiet woman, Gelia, walking ten paces to the left, without speech. All here have had an excess of good days.

We set out broken on the path of death and dust — human life. Here we wait and wade. Wait and wade. Into oblivion. Into the accursed hue. The birds are lost. The memory of them is vague, like the madness I imagine waits for me. I've lost my love for this scarlet world.

Swinging on frail threads, floating over us. One thousand bodies, perhaps two. Skin that would be green is white, soaked with the water we know as sacred. It keeps them. It calls us to them from the farthest reaches of the dunes.

I look to one man, the closest hanging above me. Dried vomit clings to his extremities. Castrated, colorless — two gaping voids where once his eyes were.

The bodies drip white paint. Busiris has taken to a woman's corpse, with child. A mass of larvae erupts from her pregnant stomach with one faint poke to the skin.

Dalton spits into his palm and rubs the phlegm on the soles of the Eromaeon's feet. We know this blessing.

"Once tormented, life is distilled to an abbreviated grievance."

"Is there not some way around this, some detour?" I ask. Dalton looks to me with rage and I fall silent. I would not annoy him for the least of conveniences. Even this, they would remember from on high.

"The sky is as red as the old years," they say. "The Meiser can sense everything!"

Great mountains bleed into the valley below. The skies turn to blood. Red rivers bleed out to a forgotten sea. No one has ever seen it, but they say it washes clean the wounds of men.

Might the Meiser be flesh and blood? Or a gnome of rancor, built for no human eye? A rumor rode from other villages, far from Hule, that a horrid thing fell from the sky and spoke to them without sound, and then disappeared into the sand. At times of aggravation, it becomes a giant, pulling itself out of the den of the swarm with great gaunt hands. Up from the sand, into the sky...

And the swarm! To pursue the memory is to pursue that familiar delirium of a forgotten world. Savage beasts that would not hide their wings, living as men until the moon shattered. With one long parting look to logic in a secreted haze, the villages fell to them. Their nest, a subterranean slime pit, hides far beneath us. There they wait. There they writhe.

Meteors scar the night sky, bleeding clouds of fire behind them. A broken moon quivers behind the fury. Scattered rocks, as omens, pull closer from the point of birth to our world. A tarnished globe, plummeting under the black protean gloom. Space — and all kings it cradles in our senses. Lungs, tongues, trash, and terror. All things familiar in this monstrous array. There is no juice so bitter as that of the dying body. The resurgence, thick with bleakness of the brine.

Thoughts drift to a dream of flowers, enchanted winds, words spoken, only to be heard in the strangest of places. The imagination haunts, as it perhaps should, after deep study and hours of bereavement. I require a degree of rest.

A sound; faint whistling from the strange mist, gathering ever thicker around my bloody collar bones. Without internal motion, save for the dribbling of bodily muck into the green abyss, I hang, suspended over the mythic eternal — indefinable nothingness. This is my condition, within a dream.

I think the end must be coming. I've lifted the shards of myself in search of the way out. Curse this place of enchanted despair, and the years of measured days! God is gone, and I am on the road again. We march on.

The structure speaks to the otherness below. One could count thousands of the strange, crooked boxes that form the basis of its structure. It is enormous — a damaged pupil in a bleeding eye. The building of the deepest hue — black designed to absorb all light, in rigid blocks piled askew. No windows, and no doors, save for the secret entrance beneath the piled stones.

The mountains encroach, painting jagged horizons of black against burnished skies. Thoughts of hellfire plague every step. Red fog rolls in from the valley, blurring every man from knee to toe.

The vaulted halls, splendid in ornament, wretched in deceit. It has the look of an earnest pleasure garden — or the entry parlor of one. I would remember, as I frequented them in youth, if only for gentle observation. A purveyor of life, married to avoidance, sipping the pleasures of the body through the mind alone. I could only betray myself as lightly as this, after the coming of the swarm. She. She. She.

Margaerta, deep in the mud.

Her copper hair soaked in blood. The girl of no earth. Her face mutilated by the passing tendrils of the swarm. Her heart ripped from her chest, for what? I dare not imagine. Corpses strewn about the village shared this dismal fate. An open chest, freed of the heart.

I know of eternal despair. Of mourning. How it teases the mind. Can man cradle madness in memory alone? I grow weary of false men in quiet places. Even myself. There is too much time to think in these conditions.

Gelia's long fingers reach up to untie the sheath from her mouth. Scores of red dust fall from the black fabric as she lowers it from her face. I will avert my eyes before she sees me so unnerved. I fear the strength in her would take it as insult. And why shouldn't she? She crossed the land with as much fervor as any. And she did so, having been here before.

She has the look of the girl of no earth — there, in the enormous grey eyes. But none of this would matter, if not for memory of Margaerta. I lurch, and she raises her brow. Everything around us is madness. Two bodies wonder why they are separate and anguish over time. I imagine her — the spirit — returned to me, and feign a cosmic kiss to the air. I seal myself a river in this kiss. Without faith or feeling. Only the tenderness of a hurting heart as the others pass through the door and into the depths of the accursed underground.

We descend into the bitter depths with little light, save for the glow of lichen looming overhead. Black rock intermingling with organic tubes.

The farther down we travel, the more it breathes, this horrid place. There is no sign of life yet. At the point of exhaustion, hissing rolls into the atmosphere. Fetid mist brings on deep delirium. We are on our knees. On our knees...

A long wooden table, stained black, is large enough to seat hundreds. Our eyes, caked in phlegm, struggle to open. We are tied into strange, mangled chairs.

"Our villages send their candidates in the off-season," Dalton says, seeing me look around for other unfortunates. "To be sure we receive the fullest attention."

Gelia takes the seat across from me. Our eyes meet in a singular daze. I pull away. She continues to stare before our eyes turn to the cloaked servers lurching into the hall. Colton lets out a whimper at the sight of the silver plates.

Gelia whispers something unintelligible, leaning close to me across the table. She leans back again.

"Enough of your ancient drivel!" Dalton bangs his fist on the table. The men are nervous. The servers stand to the right as they place their hands over the plate covers, ready to reveal our dinner.

I wonder now what the chamber will do to him. I wonder what it has in store for me. They say that when you leave (if you do), the only memory you have is of those horrible hours.

The covers lift. On each plate sits a mass of charred meat - pure black, powdered in ash — we are expected to eat.

"He will pull the pink," Gelia says to me.

Busiris and Bostro have already made way with the cutting of the hocks. The smell is putrid. I look up from my plate to see Gelia laughing.

"Is this the first of their torture?"

"Overcooked dinner? My, have you seen so little of pain?"

I look away again, not bothering to answer. I have seen pains to rival the room of red night. There is no doubt of it. But I have borne them in such a way as to live. This she will not understand, and so it is perhaps best that we meet in such a way. We would not find ourselves at ease outside these walls.

She chews with expectation. Her fingers reach to the back of her throat. The sound is slimy — the mechanical wetness of experience. She pulls. The lanterns bearing down on us illuminate a single strand of white. A hair, dangling between her fingers. She watches it with knowing eyes.

"What?" I ask. She motions to my plate. I look down on the black hock of meat. Fingers jammed down throats proceed with pulling. From the depths, strands of every kind emerge. Black, gray, purple, green...

He will pull the pink.

And I do. From the soreness of my throat, I pull a long, pink strand — a color that makes no sense to my eyes. Glistening, garish. My stomach turns. The servers come around to gather the remnants of the meal. I give them the plate and goblet, satiated by disgust.

"You would not drink?" Gelia adds, downing the brown liquid. A loathsome concoction of desert herbs, no doubt.

"I would not drink their hell juice, no."

"Then there will be a price to pay for it."

"What price is any worse than what will already become of me?" I ask, the weight of fatigue pulling me down into a half-slump.

"The juice was a numbing agent. Given with mercy."

I swallow hard.

We are escorted to sleeping chambers for one night of rest. My limbs grow weak in this labyrinth of gloom. One might dream of random things, and find some undercurrent of truth; a strain of allegory in an otherwise ceaseless cacophony of mental anguish.

Must the devil get into my head tonight? Where blood is equal currency with thought? From the depths of the mountain. Like the harvested swarm, learning best to be men. Murky sea, milky sea, the multitude calls, and I am deeper — still in the ache of dreams...

It begins with the plummeting of my body through a damp tunnel, down from some impossible door. A void of black rock — the path growing smaller with each step. I've curled from full height to a guided crouch, unnerved by the noiseless path ahead. I trip and smash my face on a hard slate. The end of the passageway. Searching hands fall only upon skeletons — others lost in the attempt to flee, perhaps downed by their wounds from above.

At the point of giving up, I move aside the mortal remains and find a hole in the wall big enough for me to crawl through. Burrowing down into the rock, I feel less of a worm than above. There is something of a peaceful honor to dying in one's own way, rather than by hands held against the world.

A sliver of light illuminates my filthy arms, reaching out to the next swath of black rock. The narrow path has turned upward. There is a question of remaining strength in my upper body — if there is any left, or if I am destined to die with the light on my arms only. I pull and pull. Up up up to the light. It is a light I have not seen. Not scarlet, or red in any way — but a gentle yellow.

As I pull myself out, leaving the burrow of the mountain, I find myself in a cave. A gentle sound stirs outside. Limping forward, blood continues to seep from my gut, caked in the black dirt of the mountain depths.

With my hand on my stomach, I walk to the edge and see what very few have ever seen in this world. A vast ocean of milk white, as far as my eyes will take me. If I were to have wings to soar over the distance, I believe that I would find nothing but these waters from here to the ever after.

I look down and note that the water is shallow. No deeper than two meters, perhaps. The gentle ebb shifts in stages, revealing the ocean floor — populated by what may be millions of shards of pearlescent glass.

There is no land, or so says my wandering eyes. With the sea floor being so shallow, I could walk to some forgotten distance. As I think this, numbness cascades through my insides. Blood continues to ooze. I know in this moment that there is little chance of life for me beyond this precipice.

As my flesh commits to the surface, I am not within myself. I feel, rather, that I have become a wondrous multitude. My body breaks into ten thousand pieces. I have no eyes of flesh to look upon the wall, though I can still see. In these depths, the art of my existence will not cease. Frightened awake by the rocks above, echoes and delusions possessed my mind. I am now one of fractured millions, and the haunt of missing limbs is far from my mind.

I promise my pieces magic in these depths. I promise to succeed in the fullness of my flesh over the waves. To think that time might wait for me to reassemble – to emerge again from waters without birth – sets the roots of deeper vision in my hardened gut more than any earthly thing. I will watch the mountainside from this place, in wait for those who seek this painless rest. To this liquid life, I now surrender. I can hear her there.

He will pull the pink.

I choose not to shame my companions by looking at them now, but I know what I would see. Dalton's ocular veil, dissolved. A quiet apprehension in both Busiris and Bostro, seen only in their sloped shoulders and downcast eyes. Colton sipping up the remnants of his drool, the last of his twitches slowing to a mild turn of the head. Gelia is another matter. She stands in honor before the door, with more scars and haunts than the best of men.

My worry is not of life after death. I have come to a silent worship of an undying light; an everlasting current of energy connecting all life. This is all I can commit myself to as it comes to belief in my earthly incarnation. But my concerns do not lie with it. Rather, they lie with the fate of the universe itself.

Are spirit worlds bound together by some cosmic strain, or are they planet-bound, doomed to the inevitable annihilation that will devour their worlds entire? It is during these gloomy wanderings of the mind that the organic door, caked in rust, creaks open.

I am surrounded by enormity — a decadent fracture in the subterranean hall. A cavern fit for giants. The ceiling is so high that it is drowned in shadow. The walls are sinking in, bordered by sculptured beasts with horns over every orifice, bulging in obscenity. Deep, deep red consumes my mind. Even my ill-clotting blood. Winding, velvet carpets beneath breaking toes. The ceiling tilts overhead — paned glass set into stone. Everything is peculiar. Every dressing, every chair, every surface wails with the infernal blessing of the Meiser. Every reliquary bursting with the dormant pride of slain giants. This decadent décor, we have all seen it in the forbidden books. Couches with carved ornament on gilded handles, curved desks with marble tops of black and blood, chairs of the finest fibers from the last slaughter of beasts. A bed, even. Fit for the erotic horrors of a star-fallen emperor who would revel in this mud. Red sheets showering down — shimmering black rods. The rot of ages covered with the glistening fall of eyes on embers. These are the things that come with first glances. Second glances reveal the anguish of our predicament.

Horrid metal — twisting, turning, gutting instruments. Ropes. Bottles of strange liquid. What looks like a strange, ambling device in the far corner. So many things that I have not the time to examine them before the turn of fortune. The door is closing behind us.

I see her, set into the wall. As though she herself were part of the ornament, carved into the rocks. A crown of death hovers over her. A pile of skulls, as a monument, breathing in and out of the visible plane, a heated mess of gutted flesh dribbling over. One single eyelid admits the burden. It shuts halfway. The other is wide. A drip of ghoulish blood berates her. Perfumed with the syrup of dead angels. Deep pink hair twists upward, intermingling with auburn wire atop her head. Her eyes are quite large for her triangular face. Red robes of rare cloth flow down to the floor. The deep v-neck of the garment leaves much of her cleavage and stomach exposed. The most horrid feature of all is her inhumanly long neck — green and luminous in a sea of glowing shards, cascading down between her breasts. Sharp teeth, long fingers. A cast of gold to the swamp-like skin, the marriage of beauty and horror. A dark doll, fit with a position beyond her capacity to reconcile. I can see myself forgiving her abuse of me in one of my delicate dreams, but that is before I have stepped myself entirely within the chamber. I am in shock, knowing death is coming.

With a greater swiftness than that of our approach, we are whisked to the center of the cavern by the beasts of the swarm. Our tormentors remove their sheaths to the sound of the screeching door — their long, humanoid locks fall down over bodies cloaked in shadow. The faint glow of mutant lichen reveals them to be extraordinarily deformed. Man or insect, one could never discern.

The woman from the wall descends. On the approach, I come to realize her enormity. Gelia throws me a fearsome look, as if to say, *Don't speak.* This is where the terror begins.

The giant slides her fingers along her scalp, lifting the crown of her head off to reveal a gaping emptiness — her skull. Insect limbs reach and pull the pulsing grey masses from the ceiling of the cavern. They appear to be hearts. Each is held close to the enormous stalactite in the center of the chamber. Warming them. Warming them...

The swarm bows to the woman from the wall, handing her the organs. She lifts the squirming masses one by one and places them in the bloody depression, closing her head again and sealing the shaft with her pink saliva. We have no time to think after this moment. It has begun.

I feel the vomit rise up, and it is black, black blood. I have known no pain like this in living. Since my birth into the broken world. Toxic bubbles burst out of tiny holes in the wall. They pop and drop down on the skin, acid. I want to spit out my soul and be done with it. I want to be cast in the white water, frozen in time above the perilous dune. Bewitched, groping for pink hair and green flesh.

The tormentors signal to each other with their strange limbs. I know such language of war. It is the way of speaking during the swarm's ascent. Our hands rush to our ears to block the wheezing screams.

Before my mind can comprehend the turn of fate, my comrades are a mess of flesh all around me. Dalton is thrown on a wall of spikes, impaled at the face and gut. Busiris is made to swallow the black poison. His body turns green and expires before my eyes. Colton's head is submerged in the festering lagoon. Bostro's jaw is ripped off to make room for the burrowing snake, which slithers down his throat and bursts out of his gut.

Gelia's face. I can see her, in my mind.

I search for her wildly in the clash — searching, *searching*.

She turns her head to me — the slowness, the grace — all familiar. I know the way bodies move at the end of time. A phantom limb drags a giant blade across her neck. Her head, nearly decapitated but for a still spine, tilts backwards. Blood gushes to the floor, trailing down her limp arms. A lifeless finger points stiffly towards...a hidden door. Jutting out from beneath a puddle of blood. I watch until her eyes forfeit the soul to the great unspoken night.

I am ruined. Ruined! The agony! The motions left and right away from swords and poison! As I look down to see I have been gutted in some way, with blood pouring from the stomach, the woman from the wall locks her hands around my neck, digging in her talons. She means to strangle the life from me with the strength of ten men, but this is not my ending day. I bend my knees and throw her overhead. The mess continues as she wavers in and out of consciousness.

Looking at her now, I don't see what I thought I would. Her face holds a compelling, human hardness. Her eyes are glassy, revealing her for what she was — something wanting, something lost. I wonder what she may have been before all of this. Was she someone like I was, once?

I drag myself out from underneath her. The latch is pulled, and I descend into the black depths of the mountain.

I can only remember the essence of myself. My face. These hands and limbs. I drag my mangled body through rocks without clothes, or light, or direction. Only the memory of the room of red night.

# of one pure will

For that which is unavoidable, one must not grieve.
There was never a time that I was not.
The Dweller in the body of everyone.
She tells me of God – the witch who made the world.
And submits to the capture of a moment, sublime.
Driving me into the dirt

HERE come the eight-string days of Autumn, dreamlike and quivering, glowing above me. The moon rolls back, as solitary and as quiet as my daughter was. Gloom moves through these villages. Willows sigh to the ground — their branches weeping as one weeps upon the death of a child. There are more ecstatic days behind these, removed from the turbulence of guilt. A blue blanket of air folds over me as I carry her across the street — fair light upon my brow, the heat within my heart.

We covered the house together with white cloth after her mother left — a choice against the usual mourning of death. She took her rightful position in the world and I take up the loss of two at once — losing the elusive mask of manhood. I walk home with my daughter, hand in hand. The dirt of the streets sweeps past our feet. I have carried her through these avenues and lanes — embracing the cheers, the torment. My own eyelids tiring from the garden of sleepless nights. Women in colorful dresses watch us pass in black and white — questioning my emptiness, estranged abbreviation, detachment.

Only some are healed by the power of closure. I have conquered nothing in this way. In the death of my first wife, the departure of my second. My daughter is so little, so aware of the comings and goings.

Sage Gould, a daughter of autumn, always sleepless and dreaming tides of elfin gladness. Weekly walks in the park become strained – an artifice for the little girl. She does not belong in the world. Every evening I walk with my daughter through the city park, through the gardens at dusk. She always remarks on the color of the glow, coolness of the breeze. My strange desperation makes me quiet.

I sit with her and read her stories. Epics, tales, and terrors to dim the fading cloud of motherhood. I hug my child, folds of copper hair flowing over my arms. I want to change her story. I cannot.

"Have we reached the end of the tale, Elliott?" She calls me Elliott, not Father. I tuck her in gently, kissing her forehead, turning out the lamp. I hear rapid knocking on the old oak door.

My first daughter, Claire, comes through the entryway, her lips blackened by root-milk, ever-ailment lurked behind her wax-like skin. I have contended with this creature of deceit in more obscure rooms of night. There is no bitterness so disembodied from the soul of man than that which resides within her. Yet, somehow, she is mine. She glares frighteningly, seeking out my little one, tales of a broken childhood glistening in her eyes.

"Does Sage sleep?" she asks, cities of calm in her deep voice. Long silence passes. This, she holds against me.

"Leave this house," I demand. A penetrating look, and she weaves her feet from me, gliding away, the bulk of her plum skirt flowing behind her, a phantom framework of resentment.

My daughter is of one pure will. An unspeakably heavy knowledge of the labyrinthian depths of life. It fades slowly, as childhood gives way to a troubling adolescence. She is haunted by the same dysphoria as her sister. I will worship no god who threads such suffering within the heart of an innocent daughter.

"I wish to die after summer, like trees and flies," she says to me, not yet fifteen. I see Claire leave the house as I arrive home from work, with a Victorian black collar standing high, concealing her neck. She weaves in and out of the city streets, like a phantom traveler, wandering afresh amid the perils of shapeless life, appearing at our door as often as my darkest daughter does. I can never catch her, predict her coming. She comes and he goes as swiftly as a bat may.

Some girls hide behind shadows of pretension, their intimate stirrings being as peculiar and dirty as the sea. Sage is no such thing. She smiles discreetly, exhausting the air without ruse. I feel some onslaught, some peril coming from the unknown place that presides over all things.

I hear Claire coming, like an orchestra of rumbling bees.

Her mother knew herself a ghost among the living at this same young age. With skin painted spectral-ivory and a penchant for silent wandering, a daughter adopts the identity of her mother. So caught up with things of nature and the divine, and yet never missing the meaning behind every human glance. She kisses the air — nocturnal purity in motion.

Claire crosses in front of me without the slightest attempt at friendliness.

"Speak, and I would understand everything." She knows me, still.

The silence of the starscape is not lost on me. I have behaved with grace, and so I die ten thousand deaths in this quiet room.

"You clipped my wings, but I have always been free. In here," she says.

There is equal motion in the snake, at both head and tail, during movement — during living. When I get the sensation that I have hurt the world, only then do I leave behind the fear myself. I can't remember the sensation of taste. The act of eating is a chore. Vomit sits at the belly in wait, a constant of uncertainty, if such a thing is, or may become. To slobber or to slumber on this haunted flight of stairs? My daughter has gone from me, and I do not know where.

I supplement sanity with the buried memory of an ancient earth. The temptation of knowledge — nature's inborn kill switch. I never had an affinity for concrete things. The particulars of the universe are lost on me. I am as gullible as I am culpable.

Even dark and dangerous things may be precious. They instruct us like no being of light can.

In my anguish to paint a perfect past, a rosy cast over my dark roots, I instead find a window into the future. Not because of some supernatural intuition, but because I will it to be. How often have we heard it said that heathen spectres long since dead may linger still? How often haunts of precocious deaths and silly riddles mock the land and deprive it of its majestic frailty? There is no frailty in darkness but our own.

The sheer density of black on black does a number on the mind so profound that it is impossible to reconcile. My candles are lost. The flames, undelivered. This is the reality of a ruined man. Living as the temple lives and breathes, where it cannot be taken down without paramount force. I am not so lightly engaged as I may have been. I promised myself heaven, so I would not be afraid to leave this world. Claire and Sage are not my daughters. They are my one daughter, lost to the disease of time and neglect, coming to me again and again.

There are conditions through which we judge our character, bludgeoning ourselves with memories and missteps. There are two ways in which to escape the absolute end. Through generosity of spirit and the willingness to continue on, step by step. A woman of ill repute cannot see dominion as necessity! She knows only the delicate touch of wind in cages. A heart of truth beats at an irregular pace: a mechanism of cosmic intervals rather than human ones. They are my daughter, a wisp of wind and memory forever out of reach, out of understanding. There is a family plot to visit, that I cannot bring myself to go to. I am bewitched by the conspiracy of this tainted nature and wish to walk the streets for a time, alone.

time disease [in the waking city]

"Love is a privileged perception, the most total and lucid not only of the unreality
of the world but of our own unreality: not only do we traverse a realm of
shadows; but ourselves are shadows."
—Octavio Paz

PALE storms linger in the white evening, glittering over concrete
and lifeless stone. He arrives in the city, accompanied by the
nightmarish fanaticism of lost time. Dark air flashes green. Fog
rips down the street from the unseen eternity. There he lives and
breathes another age. Lamp-lit by the sounds of nature, he tells himself
there will be pleasure in the panic.

In earlier years, he became a complicated mess of exaggerated
motion and sickly thoughts. Sobs of increasing madness grew so loud
that neighboring parties had no choice but to write their letters of
concern. When the heart is abandoned, vanity is only accentuated by the
bitterness. Someday, at the turning point of peace, I will rejoin her in the city,
he thought, each and every day of his confinement.

This new Providence sends waves of warm panic through his chest.
The bright morning floods into the square. For years he had longed to
return to the city, visions of familiar places soothing his fragile mind
with a decided fervor that lent itself to dreams of reemergence. The stink
of perspiration hangs on his heavy coat. Having been admitted in winter
all those years ago, he hasn't the mind to reconcile the season's air
anymore.

He lights the vigilance of the night with eyes of black. Penetrating
the atmosphere with heaviness of heart, he falls in grief from the throne

of earth, seeking time elsewhere. The anxiety of death stalks him. His heart rotten, beating in despair.

I am breaking apart, he thinks. *I do not know how to live in the city anymore.*

Walking into the distant night, tired eyes glide over every house on the long street. The air, still sticky with the heat of an ailing summer, sets off a fever of memory. Dim moonlight creeps into every crevice of his aging face. Eyes wide, mania setting in, pace quickening.

I will stay awake all night, he thinks, a breathless energy setting into him.

I want to remember.

Leisure is a form of possession. Of necessity. The neutrality of empty spaces tempted him in earnest, long before the confines of the sanatorium diminished his constitution.

Time, he thinks. Outstretched according to his eccentricities. His confinement.

There are lesser nights when he thinks upon the inevitable dark pull and quickly moves on to lighter cerebral imaginings. This becomes more difficult with age. The blindness of youth, a luxury, has long been lost to the lifting veil of internal decrepitude. Every cracking bone is a calling bell to the long sleep.

He knew beauties whose faces were eaten by worms. None so precious as she. She. She. Her anemic lips touched his heart and he couldn't keep time. This became his art and absurdity – a memory of her, in the old city. A fragile, gentle life, crying under the limitless blue. Spared the death set out for him in the swamp of nighttime fog.

There is no honor in death, he thinks. *Only grace in preservation. These are organic concepts. Love is an invention of natural life. Death, a dark inheritance of the stars.* He stands in contemplation of a bitter eternity.

Where does one begin, when describing the place where everything changed for them? Where the whole of their lives collapsed to the eccentricities of the unnatural? He remembers himself as faint and fortunate, prancing about Providence in ecstasies others denied to themselves in fear of fallen morality. There was no fear in him back then. Only now that he has before him the evidence that consequence, should it not manifest immediately, does have a way of circling back. Even the manufactured consequences of warped and warring time.

This is not the place of elder years. The former agrestic landscape surpassed by a modernity of attraction and false ideas. A vast autumnal sky, in fever, heaves over the city. Candles gleam in silent windows. The chill – serene error on this late summer journey. The neighborhood is nothing of its former self. Catapulted into a new unconscious constant.

Progress? he wonders. Far from the chasm, the chaos. Far from the despair of beginnings. He curves his head against the wind and thinks. An ear, touched to the earth, knows no worry. He will not sit to rest. Cold, gray pavement is closer to death.

He turns the corner and sets his eyes on a decrepit garden. Overturned by rabbits or some other creature, carrots and cabbage are strewn about the patch in fragments. The vegetation has a rotting smell, carried by the breeze to his already aggravated nostrils. Every smell is more potent outside of the sanatorium. Every sense exaggerated after years of being unfulfilled.

The dense gloom lessens only by the casual flight of lantern-bugs. He is sleepless. Mortal. The new vegetation has an irresistible strangeness, like the weeds one gathers in the mind when bereft of course and company.

Enough of strange gardens, he thinks.

Anxious moths float past, swarming in the bushes. Stars blink a cool, pale light over the city. A phantom congestion at the corner of Angell and Prospect. The torture of man against the wind, and memories of vanity.

Gnats buzz within earshot. The eyes of ghosts glower at his weight, his age. His anxiety. Certain information being inextricable, he walks on, spirit escorts flanking him on approach to the water. One fear, with pride, circles in his mind: *I was born in Providence and I will die in Providence.*

Cruel innocence, the trembling of unhappy hands. He is displaced in this time-wrecked familiarity. The world after confinement, transfigured. A whirling metropolis of displacement. Everything comes floating to the hollows of his mind one night in the dry pre-autumn. Delicate gloves sweep past iron fences. Rust floats down to dirt. Gentle flakes.

Fluid is his state of gloom. Never losing sanity completely, his old resolve to kill himself in the sanatorium despite this fear of death fades under the weight of erotic personal reminiscences.

Dear Genevieve! Her long, spider legs! Her honeysuckle eyes! Her beauty bolts through him, and he must wait several moments before stepping again.

There is no sky to recognize at this hour. Few animals to know. Determined to conquer this heathen sensitivity, he writhes in the mist. The dormant shards of madness flash as emeralds in the night fog. Illness reels in him, back and forth, a pendulum of vertiginous aching.

He looks up to see a lonely shape walking barefoot in the starry night, foot to foot over each wisp in the great glory of dying weather. Feeling himself perverse, he takes small steps towards the water, subordinated by the looming dread. There is intrigue there in the vast, relentless ebb. Silver rays dance on empty liquid pools. He makes no mystery of it. The familiar shape vanishes into the dense obscurity.

The silence of the firmament reminds him of his troubles. A temporary attribute of the unwillingly confessed. Seeking a sense of vigor, a fortune, he shoos the wisps of anguish as one would shameful ghosts. *Tonight, there will be laughter, familiarity! Tonight there will be life anew!* Preaching to himself feeble accomplishments of expectation, his belly aches with the secret prodding of confinement.

He licks the sky clean of gray and abandons all hope of finding her. The city pours the grief of ages into him. He knows the illusion lives as garbage. Precaution swarms within him as maggots would, after death.

There is still much to see of the city. My city!

Each flower serves as a signpost that he is closer to her — farther from that alien aggression, captivity. Half-filled with the sweet magic of the wilting season, he braves the brightness of the moon. A deep swelling of light breaking through the fog. Like a sterilized angel, blind to the nothingness that is earth living. His chest serves as a fortress of history, bleeding circumstance.

Few are truly thoughtless in silence. She could frighten the darkness away from him with the lantern of her heart, a fractured thing sputtering gold as rivers into the streets of the old city. Genevieve de Geyche! Within her, the might of untold ages. Her endless copper locks as elegant as a gathering of young birds. He inhales her former scent — cypress and a dying summer. Recall her sensitivity in the sunlight. Take in the sounds of her again. The dream returns of her pale, rotting face. Blue, bloated skin-frothing, bubbling, gone from the earth at the mouth of the Mosshasuck.

He could scrub the stain of death out from his mind's eye, and still never know the eternal calm of that moment before her fall. *But if a girl is to leave this earth from any place, wouldn't this be it?*

Into the night, he remembers the sting of affection captured in lost moments, and its power to haunt beyond the bounds of reason. His wrinkled hand grazes the rail of the bridge as it had all those years ago, cold flakes crumbling as he sweeps his fingers past, taking in the texture.

The subtlety of dawn approaches, signaled by the rustle of delicate birds. A citrine-feathered beast materializes over the waking city. Deepest bliss. What need is there for gloom? For mourning? Patience, once reflected in her dusk-dipped wings, lives on through him.

Swollen tree branches burst open, pouring maggots out like falling sand. *Maybe I wasn't ready to return*, he thinks. Fallen blossoms wither on the bridge. A quiet corner orchid gleams the light of former worlds. He bathes in the brightness of the day sun, for the first time.

Soon after returning to the waking streets, his legs begin to quiver. His head is spared as his body collapses against the concrete. Lying in a daze of unreason, city-goers — until then unseen — swarm around, watching with awe and alarm that suggests the sight of a visitor from a distant sky.

Keep calm, he says to himself. Wetness bursts from his gut. A familiar wound in his stomach gushes brown blood. Vulnerable from years in confinement, he wails for the old city.

There she is, coming this way! As lovely, as vibrant as that very day!

Genevieve emerges from the crowd, her Raphaelite hair swaying against him, picking up ruby droplets from the gushing wound and dripping them in pendulous succession over his face. Anticipation grows as her sweetness washes over him. Her eyes, swords of fondness, pierce through the time disease. She smiles, taking his hands, warmth cradling the deep chill in his chest. Further enhanced by the majesty of shadows, her femininity blooms gracefully in the open air.

Stiff and trembling in the heat, she leans over, touching his stomach. Lightning flashes, sending a cast of yellow over the street. The swift flight of nature descends. Feeling the fair breeze exceed his gladness, he hears a voice whisper from an unseen distance.

There are no rivers here! No gardens! Only your bed — a tomb of rot, piss-stained sheets, and these!

The chill of metal grows heavy in his hands. He looks down to see his fingers curled around a pair of bloody scissors.

Now he remembers her in earnest — a stranger without a name, seen only for a moment in the old city, plummeting from the bridge overlooking the river. Climbing down to the water's edge, he held this stranger as she succumbed to death, as one would hug a child on sleepless nights. Enchanted by her delicate limbs, her weary eyes — he would lose his mind in that embrace, confined to the sanatorium thereafter.

Dark thunder flies through the morning. Soon to be unconscious and lost from the earth, he lifts a hand to her cheek and smiles softly.

"Farewell, dear Providence. Your elder rivers and quiet rooms! May this phantom metropolis remain eternal by the sea. If I ran into ruin — myself, within a dream — it is as I willed it to be."

ivisou

I look for her in every friend I make, or try to make. I find myself looking for her in bookstores, or remembering albums she liked while wandering through the stacks at the record store. I have met girls like her, in a way, but there was always some key ingredient missing. Her ebullience, effervescence, enthusiasm, all the Es of wonder that live in an extroverted girl. Charlotte was most like her, I think. She could also walk into a room and demand every eye, every mind. But Charlotte was not wounded similarly, or was perhaps better at healing her own wounds. And certainly didn't try to conceal them. I miss Charlotte intensely though not as much, or not in the same way. How could it be the same? We parted amicably, and it was all circumstance. It wasn't an explosion of heat and violence like the loss of her. I wonder how much healing past her may have taken place, if not for these wicked dreams?

The bog looks so different from the beginning of that summer. Burnt up, used, fetid. It smells like death from a mile away. No one will approach it anymore without a mask. No one will approach me anymore, either. They remember us, together. They don't know what to say anymore.

I have at times paused in confusion at the intensity of this loss, because there was nothing remotely romantic or sexual about it, and aren't we encouraged to believe that platonic relationships cannot harbor the same intensity, guilt, possession, elements of romance or lust? I think it is more painful. I think women feel the pain of these losses in a particular way, though perhaps to say that it is worse than another gender is an unwise generalization. But when girl becomes sister so swiftly, and a sister is lost to eternity as swiftly, it becomes hard to believe that any loss in the history of time could have been so horrible.

It was not a teenage girl's remains that they found at the bottom of the cranberry bog. It was, rather, a strange orchestration of horror in the form of teeth and bones — exaggerated, woven into the belly of the bog's deepest dirt, mud, muck, and grime. This was the beginning of the rotting.

It was not so brown or decayed in the beginning. She once pointed out a grand oak on the hinterside of gathering water, where the cranberries grew deep gold instead of red. The shades of rot and horror were absent in this time, as I regress in the mind back to the evening vale of mist and memory.

One night we stood naked under the moon-coolness. A dare, so unaware of the black decay of eternity creeping up behind our backs. Her challenge to the night resounded to every tree and branch, to every bat hovering overhead in wait for winter. A chill sank in me then, as it does now. A mighty grief of mourning for her, for myself. But never for Ivisou, the subject of her worship.

But was she not cruel, and indifferent to the suffering of others? Or selective in her empathy? There was a coldness in her. A streak of true, perhaps very real (though I will not psychoanalyze) narcissism that we could not manage. I am thinking now of her eyes when we parted ways on the edge of the bog, after our shifts on a mid-day in November, before I returned to Brooklyn. I remember the real, true love in them. The love for a sister, for me. That *was* love. It's strange. To remember the authenticity. I know, have known love, and it has nothing to do with passion, or convenience, or the delineation between romance and friendship. I loved her as dearly as I can love another, though our friendship was imperiled by anxiety and hurt. I remember sitting outside the train station and pulling a frail wasp from my (then healthy) hair. I held it in my hands, and it did not sting me. But the sting was an ever-present threat — an inevitable horror. As was the scent of cranberries still swimming around my fingertips.

I love Wamsutta, but we are not happy together. I have no desire to psychoanalyze him either, as I think it is often an affront to a bond to do so, intent aside. Though I understand deeply what he does, how he is, what he needs, and also understand that these are not things I can easily navigate, or provide him with. I cannot wish to heal him, save him, change him, not because it is unfair but because that burden is a failure in the making. And frankly, I cannot say that I care that much. Not in a cruel fashion. I think him to be quite complete and wonderful, though so utterly trapped in his own history that he cannot see why he is not happy... But is this not psychoanalysis? He could be happy with another one, who is not haunted by the dreams of Ivisou. He was once happy with her, but stuck to me after her loss.

He does not wish for me to return to the bog, no matter the time that has elapsed since her sinking, her drowning. Wamsutta does not condone this obsession of grief that lurks in every glance, every bone. *Why return to a rotting place?* he asks, misunderstanding me. He does not linger in the recesses of time as I do, remembering every curve and corner of the bones they brought up from the bog. They were not hers. Why were they not hers?

She spoke of Ivisou like a character in a faerie tale. Swaying silently through the slurry of red, arms upraised in feigned worship, the layers of berries above her ankles, her altar of indifference. There were no darker late-summers than these, and no lighter. Dark moths flutter through my hair as I lower the window, breathe in the stench of decay from the rotting bog. I cannot remember it in this way. Even in the denouement of her descent, it was not so bold, so potent. The land is angry for our betrayal of faith. I close my eyes and think back to she and Wamsutta together. Then I think of us.

He has chosen someone every bit as wretched and monstrous as one could ever fear, and why? Because my needs bind me to those I become involved with? This would seem the perfect approach, though as my mother says, I am the perfect victim that wasn't. The ultimate contradiction. I burn the bonds of love with heat and fury. I destroy attachments in a wave of darkness so profound that I cannot contend with it, ever. It is in this way that I lost her. I fight the urge to lose him the same way, but that is not to say that it is not inevitable, or necessary. I know that I will never be happy with anyone because I have failed so profoundly. Because I will never see her again. Because of Ivisou.

Great Ivisou, matron of reflection! Come into the darkness of our lives! Enrich our breathing, our resistance to evil! Play with us, Nitka Ivisou, Ivisou! You are alive in her, and in me!

We were engulfed by the scent of them — berries dripping with the mother-blood, the riches of the land. We would make cakes and tea, gather leaves in her honor — the honor of the spirit, this phantom of defiant womanhood. She sleeps and she stirs, an elemental of the bog.

Do I surround myself and become enamored with people I project as being who I "may have been"? Yes, but why? I suppose it is what my therapist called my "pure masochism." A true and distinct element of my "*Second Self.*" But has he become aware of this *Second Self* in full? I think so, though its manifestation is vague. No...not vague, but peculiar. When my *Second Self* is not there, all can become. When it is, there is nothing but disappointment and pain.

She danced among the splendor of berries and pressed her lips to my forehead. She sang the songs of forgotten tribes — her ancestors — beckoning me to join her. I did not. My mouth, held still like the suffering landscape, only listened to this marvel of theatre-worship. What once was golden silence has become rotten. I have paid the price for such isolations of faith.

I cannot have a child, not yet, or perhaps ever. I have not lived enough, made enough of myself. I am too selfish to want to care for someone in that way, and knowing that whatever smidgen of affection and attention I get from Wamsutta would gravitate towards our child, I would grow resentful and hard. I can already feel the fury of Grandma Leilan boiling up in me, growing more ferocious each and every day. I do not want her violence to grow in me. I don't want to be a violent, selfish mother, blaming a child for the downfall of my life. I have only myself to blame. Other women may forgive themselves for such a deficit. Can I? I wanted only the chance of this bond again. A splinter of hope towards a cosmic convenience. That she may return to my heart from my very womb. But this was not her door.

The morning before I left to see the Cape again, in the early hours, I woke up in such agony in the area of the solar plexus that I could not move, and thought myself done for. I reached out to Wamsutta and his eyes opened, but I could not tell him the pain I was in, as if it would be a great inconvenience. And wouldn't it have been? There is nothing he can do but say that he's sorry. And that angers me. Not that he can't help, but that he doesn't remain silent, or hold me, or make offers of remedy... But why is it that nothing he does is good enough? Who am I to deserve such care? In these moments, I am made profoundly aware of his lack of investment in me. Of my lack of worthiness. Of course, he will not help me! I am a horrid inconvenience. All this speak of her, these mumblings of Ivisou! Ah, the laziness of this affair. But is it not me, that held myself from saying I needed help? But does he help me when I ask? Do I not plead with him to help my perspective change? But isn't that my responsibility, alone? I now know that he believes himself to be unworthy of happiness with a woman after her, that that is too much to ask.

She had survived once before the failure of common sense, but there is no safety in play. Swarms of volunteers looked for her over the following days. I returned to Cape Cod on the train, desperate for news of her. By the time I had arrived, focus had been placed upon the hinterland ridge, where once a dab of golden fruit arose and fell back as quickly as angel wings in gloom.

We reminisced about our infancy, our bond from birth, she and I. Our mothers were the best of friends, both taken too early in the cleaning out of culture from the far too pale and powerful. I saw the beauty of her mother in her eyes — and the horror. She saw the same in mine. To think! The lustfulness of other things would decapitate her life so soon, so long ago. I think to Wamsutta, and his rejection of this thought. He wants for her to be buried and dead. Forgotten. A face in a photograph with no meaning to behold. And yet, there are trials he cannot understand. It is a love he cannot find inside of me.

I am with him because I recognized him, knew him as a familiar being. He is so much like everyone I love. So much like her. To say I would be with someone better? I am unsure of what that would mean. I have a deep disgust for the affluent and ambitious. I don't want to be with a rich person. I think, rather, I should be happiest here on the Cape, as I once was. With my best friend, childish pattering in the bog waters, the swirling songs of Ivisou.

Lots of woods, lots of play. A humble, unpretentious life. It is my ongoing battle with pretension and the need to become rather than just be that weighs me down philosophically here. I want so much from myself, to become things, but I also want to sink back into the quiet nothingness of natural life. I am unsure if it is a luxury to be on the precipice of both, or a curse. I have never done well with options. But I can't anticipate anyone wanting me, with sadness, pain, enormous complexity when it comes to dreaming and things I cannot do. What a burden I am to Wamsutta. I can be alone. There is no shame in that. I do not need to be with anyone. And when I am alone, I need only be myself, and contend with my own failures, rather than imagining myself in competition with the gods of women in a small seaside town that was never meant for me. Do I not sound decided here? My laziness and fear prevent me from acting in any direction. My *Second Self* leans its head in, aiming to start mischief. I will medicate it away with pills and sleep and must attend to the bog in the morning.

I recall the hurt of hearing his story distinctly, married to awe. Awe of its beauty, horror at something I had yet to understand in full. He says only of me, "You will be haunted," and this is true. Perhaps he knew of my *Second Self* far earlier than I realized. But what a hurt it is, to know that you do not merit record in the halls of inscribed memories. Another affirmation of the lack of love. No one will write of me in awe, appreciation, or wonder. Not like her. I am not a woman who inspires such things in men, or anyone. I will be no one's muse, no one's passionate affair. I will be no one's special thing. My obituary will not be pinned to the walls of every library, every school. Unless I am resolved to be such a woman for myself, and then these trials and reflections on inadequacy may fade from relevancy with the memory of a man who could not (through little fault of his own) love me. The *Second Self* reels and roars as the wheels roll on towards the bog.

I ask myself about the pain of seeing her in pictures. It brings me to tears, sometimes rage, sometimes a deep sadness that is unlike any other. But it is not only a matter of reflecting on our separation as friends. It is also the deep devastation of knowing that men will always pick girls like her. They will always put her on a pedestal, mourn her as the great loss of love in their life. In a way, as I have. She has left a trail of broken men and women behind her as she has descended through death, even at such a young age. Friends and lovers. What might be made of this fact?

I detest myself, for being so like her in ways, so unlike her in others. I think I am in prison in myself. I think I cannot even see the horror of her sinking, of her suffering.

Like the jaw of a pitbull, my *Second Self* locks in.

Will I ever stop thinking about it all?

Someday, yes. Today, perhaps.

The *Second Self* has a grip like the most powerful of demons. I think, today, if it is not too cold, I will go to the bog, or something, as I think was my plan?

The bog is cracked now. Dehydrated. Covered in damp weeds, black pus, a pool of memory of menace of death. November. White light undulates over my shoulders, an angry invocation from the sun. There can be no pretension here. No ambition. Only the sloshing sounds of once-red meat, of life, of lusciousness. Of her.

I couldn't help but feel a melancholy invocation as I stepped in wait for the body. "Look me in the face," I whispered to the sun-bleached bones as they ripped them up from the soil. The sky is sick. As infected, as it was.

I plunged my face into the whirling water, cleared by the chemical mess into a translucent film. I could see to the bottom, a great manifestation — ossiferous evil. I had never seen such a fossil, such a creature on this earth. Had never learned of one. It was called a hoax, a cruelty of the local tricksters who had no respect for the investigation at hand. I think more of such elaborate things beneath the weight of the bog. What can see so clearly as to place a masterpiece of death beneath the water?

There were always labyrinthine pools in the bog. Spaces of intrigue and the mystical paintbrush of nature. There is no telling what one may find now in the rotting, half-dried place. I can see more, hear less. Feel more, taste less. My eyes flutter as a heavy sky pulls in. I could demand no greater interference from the firmament, blocking my view and intention in its midst.

I feel Ivisou. A creature so rich in horror and in darkness, that it cannot be portrayed in art. Only in words. In the wrong tongue, they are poison. Her eyes of opaline milk, her snarl of a thousand daggers, her serpentine lengths and lion's paws. I dreamed of her fullness, her elation. She grows tightly, distributes evenly in the features, in the face, in the fallacies of life and love and learning. There is no avenue of consciousness that may lead my heart to gladness after such a fact. Her name on the lips of she, Ivisou! Ivisou! The twelve o'clock sun burns my body, sends my bones to aching.

I pull off my skirt and sit in the dark pus of the bog. Rotten berries burrow in my skirt, stains like old blood gathering at the hem. I tear it off in the heat of mania, rolling my hips, my heart in this muck, my hands in steady worship overhead. "Ivisou! Ivisou! Can you not hear me? Where is she? What have you done with her? What have you done to me?!"

The hemispheres of my brain suffer. I fall to the fetal position, eyes erect and great and protuberant as the poison of the bog infects them. Everything stings. Everything, except my heart. There are lonelier deserts than these, in the midst of mayhem, in the eyes of men. Stars swarm in midday, a celestial phenomenon. I can only attribute it to her. I miss her so much, I think, as my lips fall to the fetid mess of the bog. I look up, eyes aslant and wondering what might become of my bones in the shallow landscape, so unlike it was. I will not have the heavy water of her tomb. The mystery of her disappearance. I will not have her face, or her eyes, the magic of life alive inside her. My anatomy swells, an aggression of organic life. My arms crumple, my eyes go still. A gold shadow, tender and sweet, crosses into the labyrinth of my mind and leaves as swiftly, darkling reminiscences of time.

She likes oleanders and long skirts, berries and pies and the intrigue of natural life. She sings and sways in the old-time vibrance of the cranberry bog. I see her, as alive as she was. I remember her, as alive as she was. I cannot hold on to myself in such a way. Ivisou the monstrous, matrician of envy, of pride, sensing my malice, my resentment. I love and I hate and it is all the same to you.

the river

THE composition of my death is as follows: a deep, beating hum from a great distance, to which I am dragged ever closer, each moment in life, aware of it only in quiet whispers on nights of great difficulty.

I can smell her body — at the beginning of the shoulders, fragrant like drenched magnolias, tendrils of dark blonde hair knotted in two disconcerting braids, dragging me out of the water. In moments, I writhe, hideous spasms rocking me forward and backward, unable to know the world around me. A dark veil clouds all being, guarding itself from a distracted end it will not realize beckons from within.

The house — a phantom dwelling — is awash with the trappings of death. They are yet to be buried — mother and father — coffins empty of their remnants, missing in the misadventures of the heroic without pause. Her coffin is white. His, black and austere. I cringe at the melodrama of the contrast, one delicate and one dreadful. It speaks nothing of them, really. Nothing of warmth or intellect. Only of death, and the quiet anxiety that builds in me.

Weeks pass under the strain of possibility. The birds rise from their nests. I hear them, as distinctly as the other sound. A low rumble from the east, vibrating through the body with a heathen might. With one ear against the chill of floorboard oak, the glee of morning light departs with the hum.

Dim rays shine down on the web, painted with hoarfrost. Water drips gently from the ice as dawn turns into day, however weakly, making way for the spider that sits in wait for the opportunity to crawl back to the center. I have known myself in such a fragile waiting. It is the condition of this day, in my home.

After unusual spiritual effort, and the decay of a bond of promise to my mother, I creep back to the feverish allowance of self-decay, in the confines of my condition.

The room is filled with yellow lamplight. Tired and uncertain, awaiting the arrival of Aunt Web. Piercing my nails against my brace and unable to hobble another step, I rest at the foot of the staircase and the door before me. I wonder about her. If she is as she was — a mere husk of the banshee I remember, and is that husk better or worse? A bead of sweat sits on my forehead. I weigh its presence, become timeless in wait for its departure from my skin.

I hear a knock — three booming accents to the ever-present hum. I tremble, stretch my fingers out to my cane, stagger to my feet, wipe the sweat off my forehead, open the door. A rainbow glimmers in the distance, the foremost trails of color disintegrating in a sea of orange clouds. A sudden flash blinds me to the image — the woman. I see Mother without life, head bashed against a rock, flesh pouring out over silver taffeta. I see Father without life in the backseat of a town car, thoughts blown into pink mist. One bullet, one second in time. And then all as it is in the present world. I am near enough to death to believe these visions.

She turns and smiles menacingly, her grey teeth barely visible beneath the mass of her inflated lips, painted in plum, coal-paint sparkling around her violet eyes. The sun freckles her hair through black net, dyed locks frizzily pinned. For years, I agonized over these features, this face. The sickness folds over me in waves.

"You are quite the same, Solomon Ward," she sneers, extending her hand so that I might kiss it. I take it in mine and shake firmly, turning my back to her in a gesture of strengthened will. She huffs and enters the corpse of my former home, through the French doors and into the parlor.

Petty to the point of choking the very air out of her immediate surroundings, Aunt Web grasps a swath of fabric from the curtain and sneers.

"Your mother... Still keeping this *hideous* yellow."

"My mother is dead," I answer, struggling to stand up straight. A piercing pain shoots through my left thigh. I flinch. Her eyes fall to the broken parts of me and lift again.

Mother never would have allowed her to visit, especially not under these conditions. But Mother is now long gone from this world, adrift in the currents of eternity I so often imagine in this confinement. Aunt Web pulls a single flower from a nearby vase and crumples it in her hand — petals weeping past black velvet.

"It is a *hopeless* condition, dear boy."

I watch as her expression shifts from bruised to elated, eyebrows painted violet, sliding up her forehead. My bones harbor a menacing ache. A familiar severity, roused by the phantom — anxiety.

"You in this dreadful house, by yourself. Thank goodness you have *me* to care for you now."

Her expression is complex. A blue shadow passes through her pupils. A memory of water — of summer. I remember Philip by the river. It is a spiritual dislocation unlike any other.

"Have you packed your things? The train departs at 7 o'clock."

"I'm almost finished," I answer, feigning politeness. My limbs are as feverish as they have always been. I open my mouth to ask something of her in the darkness of the parlor, stroking my neck in memory of blood drops. It could never be so easy as this. I am an imbecile. I am humiliated. I am...as alive as I was.

"Let us go together, hmm?" she says. I am in a frenzy of regret, and evermore is this sadness that leads me to my room. If there are words that don't quite fit, then I have heard them there, across the wild airscape I once knew, beneath the glow of silver light.

It is as though I have forgotten the journey before it has even begun. On the floor of my room, I am surrounded by bundles and unwashed clothing. With a groan, I look up to the ceiling and become engrossed in my own predicament. I have descended before into such depths — the fluid blackness of melancholy and self-denial — most often appearing in the summer months as memories of the parks and the water wash over me like shards of broken glass. I remember Philip. I remember the flecks of gold in his ginger hair, the look of stone about his cheekbones, the taste of divinity in his mouth.

Among my present difficulties, I must dispose of the painting made
that summer. It is the image of a great orange cat holding a grasshopper
in its mouth. A sight we shared that summer as we explored the lands
around the river together. It was the only way I could preserve the
natural — the memory of togetherness without the gathering of shame
and distaste. Eternity howls towards this ending.

I dress myself in guilt, glancing across the room at the mirror. At
this point looking truly fatal — in my eyes, years lost to recollections of
the river.

I need not know how she discovered us. Only that she did. Aunt
Web came tearing through the bushes — lips pursed in accusation, her
knotted hands reaching towards me. My childhood died quietly in the
blue evening. Golden clouds strung up dreamlike and warm, held in the
sky above us. The echoes of crones sounded through the grasses, telling
of time and nature, of things that are to end and begin again in darker
ways.

Astonished with the agony of myself, half-mad with the pain of self-
revelation, I whimpered quietly as she dragged me through the woods
back to my father's house. I did not want to be held so tightly by her.
Long fingernails cut into my neck, dribbling blood into the collar of my
white shirt.

She shapes for me a dark future — one that would speak to the
startling deficiencies of my form. That shames the artificial parts of
myself, the innovations of loss that I have found. I would be crucified in
want of security, but her sensitivities are without the noise of method,
and she breaks in reason when confronted with herself.

It was his gentle embraces of the soul. The tears that burst out, the
veneration of flesh and refuse as I once was. As I am. A fiendish,
glowing, evil abomination of man. Oh! The thrill of purple flowers, cold
water, longing for autumnal skies, the silent long gaze of being oneself in
entirety. I sprung hard there as I never had in the presence of another —
the deserted castle of passion filling me up — a choir singing into the
starlit evening. The derangement of my passions was no longer. The
cavern of my heart, no longer. I have loved no one so much as myself in
that condition, held only in a memory. My heart has laid long as ice in
the remnants of this derelict house.

My hair was a lighter gold back then, with the appearance of a
young elf alone in the woods. Fairer people in the condition I was born
in are not so caged without reason, but are they not without justice in

this way? In the subjective world I sense only that I am an animal without power. A hurtful thing that watches on towards others — yawning in conclusion of interest because there is no reason to be as one must be in a body that is not complete. The body of a beast is always a vile thing. A slavish, hideous prostitute of the law of organic creation. It is no wonder in this light I became so shy of lovers in my youth, leaving lofty sentiments to those who were creative in their flaws. To those who have no fear of death. To those whose individual power succeeded the horror of nature. I discontinued my cruelty towards myself in waves as the pull of erotic thirst became a frenzy. I feasted on nobody but myself, the one I could hold in peace without regret. The one domain I could control in moments. I could undress with honest emotion and fear not the cruelty of observation — not the cruelty of nature or family.

When in want of food, I would give to the starving. When in want of life, I would visit the dead. When mingling with the lustful — those who used misery as aggression — I would lie alone in the essential organization of thoughts. A weight upon my head, scrapes upon my knees, I gasp at the war within myself, incapable of hearing another's pleasure again. Faith is only sometimes overcome by failure of the body. Hampered by the victory of nature against me, of nature against man, of nature against flesh. I was caught in the passion of love making — returned to the absence of myself, to the dark shadow of observation, to the forbidden territory of deformation. I was terrified by the dragging — by the eyes of her, the brutality — that contrasted in every way with the previous moment by the river. Thou shalt not perform as I did, thou shalt not be as I was and am now, thou shalt not exist as themselves in a framework of goodness held up by the mind. From the spiteful there will always be an orgy of obliteration!

I reflect upon my own deformity, thinking myself an animal as I look into the painting. I cannot blame her for this trouble, not alone. If in her absence, the memory was allowed to fester by my unwillingness to fight it, then the dark gem truly lies within — her person being a mere living thread projecting outward. But a thread is not nothing.

The ethereal shapes of the cat were painted delicately, desirably. A mysterious animal with aspects of man is another creature, not an incomplete version of man, and in this way are they not a deformation, and this way are they not incomplete, but complete within themselves? Who am I, and what might I be? Might I be as myself, incomplete as man, complete as something else entirely? I am rich. My inner life festers with such suggestions, knowing myself the lowest form of organism. I would not snuff out such a thing. Only become hopeless in isolation. Yet the hopelessness seems so much more in the presence of Aunt Web. I wonder if she knows that we will burn, the same?

I throw the painting away.

There is an ache in me that lives deeper than reason. A large, empty space where once-vibrant colors were rubbed out. I look into the living room for the last time. The black pillars, parquet floors, maplewood furniture fading dully into the shadows of the unlit space. I wonder who will live here after us. Perhaps there will be a time of greatness for such people, though my doubts are rooted in the experience of living.

A tiny bug enters through the front window, leading with a trumpet snout and four iridescent wings. Silver water drips from its mouth. I hear the hum — an unholy melody, like an orchestra of untuned harps. I imagine that I have escaped the sorrows of my tomb through sheer inevitability. I hide from the view of earth in a silent, silver cloud.

The light of dusk crosses over my spectacles into blades of pink. Entirely unprepared for the truth of my departure, I follow behind Aunt Web despite the blindness, despite the pain in my legs displaying every instinct within myself that says *stay home*. Darkness looms over the town car sitting in wait — an automobile I have no doubt she has not purchased for herself. Did she expect me to be better? A stranger? An apparition? A grown man? I am addressed as the boy I was, fresh in life as though there has been no escape from the horrors of adult living.

Clouds amass over the station, the contrast between changing shades making me grow ill. It is a mighty evening. Great green clouds lean in overhead. Eternity breathes in this landscape. My eyes glaze over, become bodiless, traverse the great expanse without name, without suffering. I am shocked back into myself with a nudge. It happens without sound. My nostrils flare with anticipation as Aunt Web steps onto the platform.

I recall the blue waters as they once were. The flights of birds — crystalline and gentle — riding on the winds of summer. Black flies swarm from their nocturnal graves. I see the white pond in the distance. The walls singing out, covered in songs as they were. I imagine a descent into the battlements of a great city — the green decaying flesh of constructed living. An eerie wind shakes through the platform, weaving through her knotted hair — her wrath growing more venomous as I dare to look directly into her. The embodiment of compassion's inverse. She addresses me threateningly.

"Be still."

I am entirely still, already.

I hear the clamor of bells from a nearby church. It has been abandoned for thirty years. Cities are as distant in my mind as they ever were. Gold light passes over his eyelids. I am not lifeless, as I once was. Blood dribbles down my neck. She drags me through the corridor to my mother's bedroom. I hear Mother and Aunt Web arguing, their words growing louder through the walls.

I hear only, "He is *my son*." I do not want her to wound herself in defense of me. Mother with pink ribbons in her hair.

Flocks of tired geese pass over. Aunt Web is shocked at the sound. The nuisance of natural life. Notes trill through the gate. I swallow hard, adjust my brace, trail behind Aunt Web in the absence of distinction. One is best to learn to be exalted in these humiliations. Engulfed by the air of spring, a flourishing of notes in heat, I laugh, thinking such things could not happen to me, knowing full well that they can.

The landscape has grown unpredictable. The strangeness of the lands fluctuates morbidly. At once we would pass through red mist over grey grasses, completely unfamiliar to me in my travels with my parents. Another moment there would be broken walls, battlements of castles in pale light. There would be a great purple forest, a field of volcanic ash, an unimaginable lake of gold and water. Has she given me something to see such dream-like images through the train window? Is this the sheer pain of proximity to death? She sits and faces me. I reach my left hand in a pocket for a drawing utensil.

"You will not be drawing any of your obscenities here," she says to me, ripping the pencil from my hand. It has been a time since I have drawn any kind of obscenity.

What does she mean to do? Does she mean to kill me? The first reaction I have contemplating this reality is one of loss. I have lost my parents and my home, and long since lost the pleasure of good things, demonstrating only the reality of my passions through poetry and paint. I see the reflection of my eyes in the window and know myself to have been wronged by random chance. The second reaction I have is one of internal laughter, the clumsiness of my logic aimed at the absurdity of the landscape. Lands I have never seen, lands that do not exist in my home world. The third reaction is one of offense, but I am not a person of excessive violence. This is a desire of its own, and there is no room for the possession of desire in a body that has energy only for the slightest exhalation or movement. I have wronged her eternally in her eyes. I have nothing in common with the woman and there would be no way to escape.

Should I join her in stepping off the train to this unknown destination she describes with such verve and excitement? Humans change over time, though they do not change so much that the expressions on their faces do not indicate the very things they indicated way back when. I see this in her face: She is in expectation of some great redemption. She, of the lowest kind when it comes to justice. She, of the least in compassion and grace, stares through me, and I am simplified to the point of disposability. That's all I have always known. As a child, it was a source of horror and anguish. Indeed! The rejection of the self when so young and without experience is like a first death. But she is not so wretched to the usual man. In fact, she is most certainly one who takes the arm of certain minds that no longer grasp the differences of the unusual with acceptance. Only with calculation and the instilled hardness, ruthlessness, and heathen instinct.

How am I to escape? I take a close look at the critical moments of possibility, the dangers of agitating my host. I consider the uselessness of violence, the potential for other parties waiting in knowledge of my fate. My heart swells. I feel the noise of living as I have not in so long. I feel the dragging as an inner experience. Now there is only the meat of life in this woman's hands. I think myself dramatic and say it is the trauma of my parents' deaths. It makes me see things that are not real. It makes me remember as though memory were present day, but anguish is not a trick. I illustrate the bloody stage of life in my mind repeatedly. The myth, legend, lore of my passionate death in childhood. I ruminate on this ruination, the desires of my youngest self. I feel the noise rise up. I feel my hand graze my neck, and Aunt Web looks at me.

"What is it, boy?" she says to me. *I am a man now*, I think, stronger in this performance of peace and quiet than I ever was.

If one were to describe violence, it would be partial. It would take possession of reason and logic, unhindered by the pure bodily rupture that is violent experience. One cannot return to the primitive when in search of words. I am of the mind to sacrifice anticipation for escape. I have had my violence. I reach into the insignificant night, into the forward reality that might be prohibiting the panic of the usual power. It is the most human element. It is the natural element. I conduct myself in expectation because I know myself to be obliged to the natural — to the primitive — to the original aspects of organic life.

We pass by a peach orchard. Everywhere is silver grass lacing through the lands. The train puffs black smoke. Deep, frozen hours pass. I am still without flight. Perhaps some later time in life there will be some higher revelation of this affair. I fool myself in this observation, knowing myself as a sequence of small deaths. I think of a verse of Trakl's —

O the decayed figure of man: composed of cold metals
Night and terrors of sunken forests
And the searing wilderness of beast;
Deep calm of the soul.

Sickness sinks into me. I know I must return to the half madness of my youth. To stand up, to plan, to leave, to escape the inevitability of death, if only in moments. I draw strength from my original impulses. My movements — a momentary lull in the egg that never hatches — a momentary silencing of the deep hum from the great distance, calling out to me. I have lost myself and this internal living, but I may save myself yet. Black noise cries out from the shadow structures — the great citadel before a mountain. I have not seen this city before.

Surely she will fall asleep after a time, unless the alarm of her intention keeps her alert. Though what alarm may there be on my account? Might her conscience run that deep? One can never know. It is often that the act of disgrace is done with a veil over reason. If she remains awake, I may feign a headache, ask the conductor for medication. But this would require more doting, more attention. There is always the lavatory. There, though she may even accompany me to the door, I can hide away for a time. If I remain long enough, in the illusion of gastrointestinal distress, she would sit back down. She would not remain so long on foot in her high heels, especially near "acts of filth."

"How much longer might it be, Auntie?" I ask, with an air of stupidity befitting my intentions.

"Must you ask so soon? It must be three hours more, perhaps four." Her eyes dart left and back to me, a hallmark of deceit.

Strangers see light in death, see the sickness in themselves in copper shades. Those who see tears from falling eyes and think, *How sinister is this life!* may have known such pain in memory. I await the agony of death and would hold up every muscle — every drop of my own blood — to sink back into the memory of the river.

There is an ancient prayer of old. Upon notice of my father's death — the shimmer of lamentations howling, the torment of my guts begging to end the agony of loss with words — I said these verses — sobbed them — from a broken mouth.

All roads lead to this black decay. Crossing over, the birds have died as mirrors — as myself — in the mad despair of death. Deprived of my eyes, of all of those I love, because that which touches eternity when in the body of man understands no thing as itself.

Strange desperation grips me — greatly different from the usual. Within my senses, full with the helplessness of youth, I rub in the appreciation of extended living as I once did, setting aside my permanent fever. I remember the river — water against my face and legs, the feeling of splashing, late evenings painting in lavender lamp light. If I understand nothing of nature — can communicate nothing of love any longer — at least I have remembered something of my former self. And there are many stops, I think, before the last to get out of this.

Many stops before the last...

the sea hoax

IT had been said that Sophia Detti's favor in society was a dimming light; that her reach was limited to her gray inner circle: a society of elderly degenerates wrapped up in international webs of corruption. As such, the woman had no fear of lack as it came to finance. With the snap of a finger her cohorts contorted their crumbling features in assertion's inverse: To her, they were indebted in such a way that it would seem unnatural. One would think a soul would be required for such debts.

It was not long into the autumn season when Elizaveta Gallis emerged on the periphery of her sphere: a sprightly young-heart with a knack for quiet contemplation among the revelry and irresponsibility of her peers. Her vices were nothing, save for her avoidance of key frightful elements of life that rendered her into a state of doe-like shock. She did not like hot lights, insects, or bodies of water, and her career in fashion only seldom brought her in proximity with such things.

The first of this new Gothic aesthetic bled into the New York City fashion scene upon the initiation of Elizaveta's elevated reputation. Her gaunt-like limbs and sunken eyes hearkened to an age of decadence that designers had long been dying to resurrect. She was never seen without soot-like powdered eyes in the way of an Edward Gorey sketch. Elizaveta towered over her peers at a fearsome 6'2", far above the dimming and diabolical Ms. Detti, who announced her retirement on the eve of her final show, sighting a desire to spend her tiring years with her newborn son — a devil of a child who, she claimed in private, decimated her womanhood with the circumference of his ugly, asymmetrical head.

Detti envied Elizaveta with the passionate urgency she had only felt in childhood escapism. Her rival and replacement shared her floor-length raven hair, her strange eyes of brown with a glaze of citrine. What she did not share was Elizaveta's classic features: her enormous cheekbones, prominent jaw, delicate lips. She fancied ripping them, stealing them, drowning them, awash with blood, reborn in this age of decadent modernism a better version of herself. Detti carried such fantasies privately, sparing the ears of her retinue. Should they hear of such a thing, they would do away with the girl, regardless of her frailty, her young age.

The city had lost its strength in the miles of summer, floating up a corpse of towers and parks in burnished autumn decay. Elizaveta was to open the new MODERN/GOTHIC show. She did so with remarkable grace, the hallmark of her otherwise somber and worrisome physique. Having come to the attention of the infamous Russian *Irrational Dress Society*, there was a decidedly saturated and almost inconceivable shade of black introduced among the lesser greys and reds to impress international attentions. When the critics looked at the blasted hue, they were struck with a level of fright that froze them to their seats. No stranger to dark opulence, Sophia Detti took a seat in the forefront of the audience, in direct sightline of every model. They could not see her, but she was felt, the outline of her whale-bone fascinator — black gauze illuminated by the overhead light — a silhouette of dark contemplation. Mr. Bezalel came out with Elizaveta upon the last showcasing of all the looks, black-gloved hand in black-gloved hand. Something of a green flash crossed over Detti's eyes. A slight smirk of epiphany — a resolution for her own eternal reputation. She did not wince or freeze upon a color. She knew of darker things.

Three steps down from the back staircase, pink slime under-heel. Elizaveta lifts her shoe, struggling to release it from the step. The air in the back hall is filled with pink mist. She is dizzy — cannot see. Fog seeps into her brain like too many valium pills. The slime drips down onto her shoulder, clotting the sheer fabric like a leaf in mud. The smell hits her nostrils and her calm seizes. Elizaveta Gallis is screaming. She falls down the staircase, her limbs continually soaked in the mist, the slime, the oppression of substance. She cries out, a mangled echo. The top door to this stairwell is locked. The bottom door is locked. Elizaveta lies in the fetal position at the bottom step — cold concrete. Her fingers are curling down, as are her feet. Great welts grow on her shoulders, her chest, her arms. They spread to her stomach, her womb. Finally, her face becomes a garden of fetid pink pustules, obscuring her once-majestic features.

Why was she in that stairwell? they asked.

What did this to her? they asked

Is it some sort of virus? they asked

No sign of disturbance, they said

No chemicals or bacteria in the area, they said.

What a shame, they said.

A beautiful girl, they said.

What a waste, they said...

Elizaveta arrives in Messina with her partner, Paol. She comes under the cover of sheets from a private plane, her cottage-cheese-like skin unable to tolerate the intense Italian sunlight. Paol and her assistant lead her to a car for transport to the center. She is not without suffering. The heat makes breathing almost impossible. In the absence of sight from the proliferation of tumors over her face, she loses herself in this demonic sensory Oz. Everything is pink and black, gelatinous and cruel. She cringes when he calls her Elizaveta.

The facilities are clean. The lights are clear. White on white, sea blue on sea blue. It has the look that a hospital by the sea would have in her small American fantasy. The surgical resort looks out over the shores of Messina, white houses cramped up onto the hills like pale weed-blooms.

Her room is sweet, and still. Paol walks to her right, a nurse on the left, situating her on the white couch by the mirror.

"Once you are settled, our coordinator will come for you," the nurse says, handing Paol a schedule of events for the duration of their stay. "Surgery won't begin until the day after tomorrow, so we can run the usual blood, urine, MRIs and such. It isn't set in stone. We have to see how each surgery goes..."

"Thank you," says Paol in broken Italian. He is an escapee of the cult-like congregation of sadists in the *Irrational Dress Society*...an orphan of Nevsky Prospect fortunate enough to escape by means of quiet resistance and chiseled cheekbones. He loves Elizaveta like one loves a lost limb, even though she is not as she once was.

The years have done much to Elizaveta's condition. Now twenty-eight — a lifetime from her former splendor — the growths on her body have taken the form of globular, purplish-pink mushrooms. The material of this sickness is so dense that they do not know if her eyes have been crushed or eaten from within. She feeds from a stomach tube and urinates from a catheter. She is mute, but not deaf. She hears all contemplation and mourning of her condition. Elizaveta confirms her thoughts with illustrative taps of her head against the hinterwall — the only means of movement she is allowed without immense, electric suffering.

Dr. Mesa is a Colombian visionary — a visiting doctor from New Jersey in the southern reaches of the Italian coast. The facility invites the best of the best to these shores for such unimaginable feats — the dream-like conservation of life, limb, and feature for both the beautiful and the grotesque. Elizaveta is guided through her testing with precaution. They are civil, careful, quiet. They speak to Paol of jovial things in the hope that they will raise her spirits. They know not the depth of her cognition... That it has sprouted with heathen magnificence as the rest of her body has failed her. She remembers books read in childhood, first word to last. She recalls the feeling of fabric on her breasts, the removal of such from her most intimate parts. Elizaveta longs for life beyond the confines of this punishment, but the growth of herself within such a state... How does one go on after such horror...

The first surgery is minimal. Elizaveta is asleep. A medical grade glaze is painted over her protuberances to soften and numb them. Needles are inserted to remove the viscous pink liquid from the masses. They fade to grey as they wilt, post-evacuation of fluid. The second surgery is more invasive. It takes place three days later, once the masses have transfigured to a skin-like consistency. Dr. Mesa removes one mass. His suspicions are correct: her skin is intact underneath, though bloodied with tiny pinprick holes where the mass had rooted in. There will be no need for grafting, though perhaps CO_2 lasering, experimental lasering, time... It takes five day-long surgeries spread over four weeks to remove every mass. Her face is not as fortunate as her body. Elizaveta's eyes are, indeed, intact, though the sclera are a hideous bacterial green. The doctor takes note and tasks his nurses with putting her through a five-day course of the strongest antibiotic known to man.

Her facial reconstruction takes several weeks. Though no longer the beauty of her former years, Dr. Mesa moulds her so that she may be woman, may be person again. Her eyes clear slowly of the pressure and bacteria, though her sight is limited to a devilsome hue of yellow shadows. It recovers slowly. By the second month, she can see the outline of Paol's face if he presses his forehead to hers.

It is the third month, with one remaining. Elizaveta is shifting into the rehabilitation section of her treatment. The color of her skin is not quite right. Her movement is limited, as though from advanced arthritis, but there is hope with therapy. She can see more... Sphere -3.25, cyl, -0.75, axis 70. She doesn't use the air conditioning as much in her room. They are helping to build her tolerance to heat, though cautiously so. There is a question as to what will impact the healing process, given that stressful events and emotions seem to evoke a ripping of stitches, a proliferation of pink ink from the eyes.

Elizaveta is in her room. Paol has gone outside. She is walking on her own, with a slight limp. Her phone vibrates and lights up. She looks to see the following:

ALTRO ALLENAMENTO METEO
Un avvertimento per lo tsunami in
vigore per Messina fino alle 17:00.

Cercare immediatamente terreno
alto

Her limbs stiffen. The window facing the sea is slightly open, wind blowing the sheer white curtains wildly against the armchair. Elizaveta takes stunted dream-steps to the window. She can see enough to make out a shape on the horizon. Lowering her glasses from the top of her bald head to her eyes, she sees the wave — a colossal wall of water tall enough to block out the sun. Time stands still. She cannot move. The room begins to rumble violently, the roaring sound of water rushing towards the shore. She slams the window closed and stumbles backward, crying out once and closing her eyes as she falls onto the floor. A great crash shakes the room as water begins to burst through various angles of the wall. The room floods quickly.

She stands, struggling. Her wounds are wet, the gauze flapping off to reveal soaked and opening slits. Elizaveta struggles to the door and opens it with force. Water pours out of the room, but comes from no other place. Nurses walk up and down the hall casually, assisting other patients. The occupant of the room opposite Elizaveta opens her door and stands face to face, as dry as could be.

Elizaveta, soaked and horrified, her wounds gaping and emitting blood and pink fluid, stares into the face of Sophia Detti, her face faintly bruised and heavily stitched from the insertion of jaw implants, chin implant, cheekbone implants, Juvaderm injections around the eyes. She looks like Elizaveta once did. Detti smiles.

In a menacing outburst — the emotional material of years — Elizaveta chokes out an alarming howl like an animal, reaching her bleeding hands out to Detti's face. She rips her stitch-wounds open and pulls out her implants as the woman screams.

Paol comes running down the hallway with three nurses. Elizaveta is screaming on the ground, her wounds soaked and open as she tears at her own face.

"She's going to need a transfusion, quick..." The nurses open nearby closets and grab white towels, pressing them against her to still the bleeding. Paol leans down to face her.

"С тобой все будет хорошо!" he says.

A gurney is being rolled down the hall.

"Цунами..." she croaks.

"Какое цунами?" Paol says. She notices that he and the nurses are completely dry.

"Is she dead?" Elizaveta asks in English.

"Is who dead?" Paol answers.

Elizaveta looks up to Detti's doorway — her eyesight increasingly obscured by pink fluid and blood, her heartbeat growing fainter as her skin becomes gray — to see before her a blank wall. Nothing more.

electric funeral

TODAY is everybody's funeral. The warning from the sky has come. Gusts of neon light surge through the cityscape, illuminating eyes with the last feral hues of earth. The radiation pulses. Eyes bleed from the pressure, the disease of time.

She remembers the flowers as they were last night, in a spindly vase on her hotel windowsill. Scarlet moonlight shone down like blood, draping them in hell-shadow. Today, her wedding bouquet grows black, from gentle orchids to petals like trash bag plastic. Her dress melts away like slime.

This is no wedding here, but a funeral of light.

Magnus and Yulia arrive at the altar. Her brows are drawn high and dark. Like the hoof-shadow of a ram, her hair stands tall and full, from electric shock. A tuft of orange hue illuminates the front, crowning her high forehead in fire-light, the mark of a martyr.

Magnus, the strange man, falls forth, on his knees. Black hair, white beard, a tattoo of Cerberus on his temple. His neck is draped in dried hawk feathers, his robe of purest black. Eyes will not open, but are painted down, like cum, like glue.

There is but one ghost alive from the ancient world — without sustenance. Life is disposed without detail, like a funeral rite of passage. Such events have not occurred on this globe, though there have been ghosts in other places, unseen by human eyes. Darkness, dirt, and dust enter the air. Magnus has visions of an afterlife, but they are overthrown by the dark green sky. Pink light bursts forth from his skull. He is a living poem of heaven and hell — a substitute for the fantasies of fiction. Yulia takes one hand and places it on this light. Blood runs white down her wrists — attention has not been paid. Not enough, to this ritual passing.

There is no god of good or mischief who would harass love in such a way. This is a funerary offering — now a closing reward to the southern hemisphere of Earth.

Yulia remembers her trip to Egypt, traveling to the south, weighing the balance of fear, the pureness of bravery. She found a light in the soul that was heavy like a sleeping monster. If there is a place that speaks to an afterlife, this would be it. She was harassed by no ghost, no phantom, no pharaoh of the deep sands. Only herself, her hands reaching inside of herself, the overreaching sky.

Magnus holds a single coin in his palm. He cannot afford to cross the river without full payment. He fears death more than any woman would when the stories have been told and the judgments laid down. When the water has evaporated and the Elysian Fields turn to dust. He is a peasant of God. There is no place he may visit with purity. No relic he may lay his hands upon with peace. There have been riches and opportunities in life provided to him in the fullest, through the freedoms of decadence and the girls that he penetrated, but then there was Yulia — the white Ram of God — underneath the neon lights of a failing city. This falling Earth tells him he may not enter the kingdom of heaven without haunt, without dreams of death. In the night, without the villainous light from the depths of hell burning the bottom of his feet, he lights a torch for no god but himself. Here he has brought about the neon death — the Electric Funeral — the phenomenon of the last night.

There are gods. There are satyrs. There are spirits, haunters, fuckers, and dreamers. Such things are the guests at this wedding — lines of blood and gore and tombs opened up. There are no stories of death that will not be whispered as the moon turns to dust. Yulia knows and accepts this haunt of eternity. It is the disease of time to which she must honor and appease. There is no realm of living. It goes on forever. There is no dream of warning, no advanced night coming brightly.

A monster of the cosmic deep runs yellow like melted marker. This evening of hunger from the depths of time inhabits him like a poltergeist — like a hungry spirit, eating away at his bones, at his veins, at his skin — underneath like bugs. Yulia encounters herself in a shadow — in a pink puddle of neon light. Her breasts swell with milk.

In this incarnation, in this story, in this region, this house, the city — our ghosts have lived forever with guilt. *I am no princess of Babylon*, she says. *We have been deserted by God.* On a single night, spectral voices ring out. They bathe in them. Footsteps ring out of a thousand feet — creatures unknown and unseen in the shadows come forth and stand in observation of the funeral of light. Spirits leave. Spirits return. Magnus is intoxicated by the strange scent of bodies, unfamiliar to the human mind.

I should have been born earlier, she says, her hands pressed against the melting brick. Silence passes like gas, reflecting off rotting houses. A telescope slides outside a window and falls like a stick into hay. *I know no secrets of time,* Magnus says, a wonderful lizard of deceit. Powder and smells of pain fill the air. Lightning illuminates the ground as though this scene were the very first of Earth. He lifts his hands to her face. His fingers project the fright of his subconscious mind into her cheeks. Yulia steps back, removing herself from the light with the precision of a fearful animal. Soft and seizing, the abstraction of threat. Magnus is on guard as he has never been. This is his wedding day — his funeral day. He breathes bright orange light in, and out. His feet are painted blue to reflect the former sky, the former light of life. His robe is made of muslin. Calla lilies sit in his hair.

Scent guides him back to Yulia, like a lamp filled with love and urgency. They are impatient for this death, feverish for the tomb. To open their eyes become black as the soot of towers fills them up. Their tongues turn lavender blue, an endless threshold of robotic color. Seizing, scarring them. One must be still amid such a splendid colored outside world. Yulia is not horrified. There is no hideousness here, inspired by the oil of artifice in this city. It is painted by the universe. Magnus watches the undertones as though a mountain looms in the distance, blocking the greatest light source. There are bursts of sound like a plague — like a wink from the last of senses. Gasps of goblins screech out into the sky.

Yulia and Magnus are captive beneath cold stares. The intensification of the wind — force of violence, crawling of cockroaches, now white, snow, now green, now purple, now black, a degenerative fermenting complete with color. It is a carnival of sex, of death. An opening up of a deep-seated dream. It is a waste of time and silver on these people — on these human minds. She will recall it in her afterlife, the paint of a Sumerian summer. There will be a holiday of nothingness and majestic dignity. The chill of human thinking — a dark labyrinth — a glove on a hand that was broken and betrayed by human life.

Naked and breathless, they are. Fierce. They are attracted to their deaths. Sound of frogs spawning out by a million a second and then drying up. A later phase of fever rings out — there are no allowances of faith any longer. This is not a scripted attack of God. This is not a painted canvas. There is strawberry light now, in the puddles — on the city streets. There are no buildings anymore, but dark matter. *I wonder,* Magnus says, without hair, without clothing. Without jewels or the jealousy of his earlier nights.

Yulia is full of wonder, done with happiness. She is filled with her father's experiments, despite her own expectations. This is the way of the end of the world. The brightness of light, the collapse of the moon, silence in a thousand colors. Who would not set their brother here to witness? Strange things, men. Loyal to love only at the last funeral rite. It is a symbolic drama. There is a sound — a whisper, a blood drop, that knows the name of God. But they do not know any longer.

There are shapes now like legs turning into fish. The colors fade. They are not as bright as they once were. Magnus' brain is illuminated by that which looks like algae, as though the air has become the fathomless ocean. There is no salt, but all-thought, no movement. He looks to Yulia as a deep hazy fog drowns her. The air — it has become thick, like soup. They will not take the pressure any longer. They see grimaces and rage in the distance. Magnus sees a man and another holding each other until the bitter end. Yulia sees a mother and a daughter crying out into the distant night. Miles become smeared shapes, like Vaseline on a forgotten mirror. A young girl, alone, reaches out — her nipples melt, her breasts rip off like fabric. Soon they cannot see. There is no longer light in this Gothic mass murder from heaven.

To some there are chances in eagerness, but when one is clumsy, they are devoured by such affairs. This train of thought suits Magnus. He becomes a wax figure of life in the supple, bright, violent death of Earth. No one could understand such a thing at such late hours, staring with pale faces, the eternal finger on the trigger of doom. This is Yulia's wedding night. Led astray by the reeling, by the abstract venom, there will be no questions as to justice. There are no longer papers to write them on. No guns to load in vengeance. No midnight to cradle their tiredness. They once crossed breath in a shared kiss, on a couch of leather and gold. There was desperation and such love, once.

This is the Electric Funeral. A violent wedding. The buzzing of the unusual, sleepless thoughts of the god-types, the Sumerian summer, the beautiful diseases, the solidifying mass of the Earth. *Through the woods, we go*, he says, as their feet turn to mush. They have acquired each other in this mess. Fiery spirits, they will be. They are in the darkest ritual — a wrinkle in time, where nothing is so attractive as death.

Her breast heaves forward and evaporates. Trumpet sounds brush softly against that which once was an ear. A dazzling light blinds all remaining things in the Lord's path. Waxing and waning beyond the moon, beyond the sunny garden, beyond white magic light. Perhaps this is an attempt of eternity to transcend the gloom of after-hours. We are lost within ourselves, and indecisive — protesting nature, rebelling against all the elegance that is and was and will be. *Oh, brothers, I will return to repeat such things and time and space!*

The flowers melt. The moon breaks like a china plate on a marble floor. Air ignites like wood, the electric funeral pyre. There are no buildings, but antimatter, bursting black, like heathen soot. The rivers are brown like shit, they breach, a foetid rush of mess and mud. Earth is cradled in the universe, on its deathbed. There is no eye or mind to see but that of the sovereign in heaven. Dark wings, light wings, from the firmament, from the abyss. All converge with the last breath of the atmosphere. After the funeral, we all fall to heaven, reach to hell trapped in the endless ever after.

The earth is alive, for now — a graceless, wretched thing. It moves higher, rolling on the tail of a serpent. The winds chime like a slum bell.

This is the Electric Funeral. Yulia becomes the pyramid, reproaching the Knowing Mother, the Knowing Father. For a moment, they are silent, and their bodies penetrate forever — that which is wrong and evil, neon and bright.

eve, like shards of glass

I have a thousand dreams in childhood of melting into tiny spaces. These silvery reflections of youth are as real as the collected phenomena of my center life. I finish shaking, magic white light pours in through the grate overhead. Bright days glow down on rot and the tiredness of memory – old city nights, the industrial, the vulgar... Streets awash with golden skin and strange, delightful persuasions of a fading Russian district.

Dark crowds sail like amoebas through my head, disappear like dust. My father always said there was a dark rash on my forehead; the mark of a curious being. There are no more rightful positions to be taken as a working man, than that of work! I was not special to him, or any other. Except for Mother.

Eve disperses beauty into the world like water. A stain of memory sits in remains underneath my bed. That and the hilt of her brush, with which to carve, with which to center myself, to transcend.

The camp siren screams: dawn is coming. The cage door clicks, blowing snow and ash. Time to get up. In the first years, there was chatter from birds. Yellow flowers and fruit, milky and delicious, growing in the fields on the way to the Ornament. Days become darker, still. We who build for the double king know why life has left this wretched rock.

Hammers pound until the bastard twilight. Another day without sight or sound of the old city on the horizon. Each success in the construction from the Ornament brings about a haunting stillness from the other side of its walls. A black stone sheath sewn up with human hands, to hide our city from all who live beyond the reign of Ivan Isaac.

The warden's voice sounds like a hammer to the head. Sobol calls him Upyr. He watches us work — his eyes sink back like a dead man's — what a delicious fulfillment it is for him, watching the sweat and blood of our work.

I never sleep. The only noises I hear are the rattling of chains, the opening of doors. A train passing us by every few weeks. The cries of the old man in the cell beside mine.

The train passes by to the north, traveling to our city. The windows have been replaced. Black glass reflects the snowy plains angling down towards the prison camp. They travel at the speed of frozen rivers, as if to glance the horror of the Ornament reaching up into the firmament, growing, growing. Our work. My work.

We line up, the great dignity of a passing train's motor singing out the song of our internment. All rigid, walking on thin legs, we pass the icy fields and reach the precipice of the cliff rock, where the threaded bridge sways. It has lost more wood since the day before, great gaps of air opening a window to a fathomless drop into the emerald sea.

"*Oni ne ispravili eto* (They did not fix it)," Vorobyev shouts, the wind choking his voice before he can finish. The Upyr turns to him, eyes growing bright, streams of hellfire. He smiles and waves Vorobyev to the front.

"*Ty by poshel po puti Orlava?* (Would you follow the path of Orlav?)" the warden says. Orlav the miraculous, his Sunday sermons cast over us like holy light, plummeted yesterday to the limitless deep. For a moment, a circle of light travels around the Ornament, shooting out of the sea like an onyx tower, a sword of deceit. It is built to rise up like a great weed and darken the sky like so many mountains of dust.

The Upyr pushes Vorobyev onto the bridge, enamel eyes wide with fear, heathen winds prodding our mortality, our fate. It's impossible to light fire on the other side of the bridge, so ninety of us carry torches with iron feet, wrought like spikes to burrow into the ground.

Alekhin is the foreman. There is no fear in him, though his senses drown in his particular closeness to the material of the Ornament. A dream occurs in which he disappears all together under the hue of a violet moon. He is awake far before us, already clanging on the operating bells. They grow louder through the dense ocean fog as we approach.

Can you hear me, Eitan?

There is a black infinity in the space between two men. Each transcends himself, becomes broad with the cruelty of ego and time. We arrange ourselves among this construction as mice, following instructions on the perilous fringe of science. I trip, the heel of my boot dislodged from wear. The Upyr grabs the back of my neck, to whisper, "*Net vremeni dlya razoreniya, Voronin.*" (No time for ruin, Voronin.)

He barks hard curses at us. I imagine we are all feverish — like animals, forging the means of menace under which we surely will not be allowed to live. The Upyr spits his venom as we hammer and sweat. The old man, Baranov, falls, blood seething from his knees. The foreman, ever-silent, breaks his temperance to growl at him.

"*Prezhde chem on uvidit tebya!*" (Before he sees you!)

The Upyr has its back turned to us, ear turned to the faint chorus of the passing train. "*Drugiye!*" (Another), it yells, eyes wide and feasting on the northern horizon.

Baranov rises before the demented warden turns. I remember Orlav's prayer, and the first time I heard the sound of the trains. I shovel on, carry on... A devil's face becomes no paler at its end, though mine perhaps shall be, awash in a swarm of ice, like Mother, in contemplation of times before.

Young and old carry on with their worries to the point of breaking. Vast and silvery white, these skies, soon to be blotted out by Isaac's heathen ink. I knew him, once, in the time of Eve. We tiptoed past the impatience of his stirring fanaticism. His habit of fidgeting would become invisible beyond the influence of his shapeless associate. Eve never learned the name of he who filled Isaac's ears with black swarms. It happened in the grey days of latter years, when streets, once expressions of revolution, became moth-eaten and cold. In what other conditions may men of promise turn to madness?

Breakfast is charred meat, dog or goat. Whatever wandered too far beyond the gates of our city. Batteries of empty bottles flood the prison halls. Each of us in quarters of our own, coming in at midday in lieu of wind. The black maze to my cell bleeds voices of every kind. Innocent and guilty, though mostly innocent, if I am to say. Many are migrants, imprisoned with the mathematical precision of Isaac's bigotry. Others, dissidents to the reign of Ivan Isaac.

Eve hangs aslant in memory. Her being fills the heart with birdsong, stamped out by the swelling steps of horses. It will not be long until her city is lost to me. She, the primordial being of the past, etched forever beneath this skin like haunted glasswork.

She held close the memories of her imperial lover, though Isaac crept in her speech like a black caterpillar — edging in upon all of us, this epoch of terror. I sometimes find within myself a strong desire to quit this place, to find him and put an end to this.

Every evening I admit to myself that conquerors of this wear the gloves of death. At times they rise up red, like blood, committing crimes against mothers and fathers, bursting veins and sinners, all. Anatomy blackened into wax. Yet I feel a certain fullness in this crippling world — a shimmering — birds fighting for life away from our city.

I want to imagine myself and my compatriots as old men, having forgotten the perils of youth. Each hour of the night hangs fatally over me, new marks on my skin, new haunts of the soul. Some men here feel as though they are entirely free, their minds lost to the extremity of imprisonment in the north. They become quiet and irritated by nothing, feeling no pain except the very certain tension of the train song coming our way.

Who could suspect such misery of me? In the triumph of love, we roamed the black forest. There would be an offering from me, a gold band to mark our lives together. Her eyes reflected silver, her heart gladdened, complexion glossy, undulating body heat in the strange mist of summer.

We were alone. Myself at a catastrophic low. Generosity was pinned against me — reflections of her noble house far behind us in the black woods. Delicate hands, alien and pale, guided me to the forest edge. I was sober and alert, awaiting the moment of a strong smile. Never should one envision treachery accosting them in such moments. In the darkness, a gust of wind passed through. I was off my feet, the swirling sounds of madness growing enormous, like the great black morasses of the universe. Blinded by this inevitability, I fell back. I could not call out for her. Love is Eve. Oh! A great black wound on her belly as though painted with the gnarled fingers of time. A great swaying ax hacked her head off like a market lamb. I cannot account for my weakness amid such horror. There were no perpetrators to blame. Only strange sounds around us in the dark, sharp whirling instruments, the patter of horses, the liquid sounds of bleeding life. I felt myself dragged across the ground in helpless fury. I heard the murder of a stallion, cut with the same ax that downed the beautiful Eve. A great deafening slice, a flash, the pouring out of organs. It would seem that they cut the beast's stomach open.

These powerful, mysterious bodies went unseen in the woods. I heard very little after this, all sounds drowned by the massacre of flesh pouring into my ears as I was encased in the stomach of the horse. The mesmerism of entrapment... It is like Baal's womb. Dark wanderers murdered Eve, vast and murmuring nothings. My heart is filled with hatred, with shock. What god would let such evil pass upon the earth? She would say it is not of God, but the Demiurge, deprived of the divinity of the firmament. The sounds I hear are indefinable. I fall out of the stomach of the horse. Her body is gone, like the memory of birds that pass over snowfall without footprints. My hair falls in my face. I hear the clanking of chains, cold metal against my neck and wrists. I am loaded up into the carriage, and taken beyond the limits of the Black Forest and the old city, through more great woods and great plains of ice until I can see again... I see the great prison on the horizon. I, Eitan Voronin, killer of Eve in the eyes of men.

None of us have ever committed war crimes. That is to say, doing what one must do to survive is not a crime. I have stolen bread and sharpened knives from nothing. The worst of this was done in the first days, when they did not know my strength. I am not housed with the rest of them. The warden won't tell me why. We share work. I am cloistered alone in the deep reaches of the prison, alongside other solitary cells there which I cannot see. I hear only cries and screams in the night, that life might have been different.

There is dew in the air, this night. I hear ideas of escape bristling in my breast. My fury is boundless, repressed. The train passes by once a week now, always the same time of day when the sun is three hours from sleeping. I wonder of the passengers aboard such a train — windows blackened. I wonder of the deep sorrows, the gray landscape, the months and years of mourning for that which is lost in the thrush of Ivan Isaac. How does man become entangled in such things? My prayers are of silence, even among these men. Let them hear this secret; that my memories of Ivan Isaac include the memories of his ambition. I know something of that which we build — the great Ornament, the sword of the sea. Hark! The human heart gleams brighter after death.

"Might they be filled with your phantasms, Voronin? We are not given to your delusions." The foreman has grown insufferable. His daily battering, hoping for a grim end, towering overhead without merriment. This narrow person surrounds those who have been condemned for nothing. The dragon never sleeps, he says, to which I say in silence — a dragon never lived.

We take our meals like cattle, accompanied by a predilection for mourning. Each day we wonder if we have passed the black nadir, our mortal souls sweating with the anxiety of the ruin we have collaborated upon. In a land of wealth and Octobers, Mother told me a story about a girl's humor and a flash of love in her eyes. I went weeping over her, her dignified face, the black infinity within her. Mother was always afraid for me. I packed my suitcase for the old city with the memory of her in my heart — a body frozen beneath the dirt.

The Upyr leads me down the corridor. It is time for my weekly inspection of eyes, black with astonishment, the joys of torture upon seeing the first drop of blood. What follows is a complicated and vague assault. My eyes closed. I am rested. I am not hungry. I remember sitting under a small window, my father's hand upon my shoulder, telling me my mother was not coming back. I found her that night in the woods, eyes fluttering, her body buried in ice. I hunched over her, the dream of this disaster bulging through my eyes. I tried to pull her out, and out came limbs like frozen meat. A flurry of ice, shards of ice... Father screamed my name from the window. I ran into the black woods, a fantastic gesture of torment — not knowing the fate for me in his company any longer. The Upyr finishes his pleasure, throwing my clothes at me and pushing me out the door.

What could possibly be happening here? I have battled with such beasts of indifference before, in the company of Ivan Isaac. A spasm shakes my almost-human self, carrying me away to a thicker memory. The beauty of her face changed the world for me — my heart beat in a universal rhythm. Mother once spoke of the predestined on Earth — children painting the lives of others in indigo. Golden masks and moments of love unlike ever had been seen or felt before.

We are going out again, oh, that we have gone out. There is a thundering and gushing like a bomb, an unfamiliar longing in the eyes of these men. Perhaps this is the day of reckoning, the great deluge of fate. How it happened, I don't remember. Eve and I were together. Then the sounds came.

The Upyr does not let us carry the torches this time. We gather outside, wickedness pulsing, ice sparkling. Warm ghosts roll past our shoulders, a spirit visitation. How quiet the world would remain without such building. My life has been extended by this duty. I had the choice of execution upon my imprisonment. I chose the gold... I chose the gold luminous morning, to see you again in my heart and dreams, only beyond mountains in the living world.

Blue smoke puffs out of the Ornament. Like spectral wings, it is awakening. The Upyr tells us to bow down, to extend our hands to the great Magi, Ivan Isaac. He has come to inspect the Ornament. He is accompanied by a man wearing a helmet in the form of a crocodile — green snot, grinning and menacing, a blizzard of fear stirring among us. For the great Ivan Isaac to have only one accompanying party, there must be a swarm of evil in this being so fierce, so profound, that one dare not stretch their hand towards it.

I am in the back of this crowd, my usual visibility obscured by the black cloak covering my silver hair. In another stroke of bad luck, there are taller men before me obscuring my vision. The train sounds in the distance. I turn to look, and see a figure break silently through a window, a small bundle of limbs and faith tumbling out of a train car. The body is still for a moment, then struggles to stand. A person struggles and runs. Runs forever with some guilt. I am torn by this. Surely they will be captured and brought here.

There is a horrible pressing against my chest. My thoughts are all my former and present emptiness — recognizing the horror of this train refugee moving closer to the camp. My brothers make their way towards the Ornament, instructed by the Upyr. I move back in thick snow. Am I a coward? Is there saving this person, is there saving me? I think not. There was Eve and there was Mother. There were waltzes, and white sparks and air and thunder. The birth of reason and Good and Evil on the Earth. Like two veiled figures, ancient and mysterious — only they can recognize the horror unleashed by the spiraling, splintering, devil's life of love.

"Each and every one of you is known to me. I'm very satisfied," Ivan Isaac says, looking up to the great black menacing Ornament. The man is mangled. His informant, covered by a deep velvet cloak, whitelock swirling out frazzled and unkempt, emits a strange curse. A sudden flash of heat lights my soul. I can barely hear what goes on in the front of the line. The men began moving, step by step. They are filing into the Ornament in rows. The storm is stirring up — it is not so easy to see us. I stumble back, taking off my clothes, the whiteness of my skin blending in the terror of the storm. I fall back again, feet bare and freezing. I move into the wind, into the night, towards the mountains, towards the fields, snow spray flying in a frenzy, hiding me from the firmament. Snow turns to snow and ice, piercing my skin with a thousand pricks. I remember Mother, the dry ripping of her limbs up from the ice. A sound screams, and the Ornament roars up like a tunneling needle through the skin — towards the sky, the smoke of Iverness, an inverted blessing for this heathen reign. Millennia will pass under this black dome, stains of memory sinking into hearts darkened by the memory...of *before*.

a delirium of mothers

Based on a True Story

WE moved into the Rehoboth house in September of 1994, leaving the city behind us in a haze of black decay. Amariyah was walking again, delicately, with the quickened pace of an injured bird looking to re-awaken the senses. The glow in her eyes had gone out after the birth. She still called it a birth, despite the sawing, the clamping. The baby had been gone for weeks inside her, the doctors told us. It was a real struggle to get her out. "There was a heartbeat," Amariyah would say. "Kicks, and a heartbeat, and I felt the touch of the angels inside of me." She was out in the dream, the coma, on the ventilator, close to death herself. That lasted for weeks. How could she have felt a thing? "A mother loves her daughter," she said after waking. "Can feel her every sway, in the womb and out, forever."

The farmhouse was built in 1887. On the market for the first time in over a decade, it was a steal of a price in the historic town. Structural problems in the cellar and adjacent horse barn, the realtor said. "My God." Amariyah, late into the third term, her belly near bursting with mother's pride, pressing the newspaper to my hands. "This is the one! There is enough room for the cats, the dog, and more kids."

"Let's get the first kid out before planning more, yes?" I said with a laugh. I knew she wanted at least three children, and her mother to move in as well. It was a possibility I would consider, given my preference for long hours of isolated work. I had no wish for her to feel abandoned or resentful, though I was skeptical of the house. It was being sold as-is, which unearthed a suspicion in me. All the systems were working — plumbing, electricity, heat. We'd have to bring air conditioners on our own. There was no certificate of occupancy. I pressed them as to why and they noted the lower-level structural issues. "No problem," my wife said. "My cousin Alexandra is an architect. We can consult with her."

Amariyah had been sick on and off for years. Child-bearing was ill-advised for her. I had not yet encountered the fierce will of a wanting mother. The virus that came on the precipice of our daughter's birth had nearly choked the life out of the both of them. On the expected delivery date of May 17th, she had already been on a ventilator for nearly two weeks, with continual debate from the doctor as to the best time to remove the child. "There are more ways to care for premature babies these days," he said. "Not like the old days."

All this talk of care and removal being enough of a burden, I called Amariyah's mother, quarantined at their family home in New Hampshire. Her voice was deep and resolute. "Do what is best for the both of them." There was no way to know what that was.

On the morning of the 19th, her supervising nurse called to say there was something wrong with the baby. It wasn't that they couldn't hear anything, exactly, but a mass of black blood had burst out of Amariyah as her vitals were dwindling. He said they were about to do a C-section. I was not allowed to go to the hospital. Our neighborhood would be under quarantine for another two days. I sat and waited, panic flooding through me. I masked up and found the vinyl gloves in the cupboard under the sink. Told myself, "If the cops stop me, they stop me. I have to try." My hand reached for the doorknob and my cell rang. "Are you sitting down, Mr. Đorđević?"

75 Belvedere Drive. A towering Victorian homestead with ample land for farming, a large horse barn, woods. The three-floor house was painted in a fading coral, shrouded by an overgrowth of vines. Upon my first tour of the house with the realtor after quarantine was lifted, there were dozens of strange, drooping white lilies in the front garden, like angels with wilted wings. There were small statues of cherubs on the front porch, alongside ornamental carvings not usually befitting the

design of the Victorian era. The large flowerpots were cracked and housed nothing but dirt and a few mangled roots, longing for life.

The porch itself wrapped around the house, not dissimilar to the porch at my Aunt Bertha's house in South Carolina. White columns and no furniture save for one wicker loveseat, damaged by what looked like small animals or a young child's devious hand. "No one has lived here since 1972." Ms. Shelley, the realtor, unlocked the front door with a key of a variety that surely expired among locksmiths. I made a note that I would likely have to change the locks on all the doors.

The foyer was quaint. Cross-hatched wooden floors, a broken chandelier, and a standard staircase angling to the second level of the house to the left of the entryway. The wallpaper was droll. An unremarkable damask, yellowing in places. The air was slightly musty, but we had had such problems in the South. I thought of Amariyah, the scarring on her lungs, and made sure the realtor knew that we would have to install filters before moving in if we decided to take on the property. It was a decision we came to quickly, as I came to see her vulnerability magnifying in the absence of future plans.

Amariyah walked through the foyer without a sound, a slight stumble as her swollen foot grazed the curved step. Her affect had been flat since she woke from the heathen slumber of illness. She could speak, but had reverted to monosyllabic responses and strange, sharp glances to the far edges of her visual field. Amariyah had always been peculiar, hence my deep love for her. I could not fathom a lifelong venture of romance with someone less strange. We both loved cats and dogs, nature and mysticism. She loved reading, then. She hates it now.

Houses sold as-is come with the promise of elbow-grease and aggravation. We walked room to room through the house together. I asked her about painting the walls different colors, wallpaper, different lighting and furniture to suit her former liking. The efforts were great within me, to not take her ambivalence as rejection. Even amid the disinterest, I held her hand, and her fingers slid against mine in a gesture of intimacy, if only for a moment.

Amariyah had often spoken of a bench in her grandparent's woods where she would sit and read books with her grandfather. Looking out the kitchen window into the distance, there, on the precipice of a wall of oaks and cyprus, was the perfect spot for a wrought iron bench. There were some antique stores in town. I could summon her to take a look at them. No, I thought. She was too tired from the nightmares of the night before. Better to bring her about when it was assembled. There would be an enormous amount of raking to do. Two Nor'easters had moved across the property in the weeks prior to our moving in. The leaves were stacked in dune-like piles across the edge of the woods.

I found an old rake in the barn, its teeth filled with decrepit leaves of a bygone season. I pulled them out and trekked over to the edge of the woods, beginning to rake as the temperature dropped to an awakening briskness. After several sweeps, out rang a scraping sound. I cringed... Stone on metal or the like. Kneeling down to move the last of the leaf cover, I came upon a large, unusual stone, clearly out of place. It had the look of a makeshift grave, crowding upon a body no one must have cared for in life. My fingers grazed the surface. There may have been marks there once, but they were eroded. I could feel the faint carving of a letter, S. But there were no other graves. How odd, I thought. For a single grave to sit on what was once a homestead. It could not have been a family grave. Perhaps that of a cherished animal? That made little sense, since the realtor had shown us the pet cemetery on the northwestern edge of the property.

Amariyah made great effort at domestic activities, however morosely she conducted the tasks. The night of my discovery, she had cooked lamb with parsnips and sweet potatoes. No spices. She couldn't tolerate them since the loss. Some strange biological side effect, the doctor said. We sat down together and I began to tell her about my discovery at the edge of the woods. It did not strike her curiosity, though she answered questions in her usual monotone.

"It must be whoever lived here before us," she said, poking at a parsnip with her mother's pewter fork. A singular inheritance from a family soaked in poverty.

"I thought this at first, but it is no family plot, Amariyah. And you saw the pet graves when I did. We were together, remember?" Amariyah shrugged, taking a small sip of water. It was tinged yellow. I made a note to myself that we must order a filter. I took the glass from her and she looked at me with disappointment.

"Which faucet was this from?"

"I put herbs in it."

"What herbs?" I asked, astonished.

"One that makes it look like that."

She took back her drink and took a fuller sip before rising from the table. She turned to the sink and rinsed out the glass before gazing out the window overlooking the southern end of the property.

"Maybe we could make a project of this mystery," I said. "Do some research together at the local library?" Amariyah shrugged again, leaving the room without cleaning her plate. I scraped her meal onto my own plate. Tending to the house would take the sustenance of two, perhaps more.

Research was not alien to me. I had a doctoral degree in cultural heritage and historic preservation. I took to the local library and town hall, but came upon very little. Nothing of the house's former residents would be available to me until I spoke with our nearest neighbor, about a mile down the road. Mitchell Mauvais was an ancient man, nearing a century of life, and never without his fraying cowboy hat and corduroy jacket. We passed him in the car on the way into town at least once a week. He was always on his porch, smoking a cigar, his old basset hound Charlie howling at the faulty brakes in our used Ford truck.

I was driving out for medicine when I passed old Mauvais. He waved. I made a quick decision to park in his driveway — an unpaved road that reminded me of Aunt Bertha's — and got out of the car. He kept smoking, barely looking at me as I approached the porch. The hound stumbled up and wagged its tail a few pitiful times. It seems he'd been wanting for less smoky company.

"What can I do you for, neighbor? Straightenin' up that old hell house, they tell me."

"Hell house, sir?"

"Oh, you don't want to be knowin' all that." I would have let out a friendly laugh, but I was trying hard not to cough.

"Mr. Mauvais, I would be interested in some things about the property. I found an old unmarked grave in the back yard, but haven't been able to figure out who is buried there."

"That there is an old grave. You don't need to be knowin' about it. Better to fix up the house fer yer wife, ain't it?" A thick gust moved through the porch, painting the white wood with leaves. The hound made for the door.

"Forgive me, Mr. Mauvais." I left his property, unease pouring through me. When I got home that evening, I found Amariyah sitting on the floor of the bedroom, painting her toenails.

"Would you like to see what I found today?" I asked her. She looked up at me with glazed eyes.

"In the yard?"

"Yes," I answered, holding out a hand to help her up.

"Once the whispers stop." I paused.

"Whispers?"

"I hear them sometimes."

"What are they saying?" I could see she wished she hadn't told me.

"I don't know. Regretful things. Sad things."

I didn't know what to say. I changed into clothes more fit for walking through the yard and waited for her.

Three nights after I showed Amariyah the unmarked grave, she became less coherent. Dissociation had been a problem since the stillbirth. I asked her if I was supposed to gain her attention or allow her to wander in thought when that happened. She said she didn't know what was "supposed" to be done about it. That the nightmares had become unbearable, full of death and decay, and of an old woman crying in the cellar. That's why she refused to go down there with me, I thought. I could tell she missed her former energy, a zest for life and art that was unmatched in anyone I had met before her.

She usually took to bed early at night, around nine, after taking the PTSD medications the doctors carelessly told her would give her dreamless sleep. I wouldn't call it a day until three or four in the morning, using time for research and plans for fixing the house. On that third night, I started for bed around three fifteen to find that Amariyah was not there. The sheets were turned down and messy, so I knew she had been in bed for a while. Figuring she had gone to the kitchen for a drink, I made my way there, hoping to comfort her, but the room was empty. I walked to the foyer and found the front door wide open, creaking in the wind.

I circled the property, unable to see her. On my second attempt, I called out her name. She didn't answer, but the moonlight shone upon her face, which had turned towards me. She was standing over the grave.

"What are you doing out here?" I asked. She shrugged and turned back to look at the grave.

"Who do you think is here?" she asked in a whisper.

"I don't know, Riyah. Someone from way back when." I linked my arm with hers and beckoned her to the farmhouse. She came with me freely.

For two weeks, Amariyah was stranger than even her illness could account for. She began mumbling to herself inaudibly. I could make out a few words... *mother, bargain.* I strained to hear her from beyond doors, but she would take notice of me immediately and stop. I knew it was happening. She knew I knew, but nothing was said between us about it. Like an unspoken understanding of something she had to do now, to exist after all that had happened. One morning she was coming down from the attic. She had the remnants of a cobweb caught in her hair, and a handful of yellowing newspaper clippings.

"What are those about?" I asked her.

"The girl in the grave," she said.

"Oh?"

She laid the clippings out on the table, their corners falling to dust with each pressing of her delicate fingers. There was an obituary of a young girl named Sarah Hanner. Amariyah began mumbling to herself and gathered the clippings in her arms before leaving the room.

I encountered old Mauvais again on my way into town for paint. He was raking leaves in his front yard, as slowly as one would expect an elderly man to do yard work. I pulled over and got out.

"Evenin', Carter."

"Hello, Mr. Mauvais."

"How that wife o' yers?" I took off my hat and held it to my chest.

"She's...not well. Mr. Mauvais, I wonder if you could tell me about the former inhabitants of the house?" Mauvais let go of his rake and grabbed a cigarette from the front pocket of his flannel. His fingers looked like those of a mummy's, reaching for the box.

"There been several families there, son, before you and yers, several."

"I'm trying to find out who is buried in an unlabelled plot on the property."

"In the dog cem'tery?"

"No, by the woods."

"You asked me this the other day." Mauvais took a deep puff. "That'd be one o' the Hanner girls. Hung herself in the barn damn near 100 years ago."

"It's not in the town records. We found some papers in the attic, though," I said. He laughed.

"Sure, it ain't! They was poultry farmers, immigrants. Came to the land with an agreement to make use of it. They was off-record 'til that nightmare. Three daughters to 'em, and the youngest killin' herself." Mauvais shook his head, putting his cigarette out under his boot. The wind started to pick up. His old dog started howling from the porch.

"It ain't a happy plot o' land, son, but anythin' can change." With that he nodded and slowly ambled towards the house.

When I got home, Amariyah was sitting at the dining table in a strange, old dress. I asked her where she got it from.

"The attic," she answered stiffly. I'd found her by the grave at night three or four times by that point. Her speech was quieter and simpler than ever.

"I found out from our neighbor, Mr. Mauvais, that the grave is for a girl who lived here a long time ago. Over a century ago." Her eyes flashed. I continued. "It was a family that migrated here, poultry farmers."

"How did she die?" Amariyah asked suddenly, looking me in the eyes. I hesitated.

"Well, she hung herself in the barn. So says Mauvais."

Amariyah was stricken. She rose from the table and went upstairs without a word, her raggedy dress kicking up dust behind her.

In the weeks before Christmas, Amariyah took to taking long walks in the woods by herself. I had been attempting to shift my schedule so that we could go to sleep at the same time, though as a night owl, I struggled. I recommended prayer to keep her company before I came to bed, but she told me whenever she prayed, it made her delirious. One night, around the eighth of December, I went into the bedroom to find it empty again. I grabbed the flashlight and did my now-routine trek to fetch Amariyah from the grave site, but she was not there. The winds were picking up. I'd forgotten my coat on the rack. The deep chill of winter was really setting in. I put my flashlight under my armpit and my hands in my pockets, looking around. I heard the barn doors creaking, ebbing open and closed in the winter wind. I headed for the barn and found her there.

She was in her sheer nightgown, shivering, her unkempt hair blowing across her face. She stood still. I rushed to her and placed a hand on her back. She was freezing. "Amariyah," I started, brushing her hair out of her face. "Come inside."

She walked back to the house with me without a fuss. I walked her upstairs and sat next to her on the bed.

"What were you doing out there?" I asked.

She stayed silent for several minutes before saying, "I feel responsible."

"You aren't responsible for what happened to the baby. I know you think that..."

"No."

"No?" I asked.

"I feel responsible for what happened...to her."

"To who?"

"The Hanner girl."

I sat upright in momentary confusion.

"She died over a hundred years ago. How could you be responsible for something that happened before you or, hell... even your mother was born?"

Amariyah looked at me in dismay. She knew it didn't make sense, either, but she felt it. That much was certain. I reached out to hold her hand. She pulled it away.

"I think we should call Dr. Pasquierel tomorrow. Make sure all your blood and levels are okay." She sighed and nodded. She was so sick of doctors. So was I.

Dr. Pasquierel found nothing wrong with her. "Blood, vitals, ultrasound are all clear," he assured me as she re-dressed. "But I recommend, once again, that she check in with her psychiatrist and a therapist. After what happened, she needs to be on medication."

"I know, Doctor, but we moved recently, and it's harder to get an appointment with them, it's a long drive."

"There will always be a reason why not to do it, but it should be done. For her sake, and yours." Dr. Pasquierel handed me a script.

"What's this?"

"Anti-anxiety medicine. The instructions will be on the bottle. And they're for her, son, not you."

The car ride back to the farm was quiet. I parked the car in the dirt driveway. Amariyah didn't get out.

"I'm tired," she said, a rare moment where she spoke before being prompted.

"I know." She looked at me with a clarity I hadn't seen since before the birth, but her eyes seemed an unfamiliar shade, with wrinkles appearing slowly and fading away in a flash.

"I killed my daughter." I moved a strand of hair behind her ear. She looked down.

"Ri, you didn't. It was a natural thing. It wasn't your fault."

She didn't answer me. We went into the house. It was pretty late, so I holed up in my office to let some tension out with writing. Amariyah usually went into the bedroom to read for a few hours while I wrote, but admittedly, I was so shaken up with everything that I didn't check on her once we got into the house. When time got away from me again, and I was faced with a desk clock reporting midnight, I rushed down the hall and to the bedroom to check on her. Once again, she wasn't there.

I grabbed my coat and went to the grave, the first pit stop. Not there. As I rounded the hill to the barn, sure enough, the doors were open. As I approached, my pace slowed. A voice was coming from the barn. No, two voices. Slow, whispering. I walked inside after a surge of fear I couldn't explain. There stood Amariyah, nude, freezing, whispering to herself. There was only one voice then.

"Jesus Christ." I took off my coat and wrapped it around her. She seemed to be in a trance of sorts. I took off my shoes and gave her my socks. I got her to the house, sat her down, microwaved some milk and sugar, and sat down next to her.

"What were you doing out there, Ri? What were you thinking?" She took a sip of the warm milk and set it down, wiping a stray drip from her full, bluish lips with the back of her hand.

"I needed to apologize."

"There's no need to apologize, just tell me what you're feeling?"

"No. I needed to apologize to her." A cold chill crawled up my spine before a faint crackling sounded at the back of my neck.

"Apologize to who?"

"Sarah."

"Ri, Sarah Hanner died over a hundred years ago. It has nothing to do with you."

"It was my fault."

"How the fuck is it your fault?" I lost my temper. I grabbed the milk and took my own sip. It was lukewarm. The sensation of it running down my throat was more pronounced than ever. Everything was more pronounced. The sounds, the chill, the feelings.

On Monday, I drove Amariyah out to Syracuse to see her old psychiatrist. She agreed to a week-long inpatient program, so I headed home, getting back to the farm around eight o'clock. I fed the cats and dogs, and shuttered myself up in the bedroom for the cry I couldn't have around her. I drifted off, waking up late to the sound of the barn doors clapping open and shut. I got dressed and went downstairs. The front door was open, and one of the dogs got out. I summoned him back with a few treats in my pocket and shut the door behind me. I hadn't been in the barn since I retrieved Amariyah from it a few nights before. I couldn't have forgotten to shut it.

I walked into the barn, suddenly angry with myself for not bringing my shotgun. It could have been a robber, or a wolf, and I was too damn delirious to even think of it. There was nobody in there. The stalls for the horses were the same — half fixed-up since I'd started working on them. I looked up to the rafters and saw nothing. What I felt was a deep regret for telling Ri about that old grave. Some poor girl died in here unexpectedly; of course she'd overthink about some weird synchronicity in that, after she lost the baby. She must have thought she was talking to our daughter, I figured. Standing in the barn, looking up there, that made perfect sense to me. Then, I saw it. A blue light, sweeping over and through the rafters. It disappeared as quickly as it had come. I left the barn and shuttered the doors, making my way back to the house as fast as I could.

I went to visit Amariyah the next day, making the full three-hour drive through morning traffic to get to her. The doctors told me it was too early in the program for me to speak to her, but I insisted. They put us in a quiet room with a window for a wall. The kind that doctors can look through in case something happens. They'd given her a plain white t-shirt and cotton pants. Not quite medical clothes and not quite prison garb, but something evocative of both.

She was happy to see me, which was surprising. Amariyah was still burdened with a weight of worlds, but an old warmth blossomed within her. We kissed. We held hands.

"Why did you come down today, I thought you weren't coming until the fifth day visit?" she asked, though it wasn't a complaint.

"Ri, I want to ask you something. About the barn." Her smile fell. Amariyah withdrew her hand and swept it through her hair. "Did you see something in there?" She seemed relieved, pressing her hand to mine again.

"Carter," she began, her voice crackling. "Don't make me go back to the farm. Sell it, find somewhere else, please." I was shocked. She hadn't spoken to me that intensely, that directly, so much like herself in so long.

"I will," I said. Amariyah drew a few long breaths and said nothing more on the matter.

the irrational dress society

"The other shape
If shape it might be call'd that shape had none
Distinguishable, in member, joint, or limb;
Or substance might be call'd that shadow seemed;
For such seemed either; black he stood as night;
Fierce as ten furies; terrible as hell;
And shook a deadly dart. What seem'd his head
The likeness of a kingly crown had on."
-*Paradise Lost*, 2.666-73

PROLOGUE

THE long-disbanded Irrational Dress Society was an organization founded in 1912 in St. Petersburg, on the banks of the Neva. It described its purpose thus:

The Irrational Dress Society protests against the introduction of any fashion in dress that allows ease of movement of the body, or in any way tends to encourage normal health or conformity. It protests against the wearing of loose-fitting garments; of heel-less shoes; of sensible skirts, as rendering strange excellence almost impossible; and of t-shirts or day clothes of any kind. It protests against denim and cotton as ugly and disgraceful. It requires all to be dressed in elaborate garb, to seek what conduces to the otherworldly, the supernatural, to that which the common folk refer to as spectacle or deformed, seeing our dress as a duty to ourselves, each other, and the progression of society into the unknown.

The organization defined the attributes of "perfect dress" as:

1. Condemning of excessive movement.

2. Applying pressure over as many parts of the body as possible.

3. Enough weight so that warmth is excessively distributed.

4. Strangeness.

5. Departing profoundly from the ordinary dress of the time.

The leading member of the Society was Russian ex-diplomat Ermolai Krovopuskov — a vexatious man, never seen without his mangled cane and curious, lopsided wig. In 1913, Krovopuskov gave an impromptu speech on the subject of irrational dress that interrupted the intended address of diplomat Bogatyr Apollonovich on the first night of the Winter Festival. His speech was reported by newspapers across Russia and Middle Europe, with the notion of irrational dress becoming the only striking news from the event. Let it be noted that upon the conclusion of the speech, thread and needles were distributed, with which the attendees sewed their own mouths shut. The contents of that very speech were as follows...

"Let me call myself, for the occasion, a defender of the utmost and unparalleled promise of the unusual. What does such a man do? In a society without thought, without merit? Does he walk about, unseemingly? No. I look in the mirror and see myself. I do not see you. We have all been awakened by the ferocious wailings of the night, mourning beneath glass and gold. My soul was once illuminated by the promise of this land. I stand before you without the pride of your predecessors, my heart filled with the black morasses of the universe. Look around, dear friends. Are you alone? Will you find yourself alone here? To defend you from this horror, I will be your sentinel of absorption. The phantom shoulder blocking out the flood. There is a dense darkness afoot. Can you hear it? I might speak upon the black spirits in your bellies, those that come out only at night through breath and groin, but we are in a place of manners, and so I will be slow.

It is my wish for all living men on earth to reclaim that which has been scattered over the rocks of ages. That which has become a superfluous soup of memory. I have golden aspirations, those that tiptoe over swarms of convention. Hanging, perilously aslant, over any passion for the usual. If we are to swallow those ancestral eyes and see, embrace that which was repressed, buried... There may be something left of this land long after the aggravations of outer worlds. When you mix blood-like thread, sharp geometries, and harsh textures atop your everyday working suit, one may find it themselves, indeed, *on the way* to the revelations I am about to express. None of you have ever dared to be so obtuse. My first offering to you is the story of Ivan Isaac, the almost-monarch of a distant, colic empire.

None of you will have heard this offering, as it has been suppressed by your dear Bogatyr. You won't remember the slick red runway of blood cascading behind him. He descended down every staircase as a river of blood. His compatriots wore bandaged faces in solidarity with his case: that he had been wrongly accused of the slaughter of millions. Might you recall a double-breasted jacket, buttoned by the bones of the prior monarch? He made it so that women's gowns were gathered about the groin and throat, the ghoulish executor of conservatism.

There are no garments such as these today. No structural abnormality. What a shame! You, sir! With tailcoat clipped back to the collar, this hideous typicality! Were I extra long in the waist already by the suggestion of my corseted mess, I would wrap around and strangle you. Rows and rows of you, listening, all the same.

It is a solemn occasion I find myself compelled to address you all, though I extend my deepest thanks to dear Lord Apollonovich. He awarded me a prize once, upon my power. One of great obedience and pride. It was melted quite some years ago, sewed as bones into that which I wear now.

Once upon a merrier evening, I testified in public as to the admiration I had for our nation's triumph over foreign worlds. But no such thing aroused me as those late-night perusals of a devilsome hue. The heathen multitudes who hide from this very place, this night! All for want of curiosity and confusion.

Is it not true, Sir Apollonovich, that you previously expressed peace with such scoundrels, if only for their silence and conformity? Dear sir, this does not correspond with your words! You have outlawed my society for want of security, but there is no greater security than this.

One might say that the practices of myself and my compatriots predispose one to malevolence, to evil. Rather, I feel quite grounded in myself, dear Apollonovich. More than ever so, under your wing.

The time of our Passion-Bearer is growing to a close. Dear, vile Bogatyr. Have you not spread your palm atop the corpses of millions?

Twelve autumns ago, dearest Ann Dragocovich and Filip Kostantiva came to the country with a dream in mind. To weave glorious restrictions into the garb of young men and girls, an experiment to develop their attention, their acuity. If I am in so much pain as this, then what might life be at the end of the day, unclothed? A miracle of peace, even under your rule. The reports, I have here in my pockets. It is said that you split them straight down the center. That their sleeves dripped with the pinkish foam of lung-blood. The fabric they chose to wear upon their arrival to your city was delicate, intellectual. Piping details on their cuffs, a pleated skirt, a smart trenchcoat, stained with bile. You had heard their ideas before, had you not? From none other than myself?

It is quite fashionable to reject outsiders these days, is it not, good people? One would not wish to be accused of consorting with the strange! I wish to proclaim that I would hold such travelers dear, without reference to their prior worlds. Are we to be so defined by prior lives, Lord Apollonovich? Is this not contrary to the delivered addresses of the state?

I developed these patterns, these shades, these constrictions of my own accord. Based on the artistic mastery of our deceased. I hid the showroom in the bowels of the city — your city — men and women and children morphed into all shapes and sizes. Stamped with the letters of their Christian names across their foreheads, stripes and lizard skins and outrageous things!

Think now of the regeneration of life within suffering. Must it be a life of suffering, Bogatyr, or only moments? I refer to your politics in brief, because I know them too well. In your offices, there, a philosophy of life was expressed with the utmost disdain, without inquiry. Those who enabled such catastrophe, whom I have found, wear their pains upon their bodies, as should all.

I would not divide mankind between you and the rest of us. There is no gospel of reason to save the united soul.

What should a designer first think upon, when dreaming a collection? Do you remember Tyrrell Bely, the milliner from the eastern wall? How quickly captured that image of you with the splayed sleeves, the organic pustules riveting down your spine. Only once did you try on one of my outfits. Only once.

All of you, working people! Creators with hand and heart! I am one of you, and with highest honor, see your strife! The ultimate foundation of life is not obedience. It is not loyalty to a broken crown. In an era of annihilation, where is the inevitable fury? Where is the revolution? Why are you so silent? Why do you not stray! Is mankind so bent on their self-destruction?

You might think me fearless in this great charade. I feel the unpleasantness, far more than you. It is my bid to strengthen your bodies first, then the mind, then soul.

I recall arriving one day to your quarters in an outfit you declared to be "beyond tasteless" and "scientifically unwearable." And yet there I stood before you, as I do now. There was a dark architecture to the velveteen folds, blood-soaked foiling, a catastrophe of wool seeping from the spine. Only through artifice may one be so affective. I believe anyone may do this. Anyone among us in this moment. Dear Bogatyr, you have not allowed your people to explore. They have been disregarded and oppressed with the utmost punishment. That of obedience and boredom. This nation was built of monsters. Should the future choose otherwise?

Allow me to break this dreadful mood with a reflection upon romance. My beloved Vassa, always in pale gowns and ruby robes. She transformed in my company, did she not? Stumbling upon old-world tomes of terrors and torment. That which was organic became superorganic, supernatural, until the very day your knife crossed her neck, spilling blood and black pearls.

I choose to think that I am better, in this becoming. I look to my fellow man and wonder of their absent desires. What are you fighting for? Progress or status quo? If I manage to do anything this evening, it will be to convince those listening here tonight that there is rebirth in the throes of irrational dress. Techniques like that were not betrothed to the exhaustive meek and limited minds of our abyss. Be done with your cartridge pleating and bodices! There are greater things to be woven and felt. My latter darling had a black cocoon sewn into her spine that unearthed the most unsightly of supernatural wounds. Her death was the embodiment of the sublime.

I had some reservations before this address. I received word of the death of one Desya Birinov of the eastern chapter of our society. According to the newspaper, she died of a fatal overdose. What a strange and fatal flow of events. I have sharpened my eyes to such happenings for mythic meaning, presuming that all drama is in fact a work of art. You have desperately fooled yourselves, citizens! You posture on an earth that will eat you as soon as birth you.

With a deafening crash your world will cease to exist, and you follow this man! Have generations of men never cracked open a single book?

Desya had a taste for black and cream. Fabrics that spoke to her lack of territory. Deeply cut garments sewn into her flesh, wolf-like talons jutting from her brow. This is where irrational dress married with body modification and our society was elevated from the profane to the sacred. She was the queen of our revolution, Bogatyr, and now she is dead.

Revolution is a fiery maw, and I seek to open my mouth. What age must it be for all to see the seething, soaking, horrid corruption? The hallmark of my brand, my message, is irrational dress. But dress is not merely dress, dear people. These garments will split apart the essential elements, suppress the nonsense, illuminate the absolute.

Think this not my Sermon on the Mount! There are seasons for such things, and we are within them. I think myself a vintage of another world, the first of all to taste the magnificence, the uprising of the east. Like you, I praise not the explosions, the weapons, the dead bodies in the street. What a reckless world it has become.

The sensations of ease are upon you. Can you not see them? There is something richer and more fulfilling than these clothes, these hats, these familiar shapes! Imagine the sensation of living! Draping and textures and overlaid patterns that betray the minds of the usual. Embroidery and saw-cut and illusions of taste!

It may be said I am a mutation of man. My teeth were chiseled down to needles. I nourish myself on the confusion of the higher people. There is an ease of transfer through this world once one has tasted the absolute confinement of the irrational. Your hallways are my catwalk. Your sighs are my technique.

There is no literature yet to address such a craft. We are alive in the temporal, not the absolute. Sweet Bogatyr has dragged you down to the lowest incarnation of your flesh. Others have been strong amid such a charade of strength, now to be bones in a river's bed.

And so, dear citizens, what is next? There will always be suffering, deep phenomena, and death. Your children ask of such things and you reject their curiosity, for want of stillness, for want of breath! There are no true philosophers of children. None so reliable as I and these, the Society of Irrational Dress.

There are matters of the dead, of which I must reject. You are all dead. This is no error. I speak a truth hidden beneath your breast. Make no mistake — your blandness, your normality, your lack of style! They speak to the buried soul within.

I was once like you, heartless and tired. I wandered into a strange garden, quite by accident, and was winked at by a receding blossom, a colour of which no man could define, a species of which no botanist could recommend! I have always said that nature is the very essence of life, where there is no finality of style there.

I string together these truths untold. I know you are weak. Let it be no more! Look to him! I know what you see is a speckled prim! A crook of uncertainty! In doing nothing as I speak he has surveyed his end. These are the moments that the greatness of literature should preserve!

Proclaimeth yourself a mess, and I see you perfect. There are wheels turning in the cosmos that arrest at such perfection. The symphony of your resurrection is a sculpted aria on a weeping moon.

Remember tweed and black leather? Lace? The flavors of the dark feminine? Of romanticism? Imagine such things sculpted to the zenith of the abject. Imagine wears free of Euclidean geometry. Surfaces from a different plane of organic life. There is a nobility in the blood of those who wear such constructions. Whether you see them on a politician, policeman, or country mistress. Would you not stop and think? Observe? Would life not be lit with an inordinate and imperceptible something?

Your world among sweet Bogatyr is slow, so slow. He rules with longevity and absolution. The hammer and the space. Think of the complexity of great structures, of the intricacies of cerebral men. In a single second of contemplation is the universe. Might you deign to glimpse such a startling end? We are science and art, worldly and unworldy. We judge not your genitals, your duress. We believe in that which exists outside of nature. You will see our models with wooden eyes, gashed cheeks, and mismatched animals dangling from their breasts. You will see new forms of women and men. Unordinary, anything but banal! It is no longer possible to return to your former self. The wounds of Bogatyr sleep in the sinewy thread of your new body, your new soul. Yes! No disease will afflict you that may not be fought with compressions. No invention of man may accost you. No love may destroy your heart again. We are not these beasts of casual allure, we are creations of the deepest, most precise incarnation of the absolute. To wound oneself may be dangerous, but one might ask what it really is to feel alive. Nothing on Bogatyr's earth is so great as this!

You will be uplifted beyond your wildest imaginings, at the speed of the very heavens. In all truth it might be said that you are born again. Look at these ordinary women and men! You have come together to hear him, and you hear this instead! This is a heaven's assembly, a living accord of the collective soul. I see terror and splendor in you all. Your number increases with each word, each breath! Have no fear of the beauty of the abject. It is not for you to reject.

I see you move, Bogatyr! Sit, fearless leader! A prouder word has oft' been spoken here! Ladies and gentlemen and rebels of the night, see the tender soul who lies before you here! I am tour de force of anti-glamour, the illuminate-grotesque!

I have lived under your wing and breath too long. To come again to the momentous arc of your presence is a curse, but of baser things, I have always said I am the monarch. You strike them down with terror and conformity. I will lift them up with this heathen purity — with irrational dress.

Is it silence, I hear? Has life led us to such a day? Do you hear eternity in this silence? In the scraping of these hideous nails against the grain? I love what I hear. I love it. One hour, two to come, then another. We can all go forth in this heathen silence, awash with the stench of ages, zipped and buttoned and stirred up into the irrational. What has come so intimately upon us all comes only this once. But first we must cover every tongue, every lip, to assure no quivering there. As your mouth closes and we prepare the drip, remember that there is no light or dark, right or wrong. No masculine, feminine. There is no life, no death. There is only *style*.

publication history

THE WYTCH-BYRD OF THE NABRYD-KEIND
Previously published in *Lackington's Magazine*: Issue 18

IN THE WAY OF ESLAN MENDEGHAST
Previously published in *Vastarien Literary Journal*: Volume 2, Issue 1

OF MARBLE AND MUD
Previously published in *Nightscript IV*

THE VISITOR
Previously published by Ulthar Press

THE LAND OF OTHER
Previously published in *Tragedy Queens*

AS UNBREAKABLE AS THE WORLD
Previously published in *A Walk on the Weird Side*

AN ACCOUNT ABOVE BURNSIDE PARK
Previously published in *Mantid Magazine* and *The Phantasmagorical Promenade*

AS WITH ALEM
Previously published in *Twice-Told: A Collection of Doubles*

SORCERER MACHINE
Previously published in *Shadows of the Past: The Arkham Horror
Book Club Anthology*

DARK OCEAN
Previously published in *The Sirens Call Ezine*, Issue 31

ASH IN THE POCKET
Previously published in *Of One Pure Will* from Egaeus Press

FOLIE À PLUSIEURS
Previously published in *Of One Pure Will* from Egaeus Press

RITHENSLOFER (THE CORPSES OF MER)
Previously published by HUSH Media (audio)

IN THE ROOM OF RED NIGHT
Previously published in *Test Patterns: Creature Features*

OF ONE PURE WILL
Previously published in *Of One Pure Will* from Egaeus Press

TIME DISEASE (IN THE WAKING CITY)
Previously published in the Necronomicon 2017 Memento Book

IVISOU
Previously published in *Of One Pure Will* from Egaeus Press

THE RIVER
Previously published in *Of One Pure Will* from Egaeus Press

THE SEA HOAX
Previously Published in *Horror for RAICES: A Charitable Anthology*

ELECTRIC FUNERAL
Previously published on expatpress.com

EVE, LIKE SHARDS OF GLASS
Previously unpublished

A DELIRIUM OF MOTHERS
Previously unpublished

THE IRRATIONAL DRESS SOCIETY
Previously published in *Weird Whispers*

acknowledgments

T HANK you to my Mom and Dad, who encouraged my writing since I drew sloppy picture books with crayons as a young child, who allowed me to become whoever and whatever I wanted to be. Thank you to my brother Travis, who has endured the similar traumas of health and loss that make storytelling an important sanctuary. Thank you to my grandparents, four human beings of profound strength, honor, and work ethic who make me proud of where I come from.

Thank you to my husband Michael, for knowing my heart and strength, for accepting me as I am, flaws and all. Being with you has made me become the best version of myself I could dream of being. I couldn't have been blessed with a better husband.

Thank you to Scarlett R. Algee for your enthusiasm about publishing this collection, for all the work you put into making it happen, and thank you to Sean Leonard for his excellent editing. It was an absolute delight to work with Trepidatio Publishing.

Thank you to my friends, fans, teachers, and inspirations intermingled here: Lev Earle, Jeffrey Thomas, Carrie Laben, William Tea, Sonya Taaffe, Chuk Radder, Fiona Maeve Geist, S.P. Miskowski, Richard Thomas, Katarina Vorontsova, Sean Moreland, Robert S. Wilson, Livia Llewelyn, Matthew Gauvain, Todd Chicoine, Autumn Christian, Matthew Bartlett, Jon Padgett, Andrea Wolanin, Frank Difficult, Carol Gafford, The Joey Zone, Nancy Eder, LC von Hessen, Christ Benton, Rhys Hughes, Daniel Braum, John Langan, and Andreas Koerver-Stümper.

Lastly, thank you to my friend, surrogate brother/father/uncle, and mentor. Sam Gafford. Your faith in me as a writer helped me strive for success, but your faith in me as a friend and human being helped me stay alive. I miss you so much every day. I hope we will see each other again.

about the author

Farah Rose Smith is the author of the novellas ANONYMA, *The Almanac of Dust*, and *Eviscerator*. Her writing has appeared in *Lackington's Magazine*, *Darker Magazine* (Russia), *Spectral Realms*, *Vasterien Literary Journal*, *Nightscript*, *Dead Reckonings*, and more. She is a book reviewer for *Publishers Weekly* and works part-time as a literary agent. Smith is an affiliate member of the Horror Writers Association and a member of the

International Gothic Association, North American Society for the Study of Romanticism, and the Science Fiction and Fantasy Poetry Association. A native of Rhode Island, she currently lives in New York City with her husband, author Michael Cisco, and their three cats.

CPSIA information can be obtained
at www.ICGtesting.com
Printed in the USA
FSHW012115080921
84510FS